Cake and Punishment

Cake and Punishment

A SOUTHERN CAKE BAKER MYSTERY

Maymee Bell

CROOKED LANE

NEW YORK

Copyright © 2018 by The Quick Brown Fox & Company LLC.

Published in the United States by Crooked Lane Books, an imprint of The Quick Brown Fox & Company LLC.

Crooked Lane Books and its logo are trademarks of The Quick Brown Fox & Company LLC.

Library of Congress Catalog-in-Publication data available upon request.

ISBN (hardcover): 978-1-68331-571-1
ISBN (ePub): 978-1-68331-572-8
ISBN (ePDF): 978-1-68331-573-5

Cover illustration by Matthew Kalamidas/StoneHouse Creative, Inc.
Book design by Jennifer Canzone

Printed in the United States.

www.crookedlanebooks.com

Crooked Lane Books
34 West 27th St., 10th Floor
New York, NY 10001

First Edition: May 2018

10 9 8 7 6 5 4 3 2 1

A big thank you to Nancy from Fantasy in Frosting in Newport, Kentucky, for teaching me how to bake and decorate cakes for the sake of research. I'll never be able to master the flower petals.

Chapter One

"Vrrrrrr. Vrr. Vrrr. Vrrrrrrrr." The sound of the electric mixer was music to my ears. It was like coming home. "Vrrrrrrrr. Vrrrrrr." I held the mixing bowl under the whisk, blending and folding the icing to the perfect consistency.

The chocolate icing was making my mouth water, and it would've been a sin not to taste it. I stuck my finger in the bowl, coated the tip, and slowly raked it across the top of my lower teeth, making sure I got every single morsel of chocolate off my finger. My eyes closed as I breathed out a deep sigh of satisfaction. The bitter chocolate combined with the sweet ingredients to make the perfect flavor. Even heartbreak couldn't change my excellent baking skills.

The flavor of the icing was as pleasing to my taste buds as the beauty of the bluegrass field just beyond the bay window of my parents' gourmet kitchen was to my eyes. With a mug in my hand and a quilt off the quilt rack, I walked out onto the three-tiered deck. A quick cup of coffee would allow just enough time for the icing to settle and the flavor to stabilize.

Tucking the edges of the blanket around me as I sat down, I

curled my hands around the warm mug before I took a sip and enjoyed the sun peeking up over the trees in the cool spring morning air.

It'd been a long time since I'd seen a sunrise. The sun bathed the ten acres of bluegrass with dazzling light that blanketed my hometown of Rumford, Kentucky. The countryside was unblemished, not like the view I was used to in New York City.

In Manhattan, every morning I'd woken up and looked out the tiny window of our eight-hundred-square-foot apartment and peered at the fifty-one-story apartment building next to us. Any sort of sunrise was blocked by the concrete jungle of the city. There was nothing like the bustle of people walking fast on the sidewalks to get to work. Or the sound of the horns of the taxis as they zoomed past. Even the raunchy smells of the water runoff as shop owners sprayed off the sidewalk in front of their stores excited my soul. I loved all things about New York City.

But I'd always been a southern girl at heart. The open fields and the sounds of the cows in the pasture next to my parents' property had their own happy melody.

"For goodness' sakes." Mama chirped her signature phrase after she slid open the deck door and looked at me.

The sheer pink housecoat, or what she considered to be a housecoat, floated behind her with each step. Her pink low-heeled house slippers with a puffball on top clicked against the wood deck. She had a quilt in her hand.

"Sophia, you are up even before the rooster crows. The sun is barely popping up. People move a lot slower in Kentucky than that big city you're used to. Especially here in Rumford. Or did you forget, since you've been gone for ten years?" she asked.

I patted the chair next to me. "I've been back to visit since I moved."

A tinge of sadness hung in her eyes. "You've stopped in, not *stayed*. Especially during the holidays, which you know I love."

"Mama, I'm sorry, but you know that the holidays are the busiest time of year for restaurants," I said, knowing all my coworkers back in Manhattan were working on the upcoming Easter brunch menu.

The restaurant business during the holidays was a combination that Mama had never seemed to grasp, even after the endless times I'd told her why I couldn't come home. Being the head pastry chef, I'd never dreamed of asking off on holidays. Mama made restaurant reservations during the holidays but somehow still didn't understand that I worked in that industry and had to work too—to bake for people like her.

"You're home now." She pulled the edges of the quilt up around her ears.

I could have protested that I was taking off only a couple of weeks. I hadn't quit my job. I'd only quit the relationship with Noah, which meant that once I got my head on straight, I'd have to go back to Manhattan and find a new place to live.

"Let me get you a cup of coffee." I let the quilt fall around my ankles. A shiver crawled up my legs.

"I'll come in." Mama stood up and followed behind me.

"Sophia," Mama gasped, looking around the kitchen. She put her hand up to her mouth. "It's too early to be down here making a mess when you know my cleaning ladies are coming while we're at the Junior League meeting."

Mama traipsed over to the counter and stared at the dusting

of sugar, flour, baking powder, baking soda, cocoa powder, and salt. Not to mention the puddles of wet ingredients that hadn't make it into the cupcakes. A look of horror crossed her face.

Only my mama would make sure her house was clean before her housecleaner came to actually clean.

"I'm going to clean it up," I assured her before she pitched a hissy fit right there. I'd seen Mama lose her religion, and it wasn't something I wanted to see again.

"Honey." Mama brushed the palm of her hand over my dark brown hair that was pulled back tightly into a ponytail, my usual hairstyle when I baked. "I just hate seeing you go through this."

Internally I questioned her sincerity. After all, it'd been her dream for me to move home for good.

"I do too, Mama." My voice cracked. A tear trickled down my face. Mama's warm hand brushed it off my chin. "I really thought Noah was the one. We were like a well-oiled machine. When we moved into the apartment, we had the same design taste. When we went to work, his dishes complemented my desserts and vice versa. It was a match made in Manhattan culinary heaven."

I gulped back more tears.

"Last week on my day off, I'd come up with an amazing dessert that I had to get him to try. I ran it down there because I had a really great idea for an Easter dessert, and that's when I caught him and the maître d' in his office. Apparently, he was the daily special."

"I'm glad you told him to hit the hay." Mama nodded. "He's lucky I'm never going to see him again." It never failed. The madder Mama got, the thicker her southern accent got. "Don't get me started on what I'd do to him."

"That's enough about him." I grabbed a banana chocolate cupcake off the cooling rack and took a spatula out of the crock.

"What is on your face?" Mama's demeanor had turned.

She was the epitome of a southern woman. She could be so kind and gentle, but if you wronged Elizabeth Cummings—Bitsy for short—she'd rip out your heart, fry it up, and serve it to you on a piece of her fine china as you drank it down with a glass of her sweet iced tea, the one thing she could boil.

She swiped her finger under my eye. "Is that mascara? Did you sleep in mascara?"

Before I could put the cupcake and spatula down to defend my face, she'd already spit on her finger and swiped again.

"Gross." I jerked away as far as I could. "Stop that."

"Listen here, Sophia Cummings." When Mama said my full name, I knew a tongue-lashing was coming my way. She shifted her weight to the side. "You need to get yourself together. And I don't mean by eating yourself silly with all these cupcakes or being lazy and not washing your face at night. No man is worth that. I taught you better than that." She pushed the pads of her fingers underneath my eyes. "You didn't use the 'H,' did you?"

The "H" was Bitsy's code name for Preparation H. Yes. The hemorrhoid cream. She claimed that if it did you-know-what to hemorrhoids, it'd shrivel up wrinkles and bags under the eyes.

"I'll look presentable. I promise," I assured her. "Just so you know, I made these to take to your Junior League meeting."

I stuck the spatula in the mixing bowl and used the broad side of it to place the frosting on top of the cupcake. Carefully, I spread the chocolaty goodness to the edges.

Mama leaned on the counter. She looked as fresh as a daisy so early in the morning.

"I have to say that they do smell good." There was a flicker in her gold eyes and a little pride in her tone that was her way of making peace. "I've missed you mussing up my kitchen."

"I'm probably the last person who cooked in here." I held the cupcake out for her. "Go on. It's got banana in it."

"And we do eat bananas for breakfast." She grabbed the cupcake and peeled back the paper holder.

"Mmm, good." A deep sigh escaped from the depths of Bitsy's gut. "I can't wait until your daddy gets home from court today and has one of these."

Daddy was a very prominent lawyer in our small town. He made good money along with the other people who lived in their fancy gated community. When we moved here, it had been a new concept to Rumford. All the houses were massive and had an extensive amount of acreage. We had neighbors, but they were an acre over to the left and right. It was as if we lived in a neighborhood but also on a farm.

We also had the fancy kitchen equipped with the finest the builder had to offer, which I blamed for my love of baking. Daddy had questioned Bitsy's white-cabinet choice, but the interior decorator had insisted they'd be pleased. The white tile floor was shiny, and the half-moon island that took up most of the middle of the kitchen was the perfect gathering spot for conversations and homework. The restaurant-grade appliances had made my heart sing as a young girl. I'd taken every home economics class I could when I was in high school and participated in and won every single bake-off at the Rumford County Fair.

My parents had always loved my baking but thought it was just a phase. They were pleased as pie when I decided to go to college and put the baking behind me. It hadn't been until I was twenty that I realized I didn't like learning from books. I loved working with my hands and creating pastries that made people happy and smile. Though Mama wildly begged me not to become a baker, I had set off for New York City, enrolled in culinary school, and never looked back . . . until last week.

Mama had even admitted herself to the hospital when I took the job at The Manhattan as a pastry chef a year ago. She'd claimed I'd induced a mental breakdown at the thought of her daughter living in a crime-ridden city.

"I couldn't sleep last night, and baking helps me think." I quickly iced the other cupcakes and placed them neatly on one of Bitsy's silver platters. For a second I thought she was going to protest. I guess she figured it wasn't worth the fight. She shuffled over to the coffee maker, grabbed the carafe, and topped off our mugs.

"You think too much. Come sit by me." She eased down into one of the fabric, straight-backed white chairs that butted up to the glass-top table in front of the bay window. She pulled the pastel-colored place mats into a pile and stuck them in the center of the table next to the big ceramic bunny.

Decorating for every single holiday and season was in Bitsy's blood. Currently my parents' house was bathed in cream-colored items, green moss, and several Easter eggs, bunnies, and baskets in all sorts of pastels that I was sure Bitsy's decorator from Classy Southern had arranged. There was no way Bitsy was going to break a nail getting in and out of her holiday shed. Men had man caves; Bitsy had a holiday cave where she kept her decorations.

Duchess, Bitsy's exotic short-haired cat that she'd insisted she had to have after I left Rumford, was curled up in another chair. Bitsy scooped her up into her lap.

"Those turned out better than I thought with the lack of ingredients you had in this fancy kitchen." I grabbed a cupcake for myself and another for her. I handed her one before I sat down and held my cupcake in the air. "Cheers."

We tapped our cupcakes together as if we were having a fine glass of wine. I peeled back the cupcake wrapper, took a bite, and burst out in a sudden fit of laughter. Mama stopped in mid-bite. I couldn't stop laughing.

"What on earth is wrong with you?" Mama asked with a cool, disapproving tone.

"I spent the last ten years going to culinary school. Doing countless apprenticeships and worked in several small-time jobs with years of low pay. Then I finally land my dream job where for a year I've worked my tail end off. Gaining recognition and rave reviews." I held the rest of my cupcake up in the air. "Here I am. I endured all of that. All those fancy pastries and schooling to end up with this one cupcake in Rumford, Kentucky," I said, feeling bereft as desolation crept into my gut. A new anguish filled my heart. "Mama, make the pain go away."

Duchess jumped to the ground when Mama got up and dragged me into her arms. Days of sadness, bitterness, fatigue, and anger left me sobbing in the warm embrace of the woman who loved me more than anyone else in the world. Conversations and excitement about how Noah and I had planned to open our own restaurant one day haunted my head.

For a few minutes, Mama let me wallow in my misery as she ran a loving hand along the top of my head and down my back.

"Sophia, honey, you've had your moment of feeling sorry for yourself." Mama wasn't one to gloat when someone did you wrong. "You need to get your act together and tuck that crazy away because we don't have much time to get ready." Her eyes drew up and down my body. "You're gonna need some time. You know it's at the RCC," she said.

RCC stood for "put on your best outfit and sweetest smile" but really was the acronym for the Rumford Country Club. It was the only country club in Rumford, and only the wealthiest of the community could afford its annual dues and monthly fees. With those dues came the coveted bonds. Bonds were mostly passed down in the family. Sometimes, if you hit the jackpot, they were willed to you. Rarely did bonds just go up for sale. If one did, it was compared to the price of getting a kidney.

"Don't worry, Mama." I rolled my eyes so hard I hurt myself. "I'll pull out that new Lilly Pulitzer sweater you snuck in my closet with my black pants and riding boots." I called over my shoulder as I headed upstairs, "You're not so sneaky, ya know."

From Manhattan to Bitsy's kitchen. Something I'd never seen coming a week ago.

Chapter Two

Miles and miles of Kentucky's famous post fencing zipped by as Mama zoomed her Mercedes convertible around the curves of the old country roads that led into Rumford's downtown.

"Right over there was where I won my first baking contest." I pointed to the Family Feud Diner, aptly named for the feud the Bruner family had had while naming the place after they'd bought it. "I still can't believe I beat all those women in your Friends of the Library Club."

"Gawd," Mama cackled. "Do you remember their faces when they realized a thirteen-year-old child had out-baked them?"

"Do I ever." I laughed along with her. I sat up in the passenger seat and looked around. "It looks like the Beautification Committee has really stepped up."

There were some new clothing boutiques that looked straight out of Manhattan, an upscale coffeehouse, even a wine shop mixed in with the old hardware store, pet clinic, sheriff's department, and town hall where the mayor's office was located.

"We are, big time. How do you like the Garden Club's contribution to the hanging flags and baskets off the new carriage lights?" Mama asked when we stopped at the red light.

The new lights Mama was talking about dotted each side of Main Street. There was a dowel rod on each of the lampposts where a basket of fall flowers hung along with an ornamental flag.

"They are pretty," I said.

Instead of the old brick buildings that had once stand side-by-side as I remembered, each shop had taken on a life of its own. Some shops had colorful awnings with the shop's name printed on them. There were a couple of café tables inside a little fenced-in area in front of Small Talk Café. The post office even had a new facelift with its painted gray brick. The broken-up sidewalk (that I'd used to jump over, trying not to step on a crack because I didn't want to break my Bitsy's back) had been replaced with a fancy brick paved sidewalk that added to the charm of the revitalization.

"Oh, no." My heart fell into my stomach when we passed Ford's Bakery, or what had once been the bakery. "What happened to Ford's?" I asked when we passed a vacant whitewashed red brick building.

The growing ivy on the front of the building covered up most of the For Sale sign in the large front window. The old bakery could have used some fixing up like what had been done to the rest of the downtown area, though the ivy was warm and inviting.

"The Fords decided to retire," Mama said, as if I didn't remember all the times I'd spent there. "None of their children or grandchildren wanted to continue the business."

"There's no other bakery in town?" I questioned.

"No. It's a shame, too. Your daddy sure does miss their caramel long johns." She turned right on Country Club Lane.

Even though Mama was enjoying taking me down memory
lane, I wasn't interested.

*   *   *

"You've kept yourself busy, Mama," I said, changing the
subject.

It was true. Mama was an active member of the community.
She was in the Junior League, Garden Club, Friends of the
Library Club, and Volunteering Club as well as on a tennis team
at the Rumford Country Club.

"I have. I'm not gonna dry up like an old turd," she joked.

I shook my head. Mama had a wicked sense of humor behind
closed doors.

"You'll have to borrow the car and drive through town,
maybe stop at a few of the new shops. You won't believe all of the
changes in the last ten years." She was good at reminding me
that I'd been gone way too long. I swallowed back any retort.
"I'll even swing for a new bag for you."

Out of the corner of my eye, I could see Mama eyeballing
my big bag that I carried everywhere with me. It had a sketch
notebook so I could jot down my ideas for recipes as they came
to me; pens and pencils, because I never knew which one I
wanted to write with; a flashlight so I could get a good look in
all the nooks and crannies of different pastries I might encounter
throughout the day, since I believed details were very important
in the pastry industry; mints for my palate; bobby pins, because
I never knew when someone might ask for a baking hand and

I'd need to pin my hair back; hand sanitizer, because tastings could happen at any moment and I'd need clean hands; money; lipstick; and a bottle of water.

"I'm happy with the bag I've got." I patted it as the thing overtook my lap.

"You aren't bringing that into the RCC, are you?" Mama asked. I didn't need to look at her face to hear the sarcasm in her voice.

Before we pulled up to the valet at the front of the club-house, Mama gave me instructions. "Now remember your manners. The 'Yes, ma'ams' and 'Thank yous.'"

"I'm not ten." I shook my head and let the attendant open my door.

While I waited for Mama to sign us in, I couldn't help but let the comfort of the country club fill me with warmth. I'd spent many of my teenage days and nights here. Yellow daffodils curved along the sidewalk leading up to the front entrance of the Rumford Country Club house, a historic white brick mansion. Large brick stairways on both sides of the massive porch came together in the middle with an overlook at the entrance of the club.

The flowers danced in the light breeze—so jovial, as if they were taunting me, reminding me of the last time I'd stood right here with Mama as I told her I wasn't going back to college and instead was going to culinary school.

Mama had lost her religion right there for all her country club friends to see. It hadn't been pretty. She'd yelled that I'd forgotten my raising and that she'd never forgive me for shattering her dream of her only daughter growing up in Rumford and joining the Junior League.

"Now don't be going and getting no big ideas about me joining. I'm only here temporarily," I reminded her after she signed us in.

According to the RCC bylaws, everyone who came in and out of the club had to sign in or be signed in by a member. No riffraff were allowed.

The chatter of the women who'd already gotten to the Junior League meeting floated out into the foyer of the clubhouse. A waitress took the cupcakes from me as soon as we walked in.

The musty old smell that I recalled to be very potent as a child didn't hit me like I'd remembered. Gone was the maroon carpet with yellow diamonds, and in its place were bamboo wood floors. The heavy drapes that had once made the clubhouse so dark had been replaced by new windows that let the light shine in. Even the midcentury furniture had been replaced with more modern leather pieces.

"It can't be!" The southern drawl screeched across the room as soon as Mama and I stepped in. "Hold my horses. Is that you, Sophia Cummings?"

The hat that covered the five-foot-six-inch tall woman flapped with each stalking step that came toward me. A tall glass of iced tea with a lemon slice wedged on the rim was in her hand.

"It's me, Charlotte Harrington." She dragged the hat off her head.

Charlotte had a beautiful head full of ginger red hair. It was a warm color that perfectly matched her sweet disposition.

She pulled me into a big hug, and we grabbed hands and jumped up and down like two little girls

"I'd heard from some of the gals down at the Sassy and Classy Salon that you'd come back to town." She pulled back and shot me a theatrical wink. "Of course, all the rest I heard is rumor, but I'm still glad to see that you are here in the flesh." She stuck the hat back on her head, tugged the straw from her drink to her lips, and took a nice long drink. "I'm a bit sad you didn't call me yourself."

"I'm sorry. I'll do better next time," I said. The big solitaire diamond ring perched on her finger blinded my eyes. I grabbed her hand. "Don't tell me you are engaged?"

"I am." A smile curled up on her face and put a sparkle in her eyes. "I'm getting married!" She bounced on the balls of her fancy heeled shoes and stuck her hand out for me to get a better look. "The wedding's this weekend. And you have to come since you're in town."

"I'd love to. Congratulations." My voice rose. "Do I know the lucky guy?"

"I doubt it. Brett Ponder." She drew her hand to her chest. "Charlotte Ponder," she sighed, but then picked right back up. "He didn't grow up in Rumford. We met in college and he's in real estate. We are livin' in sin." She curled her lips into a heavy grin, wiggling her brows. "I'm never leaving Rumford like you. Plus, he said that Rumford is growing so fast and he'd like to be part of it." She smiled. "I'm so glad to see you."

"I'm looking forward to meeting him. I'm so happy to see you. I thought I'd only be hanging out with Bitsy's friends." I took a deep breath and realized the Junior League now consisted of people my age as well as my Bitsy's.

"Did Charlotte tell you that she and her fiancé already live together?" Mama asked, walking up to us with a disapproving side-eye focused on Charlotte before darting off in another direction.

15

"I'm sorry," I said, apologizing for Bitsy's behavior. "Old school."

Unfortunately, though time in the South had passed, not many moral codes had changed.

"That Bitsy. She's something else." Charlotte cocked a brow.

"Yes, she is," I agreed, and looked over at Mama.

She was talking to some of her friends. She pointed at me. They waved; I waved back. I scanned the room.

"Is that Madison Quinn?" I asked, seeing another of our friends.

"Yes." Charlotte batted my hand. "Yoo-hoo! Madison." Charlotte grabbed her hat and waved it in the air. Apparently, her hand wasn't large enough to get someone's attention.

Madison was too busy sitting at a table talking to even hear Charlotte. That didn't stop Charlotte from grabbing my hand and dragging me across the room.

"Sophia Cummings?" Madison stood up. Right there, attached to her left boob, was her infant child. "What? You've never seen breastfeeding?" She balanced the baby with one hand and swiped one of the cupcakes off the tray as the waitress walked by.

"I think I'm shocked you're a mom." I clearly remembered in high school that she'd sworn she'd never get married and settle down. *Children* had been a swear word to her.

"Honey, there ain't no one more surprised than me and Matthew." Her lips pursed.

"Matthew Ridge?" I asked. We'd gone to high school with Matthew, who'd thought he was hotter than a Laredo parking lot in the summertime.

"The one and only. He took me out and it was all she wrote."

Madison sat back down and gestured for me to join her. Charlotte sat down at the open chair next to mine. "I was a goner. You and I both knew he was hot, but who knew he was so romantic?" She put her hand to her chest. "Mrs. Madison Ridge."

I looked between my two good friends from high school, and it was as if the last ten years haven't hindered our friendship at all.

"How are you?" Madison asked, and tapped my leg.

She gave me the tilted head, drooping eyes, and sympathetic look that I was getting used to seeing. It was the ultimate bless-your-heart look without saying the words. She peeled back the wrapper on the cupcake and devoured it in two bites.

"Other than catching my live-in boyfriend cheating on me with a coworker at my dream job, I'm good." I laughed.

"Sophia." Her dark brows slanted into a frown. She put the half-eaten cupcake on the table. "I'm so sorry. Is there anything I can do? We can do?" Madison and Charlotte nodded at each other.

"No, I'm fine," I assured her.

"We three must get together while you're in town." She gestured between Charlotte and me. "Outside of all the wedding stuff." She ate the rest of the cupcake. "Maybe downtown for some shopping and food. You will love Peacocks and Pansies. They've got the cutest clothes."

Charlotte agreed with her.

"I'd love that," I said, hoping that we could make it happen. "I couldn't believe my eyes when we drove through town. It's so pretty and cozy. Not like it used to be."

"My gosh, Charlotte, these are amazing." Madison pointed to the cupcakes. "Did your baker make these?" Madison looked at me. "Charlotte is in charge of today's dessert. A preview of what's being served at her fancy-shmancy wedding."

"Not from my baker." Charlotte's lips turned down. "That hussy—she up and canceled on me yesterday and canceled my wedding cakes. I have no idea who I can find to bake the cakes in a pinch."

Madison's jaw dropped. "Oh, honey." She paused. "Well, the Piggly Wiggly has some options."

"That's terrible," I said, putting my two cents in. It felt so good to be sitting here with them as we'd used to. Close friendships in Manhattan were hard to have. Everyone seemed to always be competing against each other. Especially in the restaurant industry.

"Mm-hmm." Charlotte took a bite of the banana chocolate cupcake. "Oh, my stars. You're right. This is delicious."

"Thank you." I crossed my arms and leaned back in the chair. "I made those this morning."

"You're kidding me." Madison had a look of shock and awe.

"Right? Mama had enough ingredients for me to throw those together," I joked.

"No, no, no." Madison shook her head. "Kidding me as in you made these?"

"I did." I nodded. This was what made me love baking so much. It warmed the souls of everyone from the brokenhearted to the happiest of hearts.

"Then you *must* do my wedding cake." Charlotte smacked the table.

"I don't know." I shook my head and sat back up. "I don't have all the equipment I need to make a wedding cake."

"A wedding cake? You mean lots of wedding cakes."

Madison pointed across me to Charlotte. "She's invited the entire town. No wonder your other baker quit," she joked.

Only I wasn't joking. I didn't have any equipment here to make the types of cakes and desserts I'd been used to making over the past few years.

"I just knew that God had another plan." Charlotte wasn't going to take no for an answer. "My daddy pays enough money to this country club that I'll see to it that you have all the stuff you need and their kitchen to make my cakes. You meet me here in the morning."

"I don't know," I said, but she was having none of it. "I do want to spend time with the two of you while I'm here. I'm more than willing to help out, but the big responsibility of making the perfect cake . . ."

She still ignored me.

"Aren't those the best?" Charlotte asked one of the Junior League members who walked by with one of my cupcakes in her hand. She pointed to me. "My baker, all the way from a fancy restaurant in Manhattan, made them." She smiled as her shoulders danced back and forth. "Just you wait until you taste my wedding cakes."

"Aren't you Bitsy's daughter?" the lady asked.

"I am." I nodded and smiled.

"I'm Carol Bauer. I'm the president of the Garden Club. You're going to have to come with Bitsy while you're in town," she said. "We'd love to have you."

"I'll do that if I'm still here." I kept reminding myself not to get sucked into staying in Rumford for too long or Mama would have me committed to all sort of things, including volunteer work.

"Come on by the shop and I'll give you the friends and family discount." Carol spoke more with a southern twang by making her vowels more crisp than drawn out.

"Shop?" I questioned.

"I own Peacocks and Pansies downtown." Her brown eyes drew up my body. "You'd look great in our boutique clothes."

"I saw your shop on our way here." I recalled seeing the cute boutique and even thinking how much it resembled some of the Manhattan boutiques I loved to wander around in.

"I have the perfect dress for you to wear to Charlotte's wedding." She nodded.

"Wedding and rehearsal dinner," Charlotte barged her way into our conversation.

"Yes. I have a lovely dress that I can see you in right now for the rehearsal." Carol and Charlotte nodded between each other.

"You're thinking the gray one, right?" Charlotte's brows lifted.

"Red." Carol's shoulders shivered with excitement. Little did she know, red wasn't my color. "I'm excited to taste your wedding cake if Sophia is baking it." Carol's eyes squinted when she smiled. "We haven't had a good baker in town since Ford's shut down."

I chewed on the edge of my lips. What on earth had I gotten myself into?

Charlotte's eyes met mine.

"I guess I am." I shrugged.

"It's settled." Charlotte clapped her hands together. "You are baking my cake."

A waitress walked by and I grabbed the only cupcake left on her tray.

Cake and Punishment

I peeled off the wrapper and took a bite. A little sense of giddiness swept through my stomach as the thought of making Charlotte's wedding cake started to sink in. I was a baker, and seeing faces like my dearest high school friends enjoying something I'd made did make me happy. After all, you can't be sad when holding a cupcake.

Chapter Three

All night long I tossed and turned. Duchess had laid on top of my head all night, which didn't help, but it was the excitement bubbling up in me about baking Charlotte's cake that really kept me awake. It was a much-needed distraction from my life. The blood pumping in my head woke my muse. If I recalled the items Mama had in her kitchen, I'd have just enough ingredients to make Red Velvet Crunchies, one of my favorite go-to cookies when I needed some comfort. One batch made a whole bunch of cookies, which was perfect for making ahead of time, freezing, and thawing as needed. I'd load Mama and Daddy's freezer up with some.

"Let's go, girl." I peeled the covers off of me and grabbed Duchess off the bed.

We crept down the back stairs that were away from my parents' bedroom and flipped on the kitchen lights. Bitsy's pantry was a baker's dream. It was a big walk-in with lights that automatically came on with a sensor. Mama had neatly stored the baking appliances I'd bought with my own money when I worked at the RCC.

I grabbed the flour, baking powder, sugars, and salt along with the box of food coloring and gels, even though I wasn't sure how old they were. I needed the red to make the classic chocolate chip cookie resemble red velvet. I was going to have to use both the red gel and the red food coloring since there wasn't enough of either separately.

I waited to turn the oven on because the dough needed to chill in the refrigerator for at least an hour. Filling the coffee pot and turning it on would make the coffee about ready when I was finished mixing the dough. Then I could enjoy a cup of coffee in the stillness of the early morning. Really early morning.

I whisked and used the hand mixer instead of the stand mixer. The least amount of noise I could make was best. Mama would be all worried about me, and I didn't want her hovering over me while I was here. The only thing that was going to get me through the grief was baking. It always helped.

"Bitsy would die if she saw this kitchen at two AM." I spoke to Duchess as if she completely understood. She picked her head up off the chair cushion and stared at me. There was flour all over the countertops and some dusting on the floor from when I'd set the mixer too high and created a plume of dust. The front of the pink two-piece pajama set Bitsy had neatly laid on the bed—and I'd put on to sleep in—was now dusty as well.

"Mmm." The hum of my father filled the silence I was so enjoying. "I thought I smelled coffee."

I had the bowl of dough in my hands to put in the refrigerator.

"Hi, Dad." My eyes dipped. "I'm sorry. Did I wake you?"

He pulled the refrigerator door open and smiled.

"Nah. I couldn't sleep." He winked. "Like you, I've got a lot on my mind."

I stuck the bowl in the fridge and shut the door. When I turned around, Dad had already pulled two mugs out of the cabinet and filled them.

"And I haven't gotten to spend much time with you since you got back." He pushed two chairs out from the table.

"I know you're busy. Mama said you've got some big case coming up." I picked Duchess up and put her in my lap when I sat down. She purred under all that fancy fur of hers. "It seems like we are a lot alike in the sleep department."

"Yep." He took a sip of coffee. "Is that the mess of Red Velvet Crunchies?"

"You know it." I smiled at the thought that my dad knew what ingredients I used for his favorite cookies. "I figured I'd take some with me to the RCC when I meet Charlotte."

"Your mama told me about you stepping up to bake Charlotte's cake. Are you sure you're up for that?" he asked with a concerned look on his face.

"Yeah." I pishposhed. "You know Charlotte. I'm sure what she had planned is some gaudy, over-the-top, sparkly thing."

"She's definitely an over-the-top girl." Dad laughed. "But don't make excuses about why you're up baking. You always carried cookies with you."

"Something I still do." It was true. Ever since I'd discovered I was pretty good at baking, I'd started to carry examples around with me and get people's opinions. "You know . . ." I gnawed on my thought to make sure it came out the way I wanted it to. "It was about getting other people's opinions because you and

Mama would've told me that my cookies were better than Mrs. Fields'."

"They are." Dad cocked a brow.

"Seriously, what was really my validation that my cookies were good was the look on people's faces after they ate a cookie that I created from scratch, with these hands." I lifted my hands in the air and rotated them in front of me. Duchess looked up and let out a soft meow. Dad and I let out a low chuckle. I went back to patting her. "I love how cookies make people feel better. It's like a magic potion for people to talk their problems out with me."

"You've always had a knack with talking to people. Another trait you got from your grandfather and me. That's what makes our law firm so successful. The gift of gab."

It had always been fun watching Dad in court. I'd been known to give the judge a couple of cookies a time or two while I was in the courtroom. Those were fond memories, and I was sure that was the reason I'd become a pastry chef.

"You are very good at what you do." Dad reached over and patted my hand. "Do you have a plan?"

"Yeah." I took a sip of the coffee. "I'm going to head back to the city next week. There's no reason for me to run and hide when *I* did nothing wrong. There are tons of apartments. I've got plenty of money saved up to put down a deposit. I've still got my job, and I'm able to pretty much avoid Noah by going into the restaurant in the middle of the night or when he's off work. It's not like my desserts have to be made right at the time the customer orders them. It was just fun pairing the desserts to Noah's dishes."

"You are a smart and kind girl who's also pretty." Dad had

to add the last pretty part because he was my dad. I smiled. "You know, you don't have to go back. You're always welcome here."

"Dad . . ." I wondered if Mama had put him up to talking to me. "I'm not about to go to the Piggly Wiggly to get a job in the baking department. I want to create and not let anyone tell me what I can make. That's not here in Rumford."

"I'm just letting you know that this is your home and you are always welcome." He stood up and bent down, kissing the top of my head. "I think I'm going to go read in the library for a couple of hours before I have to go in to the office."

"Thanks, Dad." I looked up and took comfort in the warmth of his eyes, so thankful that he hadn't given me love advice.

He and Mama didn't understand. How could they? They'd been high school royalty in their day. The homecoming king and queen, the prom king and queen. The couple people like me hated in high school. They were the "it" couple and still were. They'd loved each other from the first time they'd set eyes on each other in the baby pool at the RCC. I was sure of it.

With another cup of coffee in me, it was time to turn the Red Velvet Crunchies dough into a warm finished product. I put Duchess in the empty chair. She curled into a tight fur ball. Once I'd retrieved two baking pans and lined them with parchment paper, preheated the oven, and rolled the dough into two-inch balls, the crunchies were in the oven making the entire house smell like cookie heaven.

There was some extra dough that I put in the refrigerator. It would last up to three days. I took a sticky note from the built-in desk and scribbled some quick baking instructions in case Mama got a wild hair and decided to use her oven.

Cake and Punishment

After the cookies were baked with a nice crackly top, I put a few extra chocolate chips on the tops for looks and let them sit on the baking rack while I ran upstairs to throw on my shorts and tee. A good morning jog was exactly what I needed to start thinking about Charlotte's cake before I met with her.

The dew was coating all of the lawns in my parents' gated community. There was a faint line of orange on the horizon that would soon fully engulf the sky. Rumford did have the most amazing sunrises.

With each hit of the pavement, my creative juices flowed. I created all sorts of different flavors to present to Charlotte—unless she'd already picked out the type of cake she wanted. I even created a mental list of items I'd need for all the fun piping that made wedding cakes ornamental and gorgeous. When it came to weddings, I knew it was the presentation that caught the eye but the inside that warmed the soul.

After I got back, I quickly showered and threw on some jeans and a nice sweater along with my old pearls. The crunchies were nice and firm. The gooey middle I sank my teeth into when I tasted one was the perfect consistency and sure to please anyone's palate. I took out a few baggies and filled them, sticking them in my bag.

I borrowed Bitsy's car to meet up with Charlotte. We were meeting in the grand ballroom, which was in a different building on the country club property than the clubhouse.

I took my time driving through town so I could get another look at all the changes. There just so happened to be an available parking space in front of Small Talk Café. I had a few minutes before I met with Charlotte, and a cup of coffee sounded good.

The café tables inside the picket fence on the outside of the café were occupied. The smiles on the diners' faces and chatter warmed any chill that hung in the air from the fall day.

"Mornin'." A southern drawl greeted me from over my shoulder as I reached for the door. "Let me get that."

"Thank you," I said to the man in the sheriff's uniform. "I appreciate it."

My face flushed. It'd been a long time since any man had held a door for me. His charming smile, good looks, and gentlemanly manners made my heart flip. *Chivalry isn't dead*, I thought to myself.

"My pleasure." He flashed that smile again. "Are you related to Bitsy and Robert?" he asked, and motioned to the car.

"I'm their daughter, Sophia." I stepped into the line to order my coffee.

"Carter." He held his hand out. We exchanged pleasantries. "How are your folks?"

"They are good." I was next in line. "It was nice to meet you, Carter."

"Mornin', Sheriff." The young girl behind the counter glanced over my shoulder as if I weren't even there. "I saw you coming in, so your coffee is already down there." She nodded to the end of the counter.

I looked at Carter again. He seemed pretty young, I thought as I looked at his side profile. He had pronounced cheekbones and a sharp, clearly defined jawline.

"That's mighty nice of you." He thanked the girl. "Good to meet you, Sophia. Please tell your parents hello." He took a step out of line and then stopped. "If you need anything while you're here, don't hesitate to give me a call."

He took a business card out of his pocket and handed it to me. I couldn't help but notice he didn't have a wedding ring on.

"Thank you, but I'm not in town long." I returned the smile and took the card.

"All right, then. You have a good visit." He winked and moved on down the counter, stopping to talk to a few folks on his way to get his coffee.

"Can I help you?" The girl behind the counter cocked a brow. The tone she used with me was much different than the one she'd used with the sheriff.

"Black coffee, please." My southern manners were slowly coming back along with the southern accent I'd thought I'd lost.

"Next," the girl said, and glanced over my shoulder. My signal to move along.

The sheriff made his rounds back through the coffee shop and gave me one last nod before he left the café.

The bold coffee was a nice surprise for a morning pick-me-up, and it got me good and alert for my meeting with Charlotte. It wasn't a gourmet coffee like the ones we served with my pastries at the restaurant, but this was a café, not a coffeehouse—or a bakery, for that matter.

When I got to the RCC, the valet took my name and directed me where to pull up in front of the old ornate building. From what I'd heard yesterday, it'd been restored when the country club had redecorated the clubhouse, and I couldn't wait to see what it looked like for a wedding.

"It's come a long way from our cotillion." Charlotte was already there when I entered the ballroom.

"You aren't kidding." Happy memories of me dancing

with my dad during the cotillion came back to me as I twirled around the gorgeous ballroom with white-and-gold-checkered floors.

Charlotte's romantic decoration elements and towering floral arrangements were dripping around the room.

"A bit over the top?" she asked, not really wanting my answer. "I know," she gushed.

"Wow," I gasped.

"I want that fairytale wedding." She let out a deep sigh.

"You've definitely taken full advantage of the room's extravagant beauty." I knew the cake would look stunning on the table in front of the window with the long satin drapes that spilled into a pool at the base of the window. I'd play on the blues and golds to decorate the most spectacular cake anyone in Rumford had ever seen. My creative mojo was flowing and I felt alive. Images swirled in my head.

I reached in my purse and grabbed my pencil and paper.

"What are you doing?" Charlotte asked when I sat down at one of the place settings and pushed the dishes out of the way.

"I have a design idea for you to look at." My ideas floated around in my head like the wind. If I didn't grab them while they were in there, they would float away and I'd lose them forever. "Unless you have something in mind." I'd completely forgotten that she'd had a baker before me. Since the wedding was so close, she probably did have a design.

"No. Bad juju from the last baker, so I want to start fresh." Her eyes narrowed. "Though I did love the almond cake with raspberry filling."

"That's easy." I smiled. Knowing that recipe by heart would

make the cake-baking process so much easier for me. Plus, it was all basic ingredients that any grocery store would carry.

The elegant shades of the ceiling's graceful, painted details reflected the romantic feel Charlotte was going for. Towering centerpieces of roses, hydrangeas, and tulips sat atop golden bird-cages strung with glittering, twinkling lights. Rich, blue table linens overlaid with delicate Battenburg lace were accented by the ten place settings of gilded crystal and china around each of the round tables. Shiny silverware lay on top of cloth napkins. The massive windows overlooking the breathtaking courtyard of the Rumford Country Club invoked memories of Charlotte and me playing while our mothers played couples tennis on the courts beyond the courtyard.

"Fairytale wedding you want"—the pencil in my hand had its own mind as it sketched across the paper, bringing my thoughts to life—"a fairytale cake you will get." I finished the quick drawing, stood up, and held the paper to face her.

"Sophia," she gasped. Tears filled her eyes. "I've never seen something so beautiful. I can only imagine what it will look like in color."

"This layer will be in gold fondant." I pointed to each layer as I spoke. "This layer will be blue like the drapes with the gold accents on the swirls." Layer by layer I told her my color vision.

It took even my breath away.

"You being here completes my vision of a fairytale wedding." Charlotte squeezed me in a big hug. "Can you believe it?"

"No. It's amazingly stunning," I said. I wasn't sure what it was; I'd not felt this creative in years and the ideas were plucking my brain so fast I could barely keep up with the mental pictures with the few notes I was able to jot down. "And seeing you this happy makes me happy and a little ashamed I've not been a good friend over the last ten years. There's no excuse. I should've come home more. Tried harder."

"All that matters is that you're here now and you're making it up to me by making my cake." Charlotte might've been over the top, but her heart was always in a good spot. "Now"—she sat down at the table and pulled a chair out for herself while I sat back down—"tell me more about why you're really here. I mean, I know you've been cheated on and I've heard all the gossip, but I want to hear the details from you."

"The gossip is probably true." Tears burned the edges of my eyelids. I blinked them back. I stuck the pad of paper and pencil back in my purse to get my mind and hands off my words. "Noah's the head chef and I'm the head pastry chef in a very upscale restaurant in Manhattan. Our works complemented each other. We had the perfect relationship."

By the look in her eyes, I could tell she was loving my very own fairytale—the one I'd thought I had.

"We even moved in together." I let out a long deep sigh. I gulped and tucked a strand of hair behind my ear. It was so difficult to talk about. "I went to work on a whim on my day off and he was in a very compromising position with the maître d' of our restaurant."

"Hush your mouth," Charlotte snarled. "Go on."

"I also found out that the entire staff and our little small circle of restaurant friends knew about it and no one ever told me. I dumped him faster than a speeding ticket."

"I reckon you better have." Charlotte slowly shook her head.

"Well, I'm glad you're here. It won't be too hurtful for you to be at my wedding, will it?"

"Heck, no." Seeing how this ballroom got my creative juices flowing was all I needed to be all in. "This will be a good distraction and will help clear my head so I can decide what I need to do when I go back."

"Go back?" Charlotte's jaw dropped. "You aren't?"

"I didn't quit my job. I took a few weeks off." The thought of seeing Noah when I got back made me sick. I chalked it up to not enough time having gone by.

"If you're sure, then I want you to get a look at the kitchen and meet Emile." She jerked her head, looking around the room. "He's the club's head chef and magnifico," she said in her best Italian voice, only it came out hillbilly style. She kissed her gathered fingertips before she exploded a wide palm from her lips. "He's always here super early getting ready for the day."

We stood up and looked around. No one was in the room but the two of us.

"I guess he's back in the kitchen, which you need to see because it's so different from when you worked here." She curled her nose.

"I loved working here. Old Evelyn Moss let me bake whatever I wanted, plus it drove Mama crazy that I was here baking her friends' desserts. She was so mad." It was another time Mama had just about had a heart attack right where I was standing.

"If you thought Evelyn was old then, wait until you see her now." Charlotte tilted her head to the side toward the offices.

"No." My jaw dropped. "Evelyn is still here?"

"Still here? She's the general manager now." Charlotte's brows lifted.

She pulled on the sleeve of my sweater. "I can't wait for you to meet Emile. A little bit of a pickle, but he loves a southern lady."

She pranced in front of me like a blue-ribbon racehorse on our way out of the ballroom and down the hall toward the kitchen.

My excitement on seeing the fully remodeled and updated modern kitchen quickly stopped when a blood-curdling scream echoed out of the kitchen's swinging doors.

"What was that?" I asked.

Rushing past Charlotte, I prayed there wasn't anyone hurt by a stove fire or a cut-off finger. I'd been around many kitchen accidents and they weren't pretty. I flung open the kitchen doors.

"Help!" The shivering girl pointed behind the steel island where the food had started to be prepped. "He's . . ."

"What?" Charlotte asked. "Spit it out."

I eased around the island and looked down.

"Emile?" Charlotte gasped at the lifeless body of her wedding chef, who looked as if he'd met his untimely demise with one swipe of his own cast iron skillet.

Chapter Four

Though I'd been living in New York City for almost ten years and among more than eight million people, never once had I happened upon a murder. I'd been back in Rumford for less than a week, gotten roped into baking my old high school friend's wedding cake, and now her chef was dead.

"This is not happening." Charlotte's reddish hair bounced, as did her shoulders with each hiccupy sob. "Please, please tell me he's not . . ." Both of us stood there over Emile's lifeless body, our eyes fixed on him.

"Dead." I finished her sentence for her, the sting of tears on my eyelids. "I think he is." I gulped back more tears and turned Charlotte away from the body. "We just need to wait for the police to get here." I rubbed her back and continued to look over her shoulder at the man.

No amount of rubbing her back and saying "It's gonna be all right" was going to help her. The truth was, I didn't know how to console her when I could barely keep it together myself. I swallowed hard looking at the skillet. My eyes shifted to Emile's chef jacket. One side of his collar was still tucked in as if he'd been putting on the coat and maybe gotten hit from behind.

My eyes moved up and down the counter to see if anything was messed up or if Emile had even tried to fight back with something. Sadly, it didn't appear that he'd had time to react to his attacker, and the only thing next to him was a white piece of paper.

"He had such great ideas for the menu for the wedding." Charlotte's voice was shaky. "Who on earth would do such a thing?"

"I don't know." I dug my hand in my bag and pulled out a bag of cookies. "Here." I stuck one in her face. "This will help," I said, and helped her to the other side of the kitchen, not only to let her sit down but to get out of eye shot of Emile.

And it did allow me to go back and look at exactly what was written on that piece of paper. Not that it was any of my business. Curiosity ran in my blood and I loved to blame it on Bitsy.

Careful not to trip over Emile's body or the skillet, I bent down and noticed the paper was a menu written in some English but mostly French. It was a beautiful language that I'd picked up bits and pieces by ear while in pastry school, since many baked goodies had French names. The delicious and fattening ones, anyways.

The menu appeared to be food that'd be served for a dinner setting and not a lunch setting, so I wondered if he'd been working on tonight's menu. There were gourmet appetizers like Champignon Portabella aux Quatre Fromages and Crêpe au Fromage de Chèvre. The main dish items seemed to be mussels, seared duck, and even roasted rack of lamb. The more I glanced at the list, the more I realized these were way too fancy for Rumford, Kentucky.

"Miss." A gentleman in a police uniform tapped me on the shoulder.

I looked around and stood up when I realized the police had gotten there.

"If you don't mind to step over there." He pointed to the corner where Charlotte and Jane, the waitress who had found Emile, were standing. "Our homicide detective will be here shortly to ask you a few questions."

I nodded and wiped back the tears that'd fallen silently down my cheek. The thought and care it appeared Emile had put into his menus was meticulous, and as a baker, it hurt to know his creations hadn't come to life. Poor Emile.

The three of us sat there mindlessly eating the entire bag of cookies I'd pulled out of my bag. We watched several men in brown uniforms come in and out of the kitchen as we waited for the detective to show up.

They were collecting evidence, taking pictures, jotting down all sorts of notes. Everything and everyone stopped when Carter from the café entered the kitchen. A few words were murmured to him before he slid his eyes toward me.

I overheard one of them say something about *bride* and *baker* and an upcoming wedding that would probably need to be canceled.

I was beginning to think Charlotte's wedding was cursed and she wasn't going to have her fairytale wedding after all. *Over my dead body*, I glared back at Carter.

I was trying to be the strong one and put on a brave face. My stomach was in knots.

"Listen to me." I bent down and got real close to Charlotte, forcing her to look at me. "You are going to have that fairytale wedding and that cake I drew for you," I said. Charlotte nodded as if she absolutely believed me; then her eyes filled with tears. "Do you hear me? Even if I have to figure out who whacked Emile."

I put the bag in her hand, and she looked up at me with mascara streaks down her cheeks and nodded, clutching the baggie to her chest.

"Did I hear you correctly? You know who, as you put it, whacked Emile?" Carter had walked up without me noticing. "Me?" I blushed. "Of course I don't. I was just saying to my friend here that no matter what, I was going to make sure she had her dream wedding."

"Like your wedding?" He arched a sly brow.

Was he trying to get personal information about me? I wondered because it was a very odd time to be asking such questions.

"She's not married." Charlotte sucked back some air. "She was just cheated on."

I looked up to the ceiling and rolled my eyes. Did we have to talk about this now?

"And she's talking about me and my wedding, Carter. This . . . this will make all the headlines on all the social pages." Her arms curled around her waist.

"No, it won't," I assured her. Not that I knew it for sure, but it was what she needed to hear right this very moment. "We are going to have the most spectacular wedding that will make everyone forget about Emile as soon as they see you and this reception." My eyes slid past Carter and over to Emile's body. I started to feel queasy.

There were several people standing over him and squatting near him. Some of them were taking photos while others were writing in notebooks and on their phones. A couple of people were taking an interest in the cast iron skillet. Some of the deputies were dusting for fingerprints. At least it appeared that way, given the little brush and black powder in their hands that they swiped along the door, the skillet, and other places around the kitchen.

Jane, the waitress who'd found Emile, had been moved away from us and was tucked in the furthest corner of the kitchen surrounded by men in suits. Her five-foot-four-inch frame slumped against the wall. She chewed on her fingernails, her blue eyes focused on Emile. "I would never wish anything bad upon anyone," Jane said calmly in a voice loud enough for us to hear. She pushed her blonde bangs out of her face off to the side. "But he wasn't the nicest person to work for. Especially to women. He had no respect for any of us, including Evelyn. He was the nastiest to her."

Carter raked his fingers through his hair and turned his attention back to me. I cocked a brow. It seemed to me that he should be spending his time on someone who knew Emile instead of wasting his time on us.

"Unfortunately, I'm going to have to ask you a few questions." Carter bent down to Charlotte; there was eagerness in his eyes.

"Now?" I interrupted. He turned his head over his shoulder to look at me. I gulped. "Can't you see she's beside herself?"

With a slow ease, he planted his hands on his thighs and pushed himself to standing. He was a good four inches taller than me. His nearness shot a dizzy current through me, making me unsteady on my feet. He reached out and took me by the arm.

"Are you okay, Ms. Cummings?" He remembered who I was.

"Yes. I'm fine." I swallowed hard and put a thin smile on my lips. He returned it with a great big toothy grin. His deep dimples nearly pushed me over the edge.

"I don't think you're fine." He snapped his fingers at a deputy and pointed to Charlotte.

The deputy rushed over to Charlotte. Carter walked me over to the island workstation just a few feet from Emile. He pulled a stool out from underneath it and patted for me to sit down. With my elbows firmly planted on the island, I rested my head in my hands.

Carter motioned for another deputy to bring over a bottle of water for me. He stood between me and the body. I couldn't help but think he was doing it on purpose.

"Drink this." He twisted off the cap and handed it to me. "It's very difficult to see a dead body," he spoke with a whisper.

A warm shiver sailed through me by the mere touch of our hands when he handed me the bottle of water. I brushed it off as a comforting gesture since he was trying so hard to make sure I was okay.

"Thank you." My voice cracked.

"You seem a little bit more together than Charlotte, so maybe you can answer some questions for me." His eyes were sharp and assessing.

My mind swirled with thoughts of the crime television shows I've seen where the detective was trying to read the body language of suspects. My heart started to race. Did Carter think Charlotte or I did this?

"I'll try," I choked out, not eager to discuss what was going on.

"How well did you know the victim?" He asked.

"Not at all. I'd never laid eyes on him until this." He couldn't possibly think I did this. "I never met him."

"What were you doing before you found Emile's body?" he asked, pulling out one of those little notebooks you'd see on TV.

"We didn't find him." I shook my head. I was quick to point that out. "Jane did." I looked at Jane, who was still huddled in the corner.

"Go through the motions," he encouraged me. "Tell me everything from the time you got here until now."

"Well . . ." I thought back to the creative streak I'd been having, but Emile's dead body had seemed to suck that right out of me. "I was drawing Charlotte's cake in the ballroom. She wanted me to meet Emile."

"Draw a cake?" His brows rose in confusion.

"Yes." I unzipped my purse and took out my notebook, flipping to the design. I handed it to him.

"You drew this?" he asked. His big brown eyes looking at me. I gnawed on the corner of my lip and slowly nodded. "Impressive."

He handed my notebook back to me. I slipped it back in my purse.

"Thank you. I take a lot of pride in my work," I said. There was one bag of crunchies left in my purse. I took them out and offered the open bag to Carter.

"What exactly is your work?" he asked as he eyed the cookies.

"I'm a pastry chef. Charlotte's baker can't bake her wedding cake. Since I'm in town for a visit, I agreed to bake it for her." He didn't need to know my life story and why I was really here.

"Visit?" he asked with a deadpan expression.

"I'm here to visit my parents," I said, wondering why he'd asked me about why I was in town. "What does this have to do with Emile?" I kept my eye contact but my gaze became glazed.

"I like to know exactly who is in my crime scene and why. Standard procedure." He looked down at his notebook, then back up to me. "You are baking Charlotte's cake today and that's why you're here?" he questioned and wrote something down in that little notebook of his.

"No. Not today. I was just taking a look around to see what I'm going to need to bake her cakes." I offered a weak smile before taking another drink of the water. Not that I was thirsty— I had to avoid his stare. "We are longtime friends. Take one. I promise they will make you feel better."

Not that I was thirsty. I had to avoid his stare.

"You and Charlotte?" he asked. He stuck his hand in the bag and looked around the kitchen before he took a bite. "You made these?"

"Yes, Charlotte and I are high school friends," I said, screwing the cap back on the bottle and setting it on the island. I continued while he took another cookie, "Anyway, we heard a loud scream and bang on our way to the kitchen for her to introduce me to Emile and for me to see the kitchen. That's when Jane ran out of the swinging door and we called you."

About that time the swinging door swooshed opened, smacking the wall.

Carter looked under his brows at a deputy who was staring at him. With his pen in his hand, he pointed to Evelyn Moss. The deputy immediately rushed over to Evelyn.

"He's dead?" Evelyn's voice escalated as she dropped down onto a stool, her mouth gaped open.

"What happened after you called me?" Carter didn't miss a beat. He turned my attention back to him.

"All this. We waited right outside the kitchen door until y'all showed up." I gestured around me. Everything and everyone was still buzzing around, in and out of the kitchen.

"Charlotte?" A man in a blue business suit walked into the kitchen. His dark eyes darted from underneath his heavy brows around the room, and when he saw her huddled in the corner, he ran over to her as if she was the only thing that mattered to him in the entire world. It had to be Brett Ponder, her fiancé.

"Brett!" She jumped into his arms, burying her head in the nape of his neck. He stroked her hair and whispered something in her ear. She nodded against his suit coat.

"What exactly did you hear that made you rush to the kitchen?" Carter drew me back to his questioning.

I let out a deep breath as my thoughts went back to that terrible moment when we'd heard Jane shriek.

"I told you. There was a gut-wrenching scream that came from the kitchen. Charlotte and I ran in that direction, and that's when Jane ran out." The image of seeing Emile after we walked into the kitchen was something I couldn't un-see. "I touched the door," I gasped when I realized my fingerprints were on the door.

"You're not a suspect, but we will need your prints to rule yours out. Or we can pull them from the criminal database." He eyes raked over me.

"I'm not a criminal." My eyes popped open, my back straightened.

"I'm joking, Ms. Cummings." He smiled, showing me those dimples again, making my heart go pitter-patter.

"Oh." My shoulders slumped. "Sophia. My name is Sophia."

"Sophia Cummings." His lips formed another grin. "Sophia the cookie baker."

For a second too long, we held a gaze. There was a familiarity about him that I shrugged off because I would have remembered those dimples.

"Sir." A deputy came over, pulling Carter's eyes away from mine. "Do you want to talk to Ms. Moss before we let her go?"

"Yep. Give me a minute with Ms. Cummings." Carter looked back at me. "Sophia," his soft voice nudged me.

"Yes?" I answered. He looked as if he wanted to tell me something. He continued to hesitate.

"I've got to go, but I'd like to stop by and question you when you've had time to calm down." His southern drawl was music to my ears—a far cry from the accent of the northern men I'd dated over the past ten years. Noah's was the worst. "Sometimes in these situations, our mind has a tendency to settle down and we remember things that we can't when adrenaline takes over our bodies. Say tomorrow?"

Maybe it was just the adrenaline from seeing a dead body that was making my heart hammer in my chest.

"Sure." I nodded.

His smile drew up to his eyes. He kept them on me as he pulled something out of his shirt pocket.

"Here is my card." He held his card out between two fingers. "Call me."

"You already gave me one this morning." I patted my purse. "Take the cookies. I think you're going to need them to get through the day."

Out of the corner of my eye, I saw Charlotte and Brett walking toward us.

"Hey, man." Brett shook his head. He had short black hair with a little bit of a curl on the edges. I could see why Charlotte had fallen in love with him. He had her curled in his arm as if he were shielding her from the world. My jealous streak kicked in and I couldn't help but be envious of the love between them. "This is crazy."

Carter and Brett shook hands.

"Crazy? We are cursed." Charlotte's eyes were red around the edges. Much brighter than her hair color. She sniffled, bringing her finger up under her nose. "The baker? And now the chef?" Little *eeps* came out of her body as she tried to breathe through her nose.

"Oh, honey. We aren't cursed." He curled her tighter against his chest, making her sob all over again. "This is crazy," Brett said again.

"Yeah. You can take your bride home, but you know I'm going to have to ask you some questions." Carter looked at Brett first before directing his words to Charlotte.

They both nodded. Charlotte dragged her face off the poor guy's suit coat, leaving a trail of tears and black streaks of mascara on it.

"Brett, this is my friend Sophia I was telling you about." She forced a smile on her face. Her eyes dipped with sadness.

"It's so nice to meet you." I held my hand out and shook it. "Though not under these circumstances."

"It's really nice to meet you." He offered the best smile he could under Charlotte's duress. "I can't wait to taste your cakes. Charlotte hasn't stopped talking about it until now."

Charlotte glared at him and turned back to me.

"I'll give you a call later." Charlotte's voice cracked.

"Come by for a beer tonight and see if she's calmed down; then maybe she can give her statement," Brett said to Carter.

"Sounds good, because I might need a couple after today," Carter said before Brett led Charlotte out of the kitchen.

There seemed to be a friendship between the two men. It wasn't uncommon for people in Rumford to know everyone. I guessed I'd been gone for so long that I barely knew anyone anymore.

"Sir." The deputy who was talking to Evelyn came back over to Carter. "She had an appointment this morning so she took off, but she said to call her anytime."

"I told you I wanted you to keep her here." Carter's jaw tensed. The deputy shuffled his feet before he walked off.

Carter's lips curled together. He turned back to me. "Sophia, it was nice to meet you this morning and see you again here. I look forward to your call." He held the bag of cookies in the air. "Thanks for the sweet treat."

"One thing." I reached out and touched his arm to stop him from walking away.

"Yes." Amusement lurked in his eyes.

"That skillet." I pointed to it. "That can't be Emile's."

"Why?" His eyes hooded. "Do you know who it belongs to? Because I'm pretty sure that's what did the job, even though there's no evidence of blood on it."

"No, but any skilled southern chef doesn't cook or bake or even have something so new in their kitchen." I sucked in a deep breath. Carter wasn't following me. Why should he? He wasn't a pastry chef. "I'm a southern baker. Emile was making southern dishes here at the RCC. That's the only thing Evelyn Moss likes to serve in her kitchen. He'd have a seasoned skillet. Even before you cook on a new skillet, you season it. But why would he even have out a skillet if he was preparing a French menu for tonight?" I looked up and over Carter's shoulder in deep thought, talking to myself. "Which doesn't make sense if he was preparing for supper here."

"Excuse me?" Carter asked, bringing me back to reality.

"I was just thinking about that menu Emile was working on before—you know." I made a gesture as if I were banging my head with something, like the skillet. "There was a menu next to his body, and it looked like a French menu for supper. I just assumed that it was for here, but Evelyn doesn't allow French cuisine. It's all southern food, all the time."

"And you knew it was French how?" His cute dimples were long gone.

"Being a pastry chef, I'm around a lot of French people and desserts." I'd leave out all the details. "And I can read some French."

He pulled out his notepad again and jotted down what I was saying.

"Back to the skillet and seasoning?" He appeared to be very interested in my knowledge, and I wondered how it was going to help his investigation.

"Seasoned skillets give extra flavor to dishes and desserts. When I get a new skillet, I rub olive oil all around it, inside and out. Then I put it in a very hot oven and bake it. This is repeated several times until the skillet looks very old, but the oil's been baked into the cast iron before you cook or bake in it," I said.

"Oh. So whoever did this might not have been a chef?" he asked.

I agreed.

"You mean Evelyn Moss?" he asked.

My stomach dropped. I reached into his bag of cookies and took one out.

"Evelyn?" I questioned with surprise, taking a bite of the cookie. "No way. I worked for her here when I was in high school."

Evelyn was a hardball, but she'd been in charge of the kitchen when I was there. She was just being the boss.

"According to the few people here from the kitchen staff, she and Emile had a very volatile relationship." He looked at Jane. Some of the kitchen staff had arrived. They were putting their chef's jackets with the RCC logo on the chest pocket over their street clothes and had gathered around Jane. She started to get upset all over again.

The employees took turns consoling Jane, either by talking to her, rubbing her back, or hugging her. Some did all three.

"Do me a favor and think back to when you worked here and how she was then. Her relationship with the kitchen staff. When you call me, you can tell me anything you can remember," Carter said to me.

I looked up and caught an unexpected look of concern on his face.

"That was a long time ago, and the only volatile relationship I can remember from then was the one between me and Bitsy." My forehead puckered.

"Your mother?" He cocked a brow. I nodded. "She's one of the sweetest Rumford citizens I know."

"You aren't her daughter," I joked, and looked down at my fingers. "Evelyn? Really?"

"You'd be surprised what a heated argument between two people can produce. Not just yelling and shoving, pushing around, but it can lead to murder." His chest heaved up and down with the deep breaths.

"Yes, I can imagine." My mind curled back to the fight

between me and Noah. I could've killed him with my bare hands that day, I'd been so mad. "I just couldn't do it and neither could Evelyn."

Evelyn a killer?

"Everyone who had issues with Emile is a suspect at this time." He shoved a cookie in his mouth. "These are great." At least I think those were the words he muffled before he ate another one. "What are they?" He rotated the cookie in front of him.

"Red Velvet Crunchies." My heart warmed as it always did when that happy face showed after someone took a bite of one of my creations. "It's a twist on the standard chocolate chip cookie."

"They aren't flat like most homemade cookies." He noticed the thickness of the cookie.

"That's one of my baking secrets." I winked as if I had some big baking secret, when in reality all pastry chefs knew that in order to make a nice, gooey cookie, you had to stack two rolled cookie dough balls on top of each other and bake them that way.

His eyes narrowed. There was a sly look on his face.

"I'll give you a call." I waved behind me as I walked out of the kitchen, very aware his eyes were on me.

Chapter Five

Sheriff's deputies and officials were hanging around the hallway and inside the ballroom, either talking to each other
about how they couldn't believe there'd been a murder in Rumford, speculating on who could've killed Emile, or on their cells
talking about the murder. Evelyn's name was on the lips of all of
them. Poor Evelyn. They'd already arrested her, held court, and
convicted her before Emile's body was even cold.

The sheriff's department was busy and their radar wasn't on
me, so I weaved in and out of the crowd to take a shortcut out of
the RCC to my car through the offices. It had been my usual
way to sneak out when I'd worked here in high school so I could
ditch out without having to stop and talk to Mama or her friends.
I walked down a long, narrow hallway with office doors lining
each side. At the far end was a door with an exit sign above it and
my escape route to the employee parking lot. I couldn't get out of
there fast enough.

"But what am I going to do? I can't just cancel all the supper
reservations or close the place down. We have members on the

golf course and tennis courts that will be here in a couple of hours to have lunch." The familiar voice of Evelyn Moss spilled out into the dead silence of the hallway from the cracked office door that bore her name on a gold nameplate.

Heavens to Betsy, they couldn't close the RCC—unless the sheriff's department wanted to have a riot on their hands. The RCC had never closed as far back as I could remember. We'd spent the better part of every week having dinner there, and that included our family holiday dinners. The members of the RCC had not only become good friends to us; they'd become family. Even Evelyn Moss.

"In the two hundred years the RCC has been open, we've *never* closed. We stayed open during the tornadoes in the late seventies. I know. I was here." Evelyn wasn't quivering in her stance of staying open. "Then there was the time the pipes in the kitchen burst because they were so old and rotted. We had to get a caterer to bring food in." She lifted up a finger. "What about a couple of years ago when we did the big remodel?" She continued to list all sorts of reasons they didn't close.

* * *

"Do you understand that I've not only got hundreds of reservations to fill, but I'm having the biggest wedding here in four days from today?" There was almost a scared tone in her voice now. "Did you hear me? Four, f-o-u-r days." There was a pause. "No. I will not cancel the wedding."

Cancel the wedding? Charlotte's wedding?

Who on earth was she talking to? I leaned a little closer, trying to figure out the other half of her conversation.

*　*　*

Not that I was eavesdropping, of course. I was only looking out for my friend's wedding.

I gulped. There was no way they could cancel Charlotte's wedding. Talk about a hissy fit. I'd seen Charlotte Harrington get a burr in her saddle, and it wasn't one bit pretty. When she hadn't made the cheerleading team in high school, she'd flipped out and pointed to everyone who'd made it, making a comment on how their mama had paid for a spot on the team. After she'd scolded everyone in the gym, she'd taken off running out of the gym, through the fields, hopping fences, not stopping until she made it to her parents' house clear on the other side of town. Mama had once told me that Charlotte had gotten her crazy from the Harrington side of the family.

No matter where she'd gotten it, she had it. And if they canceled her wedding, the crazy that family had shown wouldn't hold a candle to what she'd do to the RCC or Evelyn Moss.

I had to do something. I looked through the crack of the door. Evelyn's head was down. One hand held the receiver of the phone while her other rested on her forehead.

She wasn't speaking, but I could hear the person on the other end of the phone line doing some fast talking.

"Get me a chef. Get me one *now*." Evelyn's powerful words echoed out the door before she slammed down the receiver of the phone.

I let out a deep sigh. As much as I wanted to slip past the door, Evelyn needed someone to vent to, and I really wanted to see how we could come to a solution without canceling Charlotte's wedding. I straightened my shoulders, untucked my hair, and gave a light knock on the door.

"What?" Evelyn snapped, being her usual gruff self that I remembered.

For a second I hesitated. If I darted past the door, she wouldn't know it was me.

"I'm waiting!" She asserted with a full voice.

"Hi, Evelyn." I pushed the door open and looked around the room.

Boxes upon boxes were all over the place, along with files and binders. There wasn't a clear path or space anywhere. I glanced back at the name on the door to make sure I hadn't walked into the RCC storage room or Bitsy's holiday shed.

"Who are you and what do you want?" she spat out.

My eyes followed my ears and noticed what had been Evelyn's perfect bun perched on the top of her head was now messy and disheveled and popping out over the top of even more files stacked on her desk. From this fact alone, I knew she hadn't killed Emile. She'd have left a messy trail if she had and, by the look of the scene and the chatter of the officers, the killer had done a pretty good job covering up any sort of evidence.

"Well?" She pushed her fingers into that messy updo that no southern woman in her right mind would have ever been caught dead with in public. At least not in Rumford. She tried to fix it, but it wasn't happening. The more her fingers messed with it, the worse it fell.

She looked at me from squinted eyes as though she were trying to place me.

"I'm not sure if you remember me." I put my hand in my

purse and dug deep. Even though I thought I'd given Carter my last bag of cookies, I had to make sure.

I smiled when I found and pulled out what had to be the very last bag of Red Velvet Crunchies.

"I'd know those from anywhere." Her sullen face changed into a smile. "Sophia Cummings." She stood up. "You sure have turned into a fine young woman. How the hell are you?" she rambled, taking the bag from me and instantly popping a cookie into her mouth. She mumbled between chews. "Oh my gawd, I've missed these."

I eased down onto a chair in front of her desk—the only chair that wasn't full of boxes stacked on top of each other. There were Christmas lights hanging out of one box, Easter egg garlands draping out of another, and some Chinese lanterns sticking out of the top of a box in the corner.

"I'm sorry to hear about your chef," I blurted out. I'd never been one to have enough couth to keep my mouth shut. "I hope you're okay."

"It'll all be just fine. Finer than frog hair," she assured me, lying through her teeth. "I've got several calls in to some wonderful chefs who have begged me to work here in the past." She took another cookie from the bag. With each chew her face relaxed, releasing some of the stress.

She wasn't convincing me.

"You know, crunchies do help with stress. I'm here baking Charlotte Harrington's wedding cakes and I do know my way around the kitchen, so if you need someone to step in and cook for a little bit, I'm more than happy to help for the next few days."

It was as if my mouth took over before my brain had a chance to catch up. My mind noodled the concept I'd just offered. I'd only said a few days because I was going back to Manhattan after Charlotte's wedding. Surely I could spare a couple of days to help out.

* * *

"Poor Charlotte." Evelyn took another bite. Her eyes faded off. Suddenly she snapped out of her stare. She smiled. "I'm not sure I'm going to be able to find someone to recreate the fancy French wedding menu she had her heart set on." The smile faltered.

"What was he making?" I asked.

She looked around her desk, patted files, opened them, and finally gave up.

"I don't know. The file is around here somewhere." She picked up a couple more before she jerked her head in the air. "I know where I put it."

She stood up and walked over to the bookshelf that was just as messy as the rest of the office and pulled out a file with Charlotte's name on the tab.

"Monkfish, John Dory, Red Mullet." Her nose curled more and more with each name she read. Quickly she shook her head and stuck her tongue out. "Yuck."

She came back to the desk and sat down, eating another cookie.

"Seriously, I can help out." My mouth did it again. It spoke without my permission. I could tell Evelyn was still stressed because I'd never seen her eat so many of my cookies in one sitting. "I'm more than happy to go in the kitchen right now and help with lunch and tonight's reservations. I'm going to be here anyways working on Charlotte's cake."

Evelyn looked up at the clock on the wall. She looked back

at me. It was already well into the late morning, and any minute the first round of golfers would be in the restaurant to get an afternoon cocktail and snack before they went out to finish the back nine holes. The first set of tennis lessons would be over and the women would soon be here to eat their daily salad and drink their fancy green juice. It'd be about the time the massage therapist placed orders for her clients who had booked the spa day that included lunch.

Evelyn Moss was in a pickle and I was her answer.

"I heard you worked in a fancy New York City restaurant." She sucked in a deep breath. "I guess you know that it's really hard to find a chef with the caliber the RCC club members require."

"You mean Bitsy?" I knew Mama was hard to please and if her palate wasn't happy, she wasn't happy.

"I wasn't going to name names." She spoke with a weak and tremulous whisper. "But if that's who's in your mind, yes," she said with quite an emphasis. "Are you sure Bitsy isn't going to throw all kinds of holy hell if I take up your vacation time working?"

"Are you kidding?" I leaned back in the chair. "I've been so bored since I've been here, and plus it'd do me good to stay in the kitchen to keep my mind off . . ." I trailed off.

"Honey, I heard. You forget I walk around here where the club members think I'm invisible. Their mouths flap and gossip." She shrugged. "I'm sorry about your boyfriend and that whole cheating thing."

A smile curled up on the corner of my lip as I tried not to curse Bitsy's name under my breath. Bitsy had probably meant no harm when she told people I was home, but she could've left out the "poor, pitiful Sophia ran home to Bitsy because she needed help mending her broken heart" story. I was positive she'd told all of her friends in all of her clubs.

"Don't be. See, I can use a distraction," I said.

"If you're sure." Evelyn's eyes held a glint of wonder.

"I'm sure." I eased up on the edge of the chair and stuck my hand out over the files on her desk.

"You've got a deal," Evelyn said, gripping my hand. "You're a lifesaver." She winked. "Don't tell anyone I'm a big old softie."

"You know I won't." I smiled back at her and got up to leave. "You know I can't cook for the wedding since I'll be busy putting the finishing touches on the cake," I made sure to remind her. "But I might be able to get a start on some of the appetizers Emile had planned for Charlotte's wedding."

"I'm going to have to meet with Charlotte about this if I can't find someone to make those weird things she's signed off on, but if you want to take a gander." She offered me the file and I took it.

Evelyn stood up. She patted one of the stacks of papers in front of her. "I've got some good leads, but they just can't get here today. I'm confident the chef I've contacted will be perfect for the wedding. I hope Charlotte won't be disappointed."

"I'm sure you've got it under control." I felt as if I needed to give Evelyn a little boost of confidence.

From the conversation I'd overhead, Evelyn was trying not to alarm me, because she obviously didn't have a backup.

"I'm going to head on down to the kitchen now." I gave a slight wave.

On my way down the hall, I grabbed my cell phone out of my back pocket. Not that Mama was at home waiting on me.

She'd known I was going to the RCC to meet Charlotte. If she'd heard about Emile, she'd be worrying I was in danger and calling her would put her mind to ease.

The answering machine picked up, and I left a quick message to let her know I was going to be at the RCC for a few hours, leaving out the part about me cooking. I could hear her now: "I let you work there serving my friends when you were in high school, but as an adult with an education?"

No matter how old I was, Mama had a way of guilt-tripping me. One of her specialties.

Chapter Six

The sheriff's department was finishing up their inspection of the crime scene by the time I made it back down to the kitchen. They'd taken down the crime scene tape and pretty much left behind a fine layer of dust from the fingerprint powder on everything. A couple of people were still hovered over Jane. They were exchanging stories of Emile that made them laugh and remember the good times with him. They tried to recreate his actual tone and voice as they told his stories.

From milling around the club, I knew the general public hadn't yet heard the news about Emile, though it'd be all over town lickety-split. The click of golf shoes on the floor sounded in the distance, an automatic alarm for the staff that the golfers were on their way. Jane adjusted the apron around her waist and grabbed a couple of menus on her way out the door.

"I thought you were leaving?" Carter moseyed up to me with a smirk on his face.

"Didn't you know that I'm not only going to be baking Charlotte's wedding cake, I'm also going to be taking over the

59

kitchen while Evelyn is in limbo finding another chef? But first I've got to clean up this mess you made."

I reached up and grabbed one of the RCC aprons off one of the hooks.

"This mess wouldn't be here if there wasn't a murder." He stared at me, obviously amused. "But you can have your kitchen back." He stepped aside and brushed his hand out in front of him. "Since you're the new gal in charge, I suggest you watch your back."

A momentary panic rushed through me. What on earth did he mean by that? "Just what are you implying?"

"I'm just saying that we don't have anyone in custody and we haven't figure out yet why someone would kill such a *beloved* member of the RCC."

"Are you saying some people didn't like Emile?" I was curious because the staff seemed to have had a lot of good stories as they traveled down memory lane a few minutes before, and they were so quick to point fingers at Evelyn.

"Right now everyone only has great things to say about the man. But over the course of the next couple of hours, even days, the truth will come out. Those are the clues to the motives and reasons for killing the guy." Carter made a good point. "I'm figuring an inside job or at least someone Emile knew."

"Inside job?" I gulped and took a good look at the staff. People I knew nothing about. Employees who were strangers, and I had no idea where their loyalties lay. None of them seemed to be staring back.

"There wasn't any forced entry. The doors were locked, and we checked the member list database," he said. "I'm just telling you to be careful, that's all. I'd hate to see you get in the middle of anything on your visit home." Before members could enter the club, there was an entry gate into the RCC grounds. Members had to swipe their membership card to gain entry. Their information went directly into the RCC's database, and at any given moment, RCC security staff could tell who was on the property. Carter could've easily gotten his hands on the information.

* * *

"Jane's timeline checked out with the coroner's estimated time of death, which was two hours prior to the time she found him. Or maybe you and Charlotte," he started, but I completely interrupted that thought. I could see where he was going.

"You know Charlotte and I didn't do this. I was with you." I reminded him how I'd seen him at Small Talk Café.

"So that leaves Evelyn Moss." His chest heaved when he released a big sigh.

"What about the other staff members?" I asked, then gave some suggestions, "Like the tennis and golf pros? Or the spa service people?"

"All checked out." His words were short. "I've done my job."

"I told you earlier there's no way Evelyn would've or could've done it." I scoffed. "Evelyn seems to be hard as a brick, but she's a softie underneath. Don't tell anyone I told you. Besides, as a chef, the whole killed-by-his-skillet thing seemed so personal. And you really can't say it's an inside job." I'd seen enough TV crime shows to know that. "What if Emile let someone in? Take me, for instance." I gestured to myself. "I came in with my parents' card, so you won't find my name in the database. I'm not a member."

I asked questions that blew his theory out of the water.

"You have to think about the day. Was it a delivery day? Was it laundry pickup day? Who let them in the gate? They aren't members, so they get in here somehow."

His body shifted and stiffened after my remarks.

"You don't understand how a busy kitchen really works." I tilted my head to one side. "There are so many moving parts. Not just one person runs the show. Not just Emile. There's more than one cook, more than one waitress. All the deliveries it takes to get food on one plate."

The wheels in his head were turning.

"But you really need to look at that skillet." I pointed my finger at him and lowered my eyes. "Why would someone get so mad at him that they'd whack him?"

For some reason, the lack of seasoning in the skillet bugged me. "We don't have a motive yet. You stick to the baking and I'll stick to the investigating," he warned. "I'm just saying that you need to watch your back."

"I live among eight million people in New York City and I've never felt more scared than I do now," I grumbled, gnawing on the edge of my cheek and contemplating the rushed decision to take over for Emile.

I'd never even thought that he'd been killed over anything other than personal revenge.

"It's much easier to commit a crime in a small town like Rumford than a big city where big brother is always watching." Carter stuck his hands in his pockets and rocked on the heels of his shoes, staring at me. "Unfortunately, the RCC doesn't have any sort of video security or surveillance. Something about privacy rights, since it's so pricey to belong here. Not that I'd know."

His words weren't comforting to me, but I'd made a promise

to Evelyn, which meant I had to put my doubts and fear aside to get the job done. Besides, I had to get Charlotte's cake baked and in the refrigerator so I could ice and decorate it for the big day.

"Excuse me." A young man shoved between us. He hurried over to Jane, asking her all sorts of questions. He'd obviously heard the news.

Carter pulled the notebook out of his pocket and flipped through it.

"That's Nick, Emile's sous chef," he said. "If you'll excuse me, I'm going to do a quick interview with him before I let you get the kitchen up and running."

"Yeah, sure," I agreed.

Carter walked over to the staff, who were busy prepping for the day. I followed him. They all turned to look at us. Jane had come back into the kitchen and joined us.

"Hi," I greeted them. I told them who I was, how I was connected to the RCC, and that I was in charge of the cake for the wedding of the season. I wanted to make sure they knew me, my credentials, and that I wasn't a threat to them. "I'm going to fill in for a couple of days for Emile." I turned to Nick. "Nick, can you please go with Sheriff Carter for a quick interview and then come see me when you're finished? I'm gonna need you to give me a quick rundown of things around here."

My nerves had calmed a little bit since learning that Emile had a sous chef, which meant that Nick was Emile's right-hand man. He should be able to pick up wherever and whenever Emile needed him to. Upon death was no greater time, in my opinion.

"Sure, Chef." Nick nodded and headed on out of the kitchen with Carter.

"Why don't I show you around while he does that," Jane suggested.

"That'd be great. I'm not going to lie—I'm a little rusty around the kitchen since I've been working as the pastry chef, but I know that with you and Nick, I'll be able to run it until Evelyn gets a new chef." I followed her into the central work area. "I love the newly remodeled kitchen."

"We will help in any way we can." She tapped the fryer and started her tour of the new-to-me facility. "This is the fryer, stove, second stove, and wok station." She pointed to all the industrial appliances in a row situated under the long hooded vent. "At the very end is a stainless workstation, and next to that is just a dry storage shelf."

She turned around and showed me the double stainless steel workstations with the double sinks before she took me into the dry storage room.

"We have eight dry storage shelves in here," she noted.

"There are two doors in here." I didn't remember this room having two doors. "Did they add another door recently?"

"No. It was just blocked with stacks of boxes before. When Chef Emile took over, he wanted to make sure no one interrupted his cooking time. With the delivery men and the RCC being off country roads, they were sometimes late because they'd get behind a tractor or a cattle run, so Emile made it easy for them to just come in through the back door and drop the dry storage here."

"Without him checking the list?" I asked.

"Oh, no." She shook her head. "Chef Emile was very particular about what he ordered. Only he could place the order, but he did have Nick check off the items to make sure we'd gotten them all."

"That's good." It seemed like a lot of good teamwork in the kitchen. That was something that would have been nice for me at The Manhattan. I was in charge of all my deliveries, checklists, and anything else that went along with the desserts.

"I've worked as a waitress in a lot of different restaurants. It wasn't until Emile hired me that I really started to love the job. Don't get me wrong, sometimes Emile acted crazier than a sprayed roach, but it was one of those work environments that ran smoothly. I always knew my place." She walked out of the dry storage room and headed to the far right of the kitchen where the dishwashing station was located. "I always knew how Emile wanted it."

"I spent a lot of time in here," I joked, noticing that nothing had changed.

Jane ignored my joke and continued, "Unlike Evelyn. She hired him. She knew his process, but they butted heads on a daily basis."

On the right side was the double sink, along the back wall was the minute-and-a-half-cycle industrial dishwasher, and next to that was the rinse-off area. Above the three areas were the bussing buckets used by the busser to clear the tables.

"Evelyn is harmless." I started to go into my defense mode about her but got interrupted.

"Hey there." A young man walked into the room, grabbed an apron off the hook on the wall, and replaced it with a Rumford High School backpack. "Is it true about Emile?" he asked Jane while chomping on a wad of gum.

"Yes. Can you believe it?" Jane asked.

"Yeah. He was a jerk. Did they question Evelyn?" he asked. "You a cop?" He shot his question at me.

"Oh, no," Jane giggled. "Far from it. This is Sophia. She's going to be in charge until Evelyn replaces Emile."

"Only here a couple of days to help out. What's your name?"

"I'm Patrick." He pulled a skull cap from out of his back pocket and slipped it over his short brown hair. I couldn't help but notice the skull tattoo on his bicep. "I'm in the school-to-work program."

He put his hand in his front jeans pocket and pulled out all the contents along with the white pocket liner. He unloaded a couple of packs of gum on the counter and shoved the liner back in the pocket.

His gum popped every time he chewed.

"A high school student at Rumford?" I asked, noticing he wasn't a fan of Emile and was much bigger in stature than Emile.

"Yep." He reached up on the shelf and hooked three clear water glasses with his fingers in each hand. He lifted the lid of the ice maker and scooped up ice to put in the glasses. "Not for long, because I'm heading off to college next year. Hopefully on a scholarship."

"That's awesome. I graduated from Rumford High too." I wanted to keep my ear to the ground and keep up on what was going on in the kitchen.

Not that I was going to be there long, but staying to myself and staying out of others' gossip obviously didn't do me any good, since I'd been the last to know about Noah at The Manhattan.

"Cool." He wasn't impressed. "I can't wait to get out of this town and this stupid job."

"I'm showing Sophia around, though she worked here in high school too." Jane tried to make up for Patrick's lack of manners.

"And if I'm here, that means it's almost lunchtime. From the looks of the golf course, we're going to be swamped, and I sure don't smell anything cooking." He sniffed a couple of times in the air.

"You're right." I ran a hand down Jane's arm. "Are you ready to help me in the kitchen?"

"I don't know anything about cooking," she said.

"You will," I assured her, and headed out toward the central work area.

"Don't mind Patrick. He ain't worth a hill of beans in here but doing the dishes." She rolled her eyes. "I didn't think he was going to last long with Emile in charge, so I bet he's happy Emile is dead. You know teenagers. They never want to listen to authority figures."

"He sure didn't seem upset." I looked over the written menu that was taped up to the walk-in refrigerator. "Did Emile write this up?" The very neat and tidy handwriting didn't go without notice. Most chefs' handwriting was messy like the typical doctor's.

"Yes. That's his fancy handwriting. He made all the menus. He never strayed from it. If we sold out, we sold out and he said the members needed to pick from the other items." She took a half apron off the hook and securely tied it around her waist. She took the hairband from around her wrist and pulled her hair back at the nape of her neck into a low ponytail. "Even with the carpel tunnel he was getting in his right hand, he still insisted on writing the menu." She grabbed a tray. "Time to get to work." She headed on out the kitchen door that led to the dining room.

I'd forgotten to ask Evelyn about my time sheet, which I really didn't care about, but it would give me a reason to go back and ask her about a few things some of the staff had told me. Things like the menu and how Emile would switch up the food, not to mention how the members would send back his fancy creations because they weren't used to eating anything with a head on it or anything they couldn't make out as food.

The sound of shuffling and whispers coming from the other end of the hall made me jerk back to look after I'd reached Evelyn's office door. Patrick and a young woman were giggling and talking when they rounded the corner. She had on a tennis skirt that barely covered her, and the way she had her arm hooked in Patrick's arm looked way friendlier than a staff member helping another member out. For a split second, Patrick's and my eyes locked. His expression was deadly serious. The girl kept talking.

After a couple of knocks on the office door and waiting a few seconds without Evelyn answering, I headed back to the kitchen, barely making it back in time before Nick bolted in through the swinging door. "It's go time, people. Chef"—he looked at me— "let's go."

I nodded. I drew my finger down the menu and read off the specials.

"Chicken and Collards Pilau. Derby Pie. Company Roast and Creamy Mushroom Grits," I rattled off.

In the back of my head, I wondered about the menu Emile had been looking at when he was killed. Those food items were nowhere on the posted menu.

Nick took off and started the ovens and grabbed a couple of cooked roasts out of the freezer. The rattle of the pans, the hiss of the gas stove, and the hum of the working kitchen got my mojo hyped up and lit my insides on fire. No matter how far I ran from my problems, my heart was in the kitchen around all the hubbub and action.

"Oh, good." I was glad to see that I wasn't going to have to come up with a different entrée, since I knew we didn't have eight hours to cook the roast.

"Chef Emile always planned ahead." Nick didn't miss a beat and pulled the ingredients off the dry storage shelves. "Grab the Derby pies."

Nick and I worked alongside each other with quick, sure movements, executing dishes as if we'd worked in tandem before. Emile took great pride in his kitchen and, by the detailed notes he'd left, it showed. Nick was fascinating as he worked around the kitchen. He didn't miss a beat despite everything that'd gone on.

Jane and Patrick used the three-fold cloth napkins and silver-ware, along with the list of reservations, and got all the tables ready in the dining room. No matter what they said about Emile, they were working together, so he'd done something right.

The orders started to roll in along with more and more employees for their shifts. The key restaurant staff, from what I'd gathered from the shift change sheet, were Nick, Jane, and Patrick. If it weren't for Nick, I admit, I'd have been a little lost. Once my hands started to move, it was as if the cobwebs that'd taken over my brain the last couple of weeks were brushed away and everything started to come back to me.

"Do you think Evelyn is going to be arrested?" Jane leaned against the steel worktable on the other side of the central pro-duction station where the cooked dishes sat under the heating lamp, waiting to be delivered.

"She has to be the number one suspect." Nick put an RCC cheeseburger special and fried chicken club on the shelf for Jane to grab. "Especially after last night."

"What happened last night?" I questioned while stirring in the cream for more mashed potatoes.

"Emile saw himself as an artiste," Jane chirped in her best French accent. She even kissed the tips of her fingers and flowered them out for good measure. "Too good to make these hillbilly dishes. The RCC needed to expand their taste buds."

I laughed at her attempt to say *hillbilly* in a French accent. It just wasn't right.

"Emile thought he was too good to make southern dishes. He couldn't grasp the fact that he was the head chef of a country club in Kentucky and kept trying to make this place resemble the new hit restaurant in Paris. He made the specials all these fancy dishes that barely anybody would order because they couldn't pronounce them." Nick stirred the sausage in the Dutch oven on the stove.

"Emile would spend all weekend going over the next week's menu." Jane nodded and put the plates on a big, round, black tray before hoisting it up on her shoulder and sashaying out the kitchen door.

"But what made Emile and Evelyn fight?" I asked, and took another Derby pie out of the oven, placing it on the cooling rack.

Nick snickered and shook his head. "Emile started to get sneaky. He would make up names that sounded like southern dishes but make a French dish instead."

Maybe the menu I'd seen lying next to his body was just some new creations he'd jotted down.

I handed Nick the onions and the broth he needed to finish

the pilau before pouring it into a baking dish and placing it in the oven.

"She pitched a fit last night when a couple of members complained that they were expecting something different than a thin French pastry with meat in the middle. You know southerners love their comfort food. All fat, full of carbs, and creamy." Nick bent down and looked at the knob on the stove to make sure the temperature was set at 350 degrees.

Patrick shoved his back end through the door with his hands full of dirty dishes.

"Ask Patrick about it." Nick walked over to the fryer and pulled the basket of fried chicken out of the hot oil. "Everyone but me, Patrick, and Jane had already gone home."

"Talking about the fight?" Patrick spoke as he chewed on the gum. The edge of his lip cocked in a slight smile. "It was epic. Evelyn went craaaaaazy." He dropped the bucket of dishes on the workspace. His hand grasped the edges, and he leaned over top of it with an evil grin. "Did you hear Emile tell her that she was a nut job like all women?"

"He did?" I asked with a slack-jawed expression.

"Oh, yeah, but that's not what sent her over the edge." Nick slid Patrick a look. "When he said to her that she wasn't married because no man wanted a bossy woman like her in his bed and that a woman's place was at home taking care of kids and doing laundry was when she got that crazy look in her eye like she was going to kill him."

"Did you tell the sheriff that?" I asked.

"Sure did. Evelyn killed him. I'm sure of it," Nick noted, and Patrick stood next to him nodding the entire time.

"If she didn't, she had someone else do it." Jane caught the tail end when she walked back in. My brows knitted in a frown. The staff had even convicted Evelyn.

The rest of the afternoon, not only was good southern food baked, but the idea that Emile was killed by Evelyn had been baked and burned into each of their heads. They were worse than Bitsy's gossip circle in her Friends of the Library Club. The gnawing in my gut told me something was not right. Evelyn wasn't a killer. I knew it clear down to my bones.

Nick had a good grasp of the kitchen, so while I pondered over every little bit of gossip I'd heard, I decided to get started on Charlotte's cake. There were going to be seven tiers. Luckily, the RCC kitchen had all the different-sized cake pans I needed to get started. There was even a heating core for me to use. Since I only had a few days to bake several layers, I'd be using the heating core in the middle of each layer of cake during the baking process, which would allow each cake to evenly bake and speed up the baking process.

I kept an eye on Nick to make sure he had everything under control as I pulled out the mixer from underneath one of the counters along with the ingredients I needed to make the almond cake with raspberry filling Charlotte had picked out.

Even if Emile had been a male chauvinist, I liked how easy he had made it for me to find the ingredients. I walked around the dry-ingredient shelves with one of Patrick's bussing buckets and put in what I needed to transport over to one of the free stainless steel workstations: cake flour, baking powder, salt, almond paste, sugar, butter, almond extract, ten eggs, and whole milk.

The sound of the mixer filled the kitchen. The roar gave me joy, so much more than making fried chicken or collard greens ever would. As the ingredients mixed and folded, my shoulders fell back to their normal position instead of staying around my ears from stress. There were too many witnesses that had seen Evelyn and Emile arguing, and she'd know that.

Nick brought me out of my groove when he walked over and watched me fill the sixteen-inch round flat-edge cake pans. I had to fill four to get the eight inches I needed, since I baked only two inches in each pan.

Patrick bebopped to his own whistling and even did a little turn as he headed into the dishwashing room.

"Patrick sure does look happy," I observed, noticing all the humming and gum popping he'd been doing. When I'd had to do the dishes at his age, I sure hadn't been happy about it.

"He should be." Nick's brows rose. "Emile isn't here to bully him."

"Bully him?" I questioned. It was the first I was hearing about this despite all the gossip that'd been swirling around today.

"Yeah. Emile was good at putting him down because he was a busboy. We have at least five of them, but for some reason, Emile picked on him." Nick eyed the cake batter. "That looks really good."

"Hmm, maybe." I noodled the thought that Patrick could've reached his limit with Emile and done the deed. "Did Patrick and Emile ever come to blows?"

"Nah." Nick waved off my idea. "Of course, Patrick would threaten Emile under his breath during his shift, but he's a kid. Kids say things like that." Nick's eyes narrowed. "You aren't thinking Patrick . . ."

I didn't bother letting him finish his sentence.

"You never know. I mean, he seems like a good kid, but he's awfully cheerful today." We both looked over at Patrick doing a little dance with his backpack on his shoulder. "Where's he going?"

"He's on the high school baseball team and has practice tonight, so he's off," Nick said.

"See ya tomorrow." Patrick gave a peace sign before he stuck his earbuds in his ears and shoved through the door before I could grab him to ask him some questions. Not that I was being nosy or anything.

I couldn't forget the warning from Carter about watching my back, though. I was going to be sweet as pie to all the staff during my brief time here.

Chapter Seven

The kitchen smelled heavenly between the Derby pies and the baked layers of Charlotte's wedding cake. It smelled more like a bakery than a kitchen in a restaurant. For a brief period of time, all my sadness had disappeared and there was a sprinkle of joy that warmed my heart.

I'd gotten the four sixteen-inch layers baked as well as four of the fourteen-inch layers. All of them were lined up on the cooling rack. It was important for the layers to cool before I wrapped them in saran wrap and put them in the refrigerator.

One secret to a very moist and nicely decorated wedding cake was refrigerating it and allowing it to cool before decorating it. Fondant, icing, and any part of the decorating process adhered better to a cooled cake. If I'd had much more notice, I'd have baked Charlotte's cake a week before in preparation for decorating. As it was, this last-minute commitment didn't allow me that kind of time, so I was going to have to jerk a knot in my own tail and get it done.

"I don't get people." Jane barged through the door with a couple of full plates of the special that she'd just taken out to a few club members. "The first lunch crowd was fine with Emile being gone, but not this afternoon. The men didn't care. The women"—she sucked in a deep breath—"they've gone plumb crazy. Nearly fainted when I told them that I found Emile dead this morning."

"Why are these being sent back?" Nick took a sudden defensive tone. He wiped his hands on the towel tucked in the wraparound tie on his chef jacket while he looked the two plates over that Jane had set down on the island.

"Two of the women suddenly lost their appetite when they asked to see Emile." Jane's brows bounced up and down.

"Do you know the women?" I asked.

"Mm-hmm," she muttered sarcastically. "Ella Capshaw for one and Natalie Devin for another."

"Oh." Nick stiffened. "I forgot about them. Do you think I need to tell Carter about them?"

"Them?" I asked, and went down the line of cakes, feeling them to check the temperature.

They were cooling down perfectly. There was just enough time to bake Bitsy's favorite skillet apple pie.

"Emile was a ladies' man." Nick's brows furrowed.

"To say the least," Jane quipped. "Natalie was at her tennis lesson all morning, so she hadn't heard the news about . . ." She dragged her finger along her throat. "Ella has been at her standing massage and pedicure appointment."

"Let's get back to the ladies' man thing." I pulled the hairnet off my head because my brain needed to breathe.

I walked over to the fruit and grabbed a few Granny Smith and Braeburn apples. They were the perfect combination of bitter and sweet for the best apple pie. After chasing one of them around the island after I put them down, I retrieved the rest of the ingredients while listening to Nick and Jane give a few accounts of Emile's player ways.

If Emile was a ladies' man and I could find out which RCC members he'd seduced, then we'd have more suspects. We—as if I were trying to solve the murder. I cracked myself up sometimes. I knew I should leave it up to Carter, but I couldn't help myself. Call me nosy, call me curious; the reality was, I liked trying to see where all the pieces fit. Sorta like a puzzle.

The feeling deep in my soul was how I felt when I tasted someone else's dessert and wanted to replicate it. I'd try several combinations of ingredients until it was perfect. Emile's murder hit that nerve in me and I just couldn't stop myself.

"He could throw that French accent on our oldest member and have her in bed in a minute." Nick did his best French accent, which wasn't good.

"Was he having an affair with some members?" I asked, just to make sure I understood what I thought I was hearing. I put my hands on the counter and leaned in, looking at all the pots hanging over the island to find a good seasoned skillet.

"Yes." Jane's nose curled.

"Jane." Nick stopped her. "We don't know that for sure."

They looked at me as I grabbed a square skillet that would be perfect for my simple pie.

"You and I both know"—she gestured between them—"that there's more than just food being cooked up in this kitchen." Her brow cocked.

My tongue jutted out as in *ew*, and I jerked my hands off the counter and pulled them to me.

"Gross, I know. This stuff goes on a lot more than you think.

But Emile was so tight-lipped about it even after I saw him being all lovey-dovey with Natalie."

"Natalie?" I was shocked.

Mama and Natalie had been friends way back when. They'd even been in a few clubs together.

* * *

Why would Natalie cheat on Arnold Devin with Emile? Emile couldn't make that much money, and the Devins were loaded. At least Arnold was. I didn't mean a million or two; I meant boo-coodles of money.

"Honey, you know Evelyn and how messy she can be. Well"—Jane's hand fluttered down at the wrist—"I had to get me another ordering pad because I'd used up the one I had, and I went down to the supply closet that had things like that. You know—extra pens, pencils, menus—and when I couldn't find none, I headed on down to Evelyn's office to see if she knew where they were, thought I doubted she did." She sucked in a deep breath and continued, "Don't you know that when I turned the corner, I caught Emile and her a little too close in the small hallway, and Natalie gave me this big old smile. Then she took off down the hall with her ass swinging like church bells on Easter. Even a groan escaped from Emile." She nodded her head. "True story. If I'm lying, I'm dying."

"Really?" I could feel my face crunch up. "I thought that stuff only happened in *Dirty Dancing*."

"That's the difference between us and you." She gestured between me and her and Nick.

"What?" I felt a little offended and quickly peeled one apple after the other.

"You're one of them." Jane gestured to the door that led to the dining room.

"Far from it." I gave her a brief rundown of how my parents hadn't been so approving of my job choices in the restaurant industry, making a parallel with her. As I talked, I cut all the apples into wedges.

"What are you doing?" Nick asked.

"While I wait on Charlotte's cakes to cool completely, I have enough time to make a few of my skillet apple pies. It's so easy and good." I tossed the apples into the mixture.

There really wasn't enough time to make the crust. The refrigerator had some premade crusts, so I decided to use those. I used my fingertips to press the crust around the bottom of the skillet.

"You know," I said. There was still something that didn't click about the murder weapon. "I understand that Emile was killed by the blow to the head from his skillet, but I don't think it was his skillet."

I poured the apple mixture into the skillet and carefully put the other pie crust over it, pinching around the edges to seal in the apples.

"He used all of these dishes." Nick continued to get the lunches completed.

"Yeah, but the skillet used to kill him wasn't seasoned." I cut an X in the middle of the top pie crust before sprinkling a little sugar on top and placing it into the oven. "Think about it."

"I didn't see the skillet that killed him," Nick said. "I just assumed it was one of ours."

"I don't know what the inventory is here, but I did tell Carter that it seemed really odd that there was a skillet in the kitchen that hadn't been seasoned." I shrugged.

"Maybe he'd bought new ones," Nick suggested.

"Then Carter should be able to see some sort of inventory, right?" I asked.

"If he used the RCC's funds, it'll all be there." Nick chuckled. "That was a touchy subject between him and Evelyn."

"How so?" I asked, wanting to know if this was one of the reasons Evelyn was the number one suspect.

"She said he thought he was a million-dollar chef but was working at a beer budget club because he never stayed within the budget the RCC gave him. He added so many things to the order after she had approved the list. He'd lie to her and tell her he didn't do it, but it was in his notebook where he kept the inventory with her signature on it." Nick rolled his eyes. "Last year she had to cut the wine budget because he'd gone over so much. There was a time I hated coming to work. They fought like a married couple, not like a boss and employee."

"Did you tell Carter that?" I asked.

"I totally forgot, but if he stops in, I'll tell him."

"Maybe you don't have to just yet." I cleaned up my workstation. "I really need Charlotte's wedding to go off without a hitch this weekend, and it won't if Evelyn is in jail."

"It's true. I don't think the RCC would run without her. She might be hard, but she's good," Nick said, and went on his way fixing and preparing orders.

The afternoon quickly flowed into the evening with me barely getting a breath. The busboy for the afternoon shift was late, and as the head of the kitchen, I had to pitch in wherever I could. Since Nick knew Emile's recipes and style, I felt a lot more comfortable with him than with me at the helm and was grateful for it too, because I couldn't get the juicy tidbit of gossip about Emile and the women of the RCC out of my thoughts. If there was one, there were two, and so on.

Jealousy was a powerful motive to kill someone. Better yet, betrayal. The ultimate woman scorned. Had Emile threatened to expose their affair? Did one woman get jealous of the other?

I was going to have to keep one ear to the ground and my eyes open. Plus, I'd invite Mama to join me for a little girl talk. She'd be so delighted to spend some time talking that she'd sing like a bird and happily answer all my questions about the state of the Devins' marriage.

I stared out into the dining room through the small kitchen window as I contemplated my questions and kneaded my lower back with my fingers.

I'd forgotten how hard the long hours and the toll of a fast-paced kitchen were on the body. Luckily at The Manhattan, we had so many sous chefs and employees, our hours were pretty normal. It wasn't like the small establishments like the RCC where employees had to pull double duties.

"You look beat." Nick looked up from the chopping station where he was refilling the salad fixings. His eyes focused on my back where I continued to press into it.

"Thanks," I scoffed. "I haven't worked in a full-time kitchen in a long time. I forgot just how much toll it takes on the body. I'm going to be sore in the morning."

"We've got this." He used his knife to point around the kitchen. "Why don't you call it a night and I'll see you in the morning."

Hesitant, I looked around. The kitchen was buzzing with a couple of busboys and a few more waitresses as well as some extra cooks. Everything was under control. I just hated to leave Evelyn in a bind, but less time here meant more time for me to look into who else had a motive to kill Emile besides her.

"It's no different than if Emile were here." He went back to chopping. "Unless you don't want to go home."

"You get that from me?" I asked, grabbing a piece of the green pepper and tossing it into my mouth.

"Emile would've written you up for that." He pointed the knife at my mouth.

"I'm not Emile and he's no longer here." I smiled back at Nick and took another look around. "That was in bad taste, wasn't it?" I asked, my way of apologizing for lessening what'd happened to Emile.

"Aw." Nick brushed it off. "It'll be weird around here for a while. He was hard to work for, but I learned a lot from him."

There wasn't much more I could say that would make a difference or would make Nick feel better.

"You do have everything under control. And I might be stalling going home. I've been gone from Rumford for ten years, and it's hard to come back home when my mama still sees me as the young twenty-year-old. Plus, she's never been proud of my job choice."

"Your mom has always been real nice to us. She's actually one of our favorite members." Nick continued to chop and slice. "Actually, she always bragged about you and your fancy pastry job."

"Really?" I asked, feeling really touched.

"Yeah, she even brought in some magazine where you were featured for some important dinner."

I knew exactly what he was talking about.

"I did the New York governor's son's wedding cake. It was

sort of a big deal." I blushed. "There were celebrities and government officials who attended. It was where I met Noah." My voice trailed off.

The memory felt as if it'd just happened last night. Every time I'd told that story before, Noah had been by my side giving his account. We'd ended up talking over each other and then bursting out laughing.

My heart fell to my toes. I realized I was going to have to start leaving that little tidbit out.

"Noah?" That stopped Nick in midchop.

"My ex." I gulped. "He's the reason I'm here. I caught him with the maître d' at work."

"Caught him, caught him?" Nick put his knife down on the table.

Slowly I nodded. "In a very compromising position with the hostess."

"Man, that's rough. So you really are only here until Evelyn hires the new chef." He leaned his hip against the table and crossed his arms across his chest.

"Yep." I offered a smile to at least make him feel better. "You know, I think you'd make a great replacement for Emile." It was a perfect choice. Evelyn wouldn't have to step outside the RCC, and Nick ran the place as if Emile were still alive. "You know the kitchen like the back of your hand."

"I'm not really sure I'd want the head chef position. It's a lot of work, and I've gotten a look firsthand on how Emile was treated and treated others. I'm just not like that. I like it right here. Knowing my place and being told what to do." He wasn't up for the job.

Yet. Maybe with a little coaxing over the next couple of days, I'd convince him.

"Then I think I'm going to go, because you have this place running like a well-oiled machine." I took off the white chef's coat and hung it on one of the many hooks on the wall. I slipped my bag across my body.

"See you in the morning." He gave me the captain salute. "Why don't you take those returned meals home to Robert and Bitsy?"

"Are you sure?" I asked, knowing they'd probably not eaten yet.

It wasn't even cocktail hour for my dad. He loved his before-dinner drink. It helped him get through Bitsy telling him about her day and the new gossip going around Rumford that she'd been privy to from all her club meetings. Poor Dad.

"Absolutely. They raised a fine daughter. I'm glad you're here." His words were comforting. "They're in the refrigerator."

"Thanks, Nick." It was so nice to feel appreciated.

That was one thing about an uppity restaurant like The Manhattan. No one ever gave compliments. If things were going great, everyone kept their mouth shut. But one wrong move and the staff complained and ruined the shift.

It was nice to be able to step into a kitchen and be recognized for the hard work that I've put in to get to where I'd gotten in my career.

"I'll see you in the morning," I said after I'd retrieved the returned lunches in to-go boxes. I walked down the hallway where the offices were because I knew for sure I'd see some of Bitsy's friends if I left through the dining room, and when the name plate on one of the doors read EMILE / HEAD CHEF, I got detoured and went in.

I flipped on the light. The office wasn't much to see. The

walls were bare white. The desk was cleaned off and Emile's chef jacket was hanging on a coat tree in the corner. There weren't photos or even posters or artwork as I'd seen in most offices of head chefs. They were creative people and thrived on seeing and hearing creative things to stimulate their muse. Not even a radio was in here. No wonder it hadn't taken Carter long to go through the office.

I sat down in Emile's chair. I rubbed my hands over the desk and channeled my favorite TV sleuths, wondering what they'd do.

My eyes drew down the three drawers. I sat still for a few minutes to make sure I didn't hear anyone. The first and second drawers were empty, but the third drawer had the chef's ledger.

"Old school for a fancy French chef," I noted and took the ledger out.

He'd written the dates on the outside, and this particular ledger appeared to span six months.

Most chefs used the basic online ordering form and spreadsheets to keep up with the items stocked on the shelves, wet and dry ingredients. It was easy to print and hand off so others could take inventory.

He had them broken down into months, with the past months held together with a paper clip. Within the month, he broke them down into weeks. He'd already planned for the next three months. It seemed like a long time to plan out, which only confirmed that he was a control freak and planned on keeping his job.

Page by page, I flipped through. The ledger was definitely one to be envious of. Emile kept a very detailed account. The only thing that caught my attention was that in the last month there were some minute changes in the handwriting. According to the wait staff, Emile had recently had a bout of carpel tunnel, which would make sense for the small inconsistencies. Though I wasn't going to rule out that maybe someone had helped him take inventory since his hand hurt.

It appeared he'd been in the process of ordering for next month until I got to the last and final entry where Charlotte's name was scrolled in fancy writing at the top of the page. At closer glance, I noticed that all the ingredients to make the meat dishes Evelyn had told me he was planning on serving was listed. Not only had he planned on the fancy meats, but the appetizers and soups were also fancy. Foie gras, lobster, and Trou Normand, a pallet cleanser, were among the items it looked as if Charlotte had signed off on. There was a blank line where Brett was supposed to sign. Next to the empty line, Emile had written something about meat and potatoes.

The next line had five dollars signs, which was something you'd normally see on a restaurant website indicating the cost. I pulled Charlotte's wedding file out of my bag and began to compare the items Evelyn had on her list to Emile's list. They appeared to be the same, only Evelyn had written down all of her correspondence with Charlotte and Brett.

I dragged my finger down the dates and times, noticing that Brett had recently called her three days in a row. Next to the last entry, Evelyn had written that Brett didn't approve the menu. Did Charlotte know this?

Laughter floated in from the hall. I quickly shoved the ledger back in the drawer and walked out of the office.

* * *

Evelyn had been scarce all day, and I wanted to ask her about the wedding menu. Telling her that I'd noticed Brett didn't want the fancy food would help me lead into why he'd called so many times and if he and Emile had argued about it. Was that what Evelyn and Emile had been arguing about in front of the staff?

It was a bit surprising that Evelyn hadn't come to the kitchen to check on us, though it did make me feel as if she was confident we'd do a great job. Her office door was closed when I approached it. I lifted my hand to give it a quick knock. I didn't want to leave without at least telling her everything had gone smoothly and let her know that she could count on me and I'd be back tomorrow. Plus, I wanted to put a little bug in her ear that Nick was the answer to her needs and all we had to do was convince him.

Just as I swept my closed fist up to knock on the door, I heard voices coming from the inside of her office.

I knew I shouldn't have and it wasn't good manners, but I put my ear up to the door—but not without looking up and down the hall to make sure no one was coming. Eavesdropping wasn't considered polite around these parts.

"Ms. Moss." Carter's voice thundered through the door loud enough for me to be able to step back and listen without appearing to be nosy. "There are several eyewitnesses to the fight between you and the deceased."

"It wasn't a fight." Evelyn sounded nervous. Her voice cracked. "He always had an issue with me being his boss. It certainly wasn't a reason for me to kill him."

"Why didn't you fire him?" Carter baited her.

"Because he's Emile. All the members would skin my hide,"

she said. "He'd recently been offered a three-year extension on his contract from the club committee."

"Who is on this committee?" Carter asked.

"Arnold Devin." She mumbled a few names I didn't recognize. "Brett Ponder."

The air tightened around me.

"So instead of putting the heat on you, you figured you'd kill him and no one would ever know." Carter was relentless.

I leaned a little closer to hear her response.

"I didn't kill him. I told you that." Her voice took on a sudden stiffness. "I made our working relationship work like a good general manager does with her staff."

"You are the only one who was signed in at his time of death. It looks pretty clear to me." His voice escalated as she tried to talk, and he talked over her.

"I was . . ." Evelyn butted in, to no avail. He wasn't going to let her have the opportunity.

"There is a history of the two of you getting into arguments on a weekly basis. If it wasn't the food choice, it was the tablescapes, down to the noise of the kitchen leading out into the dining room. You didn't want to have to listen to him put you down. He didn't like women and you were at the top of his list. So you killed him."

There was a murmur of crying, and I figured it could only be Evelyn.

"I didn't kill him," she insisted. "I keep the peace with all my employees. Ask them," she said, giving Carter a wee bit of a challenge.

"Don't leave town," Carter warned. "And I suggest you get a good lawyer."

Immediately I jerked back from the door and scurried as fast as I could down the hall, hoping I'd not get caught, but hoping was a bit much.

"Did you hear anything?" There was a smug look on Carter's face. "You know this is a homicide investigation and not some sort of bake-off, right?"

"I was leaving work." I rolled my eyes.

"You were listening in on my conversation with Evelyn." He'd caught me.

"Okay, only because I think I've got someone else for you to look at." I walked back toward him. "Brett, Charlotte's fiancé, wasn't happy with the menu at the wedding."

"So he killed Emile over a little salmon tartare?" Carter laughed.

"No, he killed Emile over the price tag." I gnawed on my lip. "Though I don't know what the price tag is because it's only got the five-dollar-sign rating." His brows furrowed. I continued. "Anyways, Charlotte is pretty used to getting what she wants, and she wanted this fancy menu. Brett confronted Emile about it because Brett didn't want to come off as cheap in front of Charlotte. With Emile out of the kitchen, Brett can have his meat and potatoes at a low cost."

"First off, I've known Brett for years. He'd been sleeping on my couch that morning before I got the call about Emile's death."

Crap.

"If you'll excuse me, I need to get back to work." He darted ahead of me.

"Wait. Why was he sleeping on your couch?" I wanted to know. "I thought he and Charlotte were living together."

"We were out the night before having a little bachelor party for him. Do you want all the details of where we were in case you want to investigate that too?" He turned and started walking away.

I stalked next to him out the door and followed him across the parking lot.

"I want you to know that I'm trying to look out for my friend and make sure her wedding goes as planned," I stated matter-of-factly, realizing he was stubborn as a mule.

He clicked the key fob for his door and got into his cruiser.

"You bake the cake and I'll figure out who killed their chef." He slammed the door in my face and peeled off.

My jaw dropped open in surprise that he would storm off like that. "The nerve!" I screamed, raising my arms his way.

* * *

Carter was wrong. Evelyn Moss had been a pillar to the RCC community and Rumford itself. She'd dedicated her life to the country club and keeping the members happy. She spent more time putting out fires than creating them. The Evelyn I knew from years ago wouldn't hurt a fly. I had to get my hands on Natalie's and Ella's RCC membership files. Somehow I needed to talk to them. There might be even more women in Emile's little black book, but I figured there was no better place to start than his two most recent conquests.

Chapter Eight

"It's about time you got home." Bitsy's eyes bore into me. Her jeweled fingers gripped the old cordless phone. "I've been worried sick. I even left a message with the police to have them put out an Amber Alert on you."

"Mama, I'm fine," I assured her, and twirled around in the middle of the kitchen. Once I stopped, I handed her the takeout containers. "See?"

Dad tucked the top edges of the newspaper away from the front of his face. He gave a slight smile before he flipped it back up to finish whatever article he was reading.

"Here, extra food." I put the containers on the table and left out the part about the meals having been sent back. "And an apple skillet pie."

I put the other pie I'd made into the freezer for later consumption.

"All I knew was that you were going to the RCC to meet Charlotte, and the next thing I knew, Emile was found murdered and I thought that you got in the middle of some scuffle with the killer and was kidnapped." She shook the phone in the air between us. "I've been waiting for a ransom call. I even called Bob Bellman down at Rumford First National Bank to get some liquid cash."

Dad curled the edges of the paper down again, looking at us, his eyes twinkling with amusement.

"Kidnapping? I'm not a child," I said, knowing Mama had lost her marbles.

"I saw it on TV. It can happen at any age. And you are ripe for the picking." Bitsy was always on my side no matter what. I could declare the sky was pink and she'd agree until her dying breath.

"I left a voicemail that I was staying at the RCC today to help Evelyn out with lunches and dinner." I was touched that Bitsy was so concerned.

"You know I leave my cell in the car." Bitsy's eyes snapped open. A line formed between her brows. She put the phone down on the island and tucked a strand of hair behind her ear. "That's where a cell phone belongs. In a car in case of emeeergencies," she drew out the vowels to get the point across.

She stalked across the kitchen to the desk.

"You never know about crazies, and now that there's a killer on the loose, I've got us signed up for a conceal and carry class." Bitsy opened one of the many empty drawers of the built-in and pulled out a handgun. "This here is mine." She flung it around as if it were a string of pearls in her hand.

"Bitsy!" Dad closed the paper and got up from the table. "Put that down."

"Mama, I don't know much about guns, but I don't think you're supposed to flail that around like that." I shimmied behind the island in case the darn thing went off.

"You've lost your mind." Dad confirmed my exact thoughts. He jerked the gun out of her hands and, with a quick yank, had the barrel open. "No bullets, thank God." He looked at Mama. "Where did you get this?"

The tone in Dad's voice told me he was mad. He wasn't one to speak his mind or even get between Bitsy and me when we'd argue or disagree. But when he did speak up, you knew he was passionate about whatever it was. This gun thing lit him on fire.

Bitsy shrugged. Her lips curled in as tight as bark on a tree. She wasn't going to give an inch. Stubbornness was Bitsy's strong suit.

"I'm still going to take the class," she stubbornly declared.

Dad sucked in a deep breath. In a calm voice, he asked her again, "Bitsy, dear, tell me where you got this?"

Bitsy batted her three-layered-mascaraed eyelashes, and her lips drew to a pucker. "If you must know, I bought it from Gus down at Finders Keepers Thrift Shop." She thrust her chin up and to the side. Her eyes drew down her nose at Dad.

"Geesh." Dad put the gun in his pocket. He pulled the sleeve up on his blue button-down and looked at his watch. "I'll go see Gus in the morning. What were they thinking, selling you this?"

Dad shook his head and walked out of the kitchen. Probably to get as far away from Bitsy as he could before he killed her.

"You and me are still going to the gun class." Slowly she dragged her finger between us. "What is this nonsense about you helping Evelyn?" Bitsy tsked.

"The RCC was in need of a chef, and I know my way around the kitchen fairly well." I shrugged.

"Fairly well? I paid plenty of money to all those fancy

cooking schools for you to learn your way around better than 'fairly.'" Bitsy shifted her weight to the left and put her hand on her hip.

"Culinary school," I corrected her, but she glazed right on over that. "Pastry school after that."

"There is no way you're leaving this house until the killer is found." She stomped over to the kitchen chair where Duchess sat, unfazed by all of the fuss.

"Dad," I called after my father once Bitsy had left the room.

"Yes." He turned around.

"Do you think you could stop by the RCC tomorrow? I'd like for you to talk to Evelyn. I think she's going to need a good lawyer." It was a tall order for me to ask my dad, but it was worth it.

"I don't know, honey." Dad looked torn. "I'm so busy with my current clients, I'm not sure I can take on any more."

"It's just that all the evidence is pointing to her. And really I just need you to hold off any charges until after Charlotte's wedding," I begged.

"Isn't her wedding this weekend?" he asked. I nodded. "So only a couple of days I need to ward off the law?" I nodded. "I'll think about it."

"Thanks, Dad." I gave him a quick kiss on the cheek. I was asking a lot of him, and I respected that he was going to take some time to think it over.

"See you in the morning." He looked at me. His eyes dipped on the edges. "I'm going to need you to be careful."

"Okay, Dad." I hugged him before I answered the ringing phone.

When I saw Madison's name scroll across the screen, I scurried out to the back porch to answer.

"Hey there," I said, sitting down on the top step of the deck stairs.

The sun was still midsky, and it would be another hour before the sunset lit up the sky in brilliant oranges that would be mixed in with the white fluffy clouds. There was nothing as gorgeous as a Rumford sunset.

"Oh my God," Madison gasped through the phone. "You're alive!"

"Of course I'm alive. Why?" I looked back over my shoulder at the sliding door, where Bitsy stood looking at me as she raked her nails down Duchess's fur.

"My mother called and said that you'd been abducted by Emile's killer." Her words made me cringe. It was then that I realized my Bitsy had called everyone she knew about my disappearance that never was. "Not that my mother wasn't worried about your disappearance; she was worried about the Garden Club meeting being canceled since the annual flower show is coming up."

"Well, you can assure your mother that I'm just fine. I stayed at the RCC to help out in the kitchen." I chewed on whether I should tell Madison about Evelyn being the number one suspect.

"You helped in the kitchen? So did you see Emile?" she asked.

"As a matter of fact . . ." I pushed the image of Emile's body lying on the floor of the RCC kitchen out of my mind. "Charlotte and I were there when Jane found him."

"Jane?" she asked.

"The waitress. When she got to work, she found Emile." I wasn't sure what I could or couldn't say about the crime scene. I mean, Carter had never said to keep anything hush-hush.

"Charlotte," she whispered. "Is she just devastated? I guess the wedding is canceled."

"She is very upset. But her wedding isn't canceled." I had to put a stop to any nonsense that might get around the gossip circle. "Evelyn has a really great chef on the hook and I've started the cakes. It's all a go."

"Still." And *there* was the southern pause we did when we formulated our own opinion of the situation. "I need to go see her. I am in the wedding."

"I think she's just happy at home with Brett." There was no need to bring unnecessary attention to an already crazy situation.

"Sophia." The sarcasm spilled through the phone. "You don't know anything about being a best friend. She doesn't want a man to listen to her groan and moan when he'll just tell her everything is okay. We need to help her beat it to death. Make her feel better. I'll be over to get you."

It wasn't enough to just talk about something bad that had happened to us. We had to toss it out the window, run over it, and then back over it for good measure.

I pulled the phone from my ear and noticed she'd hung up the phone.

If I was going to have to go over to Charlotte's and help her beat the situation into the ground, then I was going to need to take some brain food. The Berry.

"Mama," I called into the family room. I walked over to the refrigerator and opened it, pulling out the fruit tray.

Instead of buying the fruit and cutting it up, Bitsy purchased multiple fruits trays that were already done for her. She claimed that she kept so many because she liked to be able to pull out something fast for people who just stopped by to snack on. Around these parts, no one really called to announce they were coming by. Most times they didn't even know if they were stopping. Usually they'd drive by and get a hankering to stop. It was those times that Bitsy would never be caught unprepared. She said it was good southern hospitality to have a bit of food to offer.

As a child, it had killed me to stare at the boxed coffee cake that sat on the counter waiting for company to stop by. As soon as someone other than Bitsy and Dad walked into our house, I immediately asked them if they wanted a piece of the cake. They thought I had really good manners and complimented Bitsy, but we both knew my real motive. "Did you call me, sweetie?" Bitsy eagerly asked.

"Isn't Natalie Devin in your Garden Club?" I asked and pulled out the prepackaged caramel dip Bitsy used for her quick fruit presentations.

"She is. Why?" Bitsy put Duchess on the floor and scooped some kibble into her bowl.

"Is she still married to Mr. Devin?" I was drawing a blank on his name suddenly, but Bitsy would love that I was calling him "Mister."

It never failed and no matter my age, Bitsy always reminded to me address her friends as "Mister" and "Missus."

"Arnold Devin." She nodded and smiled. "Such a nice man. And a nice couple."

I stuck the caramel in the microwave and took the salt and Dad's mixed-nut can out of the lazy Susan.

"Are you making The Berry?" Bitsy's voice rose in excitement.

"I am." I took the caramel out of the microwave and added some salt to it while mixing at the same time. This wasn't the usual way I liked to make salted caramel, but in a pinch, this had to do. "Madison is on her way over to get me. We are going to Charlotte's house to make sure she's okay."

"About that." Bitsy eased down into one of the island chairs. She watched as I used the bottom of one of her cocktail glasses to smash the mixed nuts. "I've been thinking about you and the RCC. I think it's best you just stay far away from there. If you insist on still doing the wedding cake for Charlotte—if there *is* a wedding—then your father and I will buy every piece of equipment and all the ingredients you need."

"It's temporary." I pulled out one of Bitsy's pewter platters. "Plus, it's for Evelyn. I feel like I owe her since she gave me a chance in high school with a job there. She encouraged me to bake."

"Sophia"—Bitsy poured on her sweet voice—"that woman doesn't have all her chairs in the parlor. If the police think she did it, then . . ."

"Who told you that?" I asked.

"Nora Kincaid. You know, Carter's mama. She and I've been friends for a long time."

I had to question Bitsy's definition of a long time. There was Webster's definition and then there was Bitsy's version. Same words, different meanings. A long time for Bitsy meant at least two weeks.

"Well, he's wrong," I informed her. "Evelyn didn't kill anyone. Besides, I'm only going to work there for a couple more days until a new chef is hired, which I'm hoping will be the sous chef, Nick." I arranged the strawberries on the platter in a heart shape. Charlotte would get a kick out of that. "Besides, I'm not really doing anything but making sure things run smoothly."

As I dipped the strawberries in the salted caramel and rolled them into the nut mix, my mouth watered. It was a spur-of-the-moment recipe I'd made years ago when Bitsy was in a pickle and needed a quick snack for one of those drop-in guests. When the guest had asked what it was called, I'd blurted out, "The Berry." It was a hit.

"Why did you ask about Natalie?" Bitsy brought the conversation back around.

"I thought I saw her today having lunch in the RCC dining room." I failed to let her know that the dinner she and Dad would feast on was actually Natalie's lunch after she'd sent it back, too distraught to eat. Maybe she was the one with no chairs in the parlor.

"You probably did. She lunches there daily after her tennis lesson." Bitsy took a strawberry and popped it in her mouth. "Mmm, mmmm. Still delicious."

"You are going to ruin your supper." I pointed over to the food container.

"I have a wonderful idea." Bitsy had that look in her eye. That look that told me it wasn't an idea but a done deal.

"I don't like that look on your face," I noted, rolling the last two strawberries.

"My Garden Club is having a meeting tomorrow. We are going to be discussing the flower show. Why don't you make your fabulous Blueberry Buckles? The girls will love it," Bitsy said.

Under normal circumstances I'd immediately have said no, but with Evelyn on the line for murder and Charlotte's wedding on the chopping block, this wasn't a normal circumstance. There was a lot of gossip that went on at the Garden Club meetings, and surely they'd be talking about Emile's death. Plus, I wanted to get in front of Natalie Devin to see exactly how well she'd known him.

"Let me ask Nick if he's got everything under control for tomorrow," I said.

Quickly I texted Nick to see if he was able to handle the RCC lunch reservations for tomorrow because I had something I needed to do for the wedding. It wasn't a lie. I did need to prove that Evelyn hadn't killed Emile so Charlotte's wedding wouldn't be canceled. He assured me he could and said he'd see me tomorrow afternoon. Madison followed up with a text saying she was in the driveway.

"It's settled." I grabbed The Berry and kissed Bitsy on the cheek. "Can you go to the grocery and grab the items I need for the Buckles? The recipe is in your recipe file in the pantry."

I grabbed my bag.

"Give Charlotte my love. And don't talk to strangers! Or killers!" Bitsy yelled as I walked down the hall and out the door.

Chapter Nine

"You know, there hasn't been anyone who's ever lived up to your baking abilities since you left." Madison munched on a strawberry on our way over to visit Charlotte. "Say . . ." She gripped the wheel of her parents' old wood-paneled station wagon and took the curvy roads back into town. "What are you doing Monday?"

"I plan on being in my new apartment if I can steal some time between now and then to check out what's available on the Internet listings." It was on my to-do list.

There was no way I was going to be able to afford my own apartment in the city without Noah paying half. I was either going to have to settle for a roommate I didn't know or sign a sublet until I could get my feet back on the ground.

Not that I was financially struggling. I wasn't. I made good money and I invested most of it. Maybe my issue was that in the back of my mind I wanted to open my own bakery, but I had nowhere near that kind of cash. *Yet.*

"Oh, I can show you several. There's some in town, or there's that new development that used to be the Jacksons' farm, but that might be too far out." She didn't quite get what I was saying. "Regardless, I want you to stop by a couple of my showings, a few hours early of course, and put some of those crunchies in the oven. They say that if you make a home smell like fresh-baked cookies, it helps sell it, and I sure could use a sale."

"I don't think you understand." I scooted around in the seat of her swaggin' wagon, as we'd affectionately called it back in high school when her parents had let us borrow it. "I'm going to be back in New York on Monday. I've got a job," I reminded her.

When had everyone in Rumford lost their minds? Why was it so hard for them to believe that I was going back to the city and I was just here for a mental health break? That sounded much better than a semi-emotional breakdown, which I'd probably had.

"That's ridiculous." She laughed me off as if what I said was the funniest thing she'd ever heard. I looked at her with a straight face and she looked at me. "Oh, you're serious?"

"Yes. Why would you think I was staying here?" I asked.

"Because you've decided to do Charlotte's cake and you said you were filling in at the RCC as a favor to Evelyn, so I just assumed. That's all." She shrugged and suddenly became silent.

"I'd love to give you some Red Velvet Crunchies dough, though, and you can put them in the oven at your houses—I had no idea you were a real estate agent. I thought you were holding down the fort with your young'uns." I smiled at my friend, who didn't return the gesture.

"Aw, that's okay. I was just thinking that if you didn't have anything to do, I'd pay you to use your skills before you opened up your own bakery." She let out a sigh.

"Bakery?" I laughed. People had no idea how much money

or planning went into opening a bakery. Ever since I'd seen the empty display window of Ford's Bakery when Bitsy and I had driven by, I hadn't been able to get the image of my own fun, more modern sweets in that window out of my head. The seed that had been planted by Bitsy and my friends had been watered by my own mind, and I couldn't shake the feeling I got inside when I pictured the residents of Rumford smiling after they took a bite of something I'd created.

"They didn't go under, silly," she said. "They retired, and let me tell you, you'd have a well-developed customer base full of pent-up demand. Now everyone has to go to the grocery store to get a doughnut hole. But I'm the listing agent on the bakery if you're interested."

"Interested?" I whispered, not affirming or denying that it sounded good. I wasn't sure this was the right time. Besides, I had my dream job. At least I'd thought I did a couple of weeks ago.

"Just let me know if you want to see it." Her lips grew into a smile.

* * *

We pulled up to Charlotte's house, and I saw a Rumford Sheriff's Department squad car. "Carter." I cleared my throat.

"He's here all the time." Madison threw the swaggin' wagon in park. The car moaned and groaned, then backfired a couple of times when she turned off the ignition. "He and Brett are best friends."

No wonder he'd taken offense when I'd accused Brett of killing Emile, though I'd yet to cross him off my list.

"If I sell one of those listings, Matthew and I will have

enough saved so I won't have to drive this hand-me-down any-more. Don't get me wrong. I love that my mother and father gave it to us, and there's really nothing wrong with it since it's never seen the roads outside Rumford city limits. But come on." She smacked the seat between us. "I made out with a guy in high school right here before I started dating Matthew. Not a good memory to relive when I get in here with my two kids and one of them is attached to my boob."

"Oh, Madison," I laughed. She was still just as funny as she'd been in high school. It was so refreshing to be back around people who were genuine and not nice to you only because they were trying to move up in the world. "You'll never change."

"Why should I?" she asked and pulled the keys out of the ignition. "Maybe you need to look at why you think you need to be different than who you really are."

She got out of the car, leaving me there with her words hang-ing in the air. It was a long few seconds of her words swirling around in my head before I heard her yell.

"You comin'?" She stood at the front door of the small gray Cape Cod.

She didn't wait for me to get out of the car before she waltzed right on in. I grabbed the platter and stood on the sidewalk fac-ing the house. Charlotte lived in an older community of Cape Cods. They were a unique development that dated back to the 1930s. From what I could remember, they'd been nearly falling apart or condemned when I'd left ten years before.

Not today. Even with the sun setting, I could see that the houses had been brought back to life. As far down the sidewalk as I could see, a treescape had been planted along both sides of the street following the sidewalk. There was a letter-styled steel mailbox in front of each house. Even though they were clapboard, each one was painted differently and reminded me of Rainbow Row in Charleston, South Carolina.

"Are you coming?" Charlotte's arm was extended, holding the door wide open.

"Yes." I smiled and took the first steps up to the door. "Everything looks so different."

"Brett has really done a great job with it." A thin-lipped smile was planted on her face. "The old neighborhood wears a new face."

"I thought he was a businessman," I said, stepping up onto the small front porch. A small dormer hung above the door, and the cutest carriage lights were attached on each side of the door.

"He is. He takes run-down areas in different towns and has investors as well as contractors he works with to bring those areas back to life. Ya know, malls, neighborhoods, things like that." She took the platter as I handed it to her. "Yum," she sighed, looking down at The Berry. "I've missed your fun food." There was a sadness in her voice that moved up to her eyes.

"How are you?" I asked as we stepped inside her cute house.

"You know." She hemmed and hawed. "I'm not sure what we're going to do." She shook her head and walked into the family room just to the right of the door. The room was painted white and had a nice white brick fireplace along one of the shiplap walls. The bamboo floors added a nice dark touch to the light space. The airiness continued with the two light brown leather loveseats and pallet coffee table. Charlotte's wedding journal and all sorts of wedding magazines were stacked on the table.

"Your house is adorable." She'd obviously done a lot of work.

"We knocked out that wall so the kitchen would be bigger."

She pointed to the large island with three fairly large round white pillars that made the delineation between the two rooms.

The side of the island that was in the kitchen area had three stools pulled up to it.

"I'm impressed." It was refreshing to see how they'd brought the old house back to life.

The sound of people talking filtered through the screen door off the kitchen.

"Grab a beer out of the fridge and come on out." Charlotte held the platter in her hand and tilted her head toward the back door before she walked out.

The refrigerator door hung open as I bent down and looked at the selection of all the different beers. Charlotte and Brett obviously had a healthy taste for different kinds. Carter's head peered over the refrigerator door.

"Carter." He'd startled me.

"I suggest the Blue Brew." He cocked his head.

His smile was contagious, and I returned it. I glanced back at the beer and drew my eyes down to the Blue Brew.

"Only because you recommended it." I grabbed one of the blue bottles and stood up.

"Here. Let me." He reached for the bottle and twisted off the cap before handing it back to me. His brown eyes were as clever as a terrier's.

His brown hair was a little more muffed up than it'd been this morning. A five o'clock shadow was tickling his jawline and above his lip. My heart quickened when I imagined what it would feel like against my face.

I gulped and blushed.

"Thank you," I whispered, and quickly took a swig. "Coffee

this morning. Cookies in the afternoon, and now a beer. We have to stop meeting like this."

"I don't think so." His gaze gratified me. "I've enjoyed our little meetings."

Was he flirting with me? He grinned at me, making me speechless.

"Did you ask Brett about the menu?" I asked.

"No, because I told you that he was at my house at the time of the murder." His slow southern drawl became much slower, as if he were trying to speak as if I didn't understand him.

"I'm just saying that you should explore all people." Not that I was going to talk him into it, but he needed to have more suspects than just Evelyn. "So you don't have any more leads?"

"I didn't say that either. And I am looking into the possibility of the affairs Emile might've had." At least he was doing something.

"What are you two doing?" Brett walked in and shoved past us to the refrigerator. He grabbed three beers. "Come on. I'm not going to listen to this all night by myself. Charlotte is talking all sorts of nonsense about canceling the wedding."

"Say, Brett." I turned to face him. I was fully aware Carter was still looking at me. "Since I've been taking over for Emile, I saw your wedding file. I'm going to need your signature on the food contract." I snickered for a cover-up. "I'm so shocked y'all're having a French menu."

"I'm not signing anything with a French menu. I told Emile that. I told Evelyn that and I told Charlotte that." His eyes bore into me, his jaw tense.

"You told Emile?" Suddenly, Carter took an interest.

"Yeah." Brett's lip curled up. "Last week when we met for

our final menu preparation in his office, he tried to get me to sign off on some papers, but I told him I wasn't going to eat food I couldn't even pronounce. Especially since I'm paying for it."

"When was the last time you talked to or saw Emile?" Carter asked.

"Why?" His brows crunched together and he extended a flat palm to Carter. "Wait. You can't possibly think I had anything to do with this guy's murder?"

"I think he should check all possibilities." I shrugged.

"Since when did you get a partner?" He looked between me and Carter, finally settling his stare at Carter.

"I'm only asking because I'm going to make your food and I wanted to get started on it tomorrow," I lied.

"Or you can just answer my questions about the last time you saw Emile." Carter was a little sterner this time.

"The last time I saw him was that day. I was with Charlotte and Evelyn too. We had a meeting in the ballroom. The rest of the week I've been at work or here. I've been around plenty of people who can verify. Is that all?" Brett asked.

"Hey, man. It's all part of the job." Carter smoothed it over as best he could.

Without looking at them, I headed outside, where Charlotte and Madison were huddled under a quilt. It looked like Madison was comforting Charlotte.

The back patio had a built-in fire pit in the middle. There were several Adirondack chairs placed around the pit as well as a bench. At the end of the bench, a few blankets folded in a stack. There were a couple of tables with some finger foods and The Berry.

I took a small plate and put a couple of snacks along with a strawberry on it before I went over to the bench to sit down. It was probably the best place to sit to avoid Carter. He made my emotions confused, and that bothered me. My heart hadn't skipped like that since I'd met Noah. In some weird way, I felt like I was cheating on Noah, even though I knew we weren't together anymore. Maybe it was because I'd not been in a situation like this in years and was a tad bit uncomfortable.

"I'm glad to see you aren't missing." Carter drew the beer bottle up to his lips. There was a vivid smirk on his face. He handed me his beer to hold while he moved the blankets to a chair and sat down next to me on the bench.

Well, my plan didn't work. My body stiffened when I handed him back his beer.

I turned my head to look at him. The fire flickered, making the gold specks in his brown eyes stand out. "I'm guessing Bitsy called you."

"Every hour." He grinned. "You're lucky you have a caring mother."

"I know." I tried to put the sweet tone of his southern drawl in the back of my mind as I talked to him. He was every bit the southern gentleman I'd always imagined I'd end up with when I was growing up. That was before I met Noah, who was so different.

Noah was suave. Worldly. He was very opinionated, which made him seem so smart.

"You should've called her." His brow rose.

"I did! I called her cell phone. How was I to know that it was in her car?" I asked.

Carter threw his head back and laughed. I enjoyed watching him get a kick out of it, since he knew I'd driven Bitsy's car that day. I also noticed my friends were looking at us with smiles on their faces. I refused to look at them.

"When I went back to the office, my secretary said that your Bitsy had called her a million times to report a missing woman and insisted on an Amber Alert. Bitsy had a hard time understanding that the law states a person of your age needs to be missing for twenty-four hours before we can do anything and you'd need to be a missing child for us to put out an Amber Alert. Unless you were sick, mentally ill, or a harm to society. Those are special circumstances. Bitsy insisted this was a special circumstance because apparently you aren't in your right mind since you were cheated on recently." His smile faded, his eyes boring into mine.

"Oh, shit," I muttered. "How embarrassing."

"He's a jerk. And I'm glad he did or I'd never have gotten to have this beer with you." He clinked his bottle to mine. "Cheers."

"Cheers." I held his gaze.

It was refreshing that he had said those kind words even though he was probably thinking I was a freak. I was sure of it. I put the notion that he'd been flirting with me out of my head, knowing he was just being nice out of pity for the girl who'd run back home after her heart was broken. Not to mention seen the dead body of a murder victim.

"How is the investigation going?" I had to change the subject, though I wasn't sure it was the best topic of conversation.

"Going." He sucked in a deep breath and leaned his forearms on his knees, bending his body over. He stared at the fire.

"Do you have any suspects?" Brett asked. Charlotte and Madison watched the men.

"Unfortunately, it's not looking good for Evelyn Moss." Carter took another drink from the bottle.

"But without Evelyn, I can't have my wedding." Charlotte gave him a hostile glare.

"I'm sorry, Charlotte. You know I don't want anything to happen to your wedding, but I've got a murder case to solve." Carter wasn't budging. His southern manners went sideways as he let Charlotte cry in her beer.

"There is no way Evelyn killed anyone," I chirped up.

"And you are now a detective?" He looked at me as if I'd overstepped my authority.

"No, but I know her and I know that Emile wasn't all that nice to everyone." I probably said more than I should.

"I didn't know you knew him." His words had a bite.

"Brett, do something." Charlotte stood up and threw the blanket on the ground before she marched back into the house.

He gave Carter a look.

"Did you have to bring this up again, man?" Brett shook his head. "Great." Carter chugged back his beer and stood up. He set his empty bottle on one of the tables. "Have a nice night, ladies."

Madison and I gave a slight wave and watched as he walked out the gate of the backyard, not bothering to say good-night to Brett and Charlotte.

"That was uncomfortable." Madison walked over and sat down next to me.

"Yeah. I wouldn't've asked Carter anything if I'd known Charlotte was going to get upset." I stared at the flames and tried to wrap my head around the fact that I was wondering when I was going to see Carter again.

"What about him?" She gave me a wry smile. "That was awkward too." After I gave her a strange look, she said, "Your and Carter's little flirt session." Madison tucked her legs up under her and tucked a blanket up under her chin.

"What are you talking about?" I snorted, trying not to ask her if she really thought he was flirting with me. I wasn't a teenager anymore.

"Are you kidding me? He is smitten with you," she said. "He even looked at you with those eyes. Just like the first time he laid eyes on you."

"What eyes?" I giggled, trying to hide that teenage girl that seemed to pop out of me every time I was near Carter. Then I realized that Madison hadn't been at Small Talk Café the first time Carter and I'd met.

"Oh my God." Madison drew back. Her jaw dropped. "You are interested in Carter Kincaid." She shoved me to the side in a playful way.

"Stop it. We aren't sixteen." I brushed her off. "But you really think he was flirting? I thought it was just me."

"Talk about me not changing. You still have all the men falling over you," she teased.

Carter was interesting, but no one needed to know that. There was some chemistry between us. There was no denying that. "I'm here to figure out a way to get Evelyn off the hook and get Charlotte hitched. Besides the whole expensive menu, I think Emile was having an affair with some members of the RCC. Carter needs to look into them."

"Like who?" Madison asked.

"You can't say anything." I reached over and grabbed another berry. I took a bite of it. "Natalie Devin, for one."

"Shut up!" Madison's jaw dropped. "Not that I'm gossiping, but I'd heard her marriage was falling apart."

"I need to find out if they were having an affair. If it's true, she or her husband could've killed Emile. That's a huge motive." I drank the last bit of beer in my bottle and set it down on the brick wall of the fire pit.

The flames jumped around when the light breeze trickled across the backyard.

"And exactly how do you think we are going to figure out if it's true?" Her face shadowed in and out in the flickering firelight.

"We?" I asked and scooted a little to the right so I could get a look at her face to see if she was serious.

"You haven't been here in ten years, Sophia. There's a lot of gossip you don't know that could help." She cocked a brow. She wasn't playing.

"You're right." It might be helpful to have someone to knock ideas around with. Not really a bad idea. She'd be able to keep a secret better than Mama.

"I'll help, but I have one condition." The smile on her face told me she wanted something from me. I'd seen that face many times before.

"What?" I cautiously asked.

"I need you to stay for another week and bake those cookies at my open houses." She drove a hard bargain. "Plus a cake for Bryce's second birthday party next weekend."

"I thought you said Monday." I clearly remembered her saying something about Monday. "Besides, I can't use the RCC kitchen past this weekend."

"I have a few houses to show next week. And I've got a space for you to use for Bryce's cake. A Big Bird cake." She put her hands in the air. "One that stands."

"But . . ." I started. She was slicker than snot on a doorknob.

"Shhhhhhh." She put up a finger and wagged it between us. "Remember, I have a lot of ins and outs of places where we can get some information."

"Like what?" I asked.

"I've got to go to Natalie Devin's house about a possible listing," she said.

"I can go with you. While you're talking to her about the listing, I can make an excuse to leave the room and snoop around." It sounded like the perfect in to me. "You can go to the bathroom but snoop around instead."

"Do you even know what you're looking for?" She looked at me as if I'd lost my mind.

"Notes, cards, letters from Emile. Check her computer or something. I don't know. Research it," I suggested. "I can't do all of the figuring out."

Chapter Ten

"Your phone is ringing," I said, and patted the space next to me. The cold sheet under my hand sent a shockwave reminder that I wasn't in my dream back in NYC in my apartment with Noah next to me.

I slid my hand down the sheet until it hit a warm and cuddle-up Duchess. She purred with each rub until the phone buzzed again.

"I guess I wasn't dreaming about the phone." I rolled over to my right and saw Madison had texted me a few times.

After I'd gotten home last night, I'd made the Blueberry Buckles and headed up to bed. The beer was a much-needed sleep aid. Bitsy had left me a note to be ready by ten AM so we could leave for the Garden Club. Apparently Madison had different plans.

I scrolled through a text message Madison had left an hour before. The last text said to hurry up because she was downstairs with Bitsy.

I peeled back the covers and slipped my feet into my warm house shoes.

"If I've got to face her"—I grabbed Duchess, talking about Mama—"then you have to face her."

I couldn't be sure, but I think Duchess had been by my side since I'd been home because she was tired of Bitsy falling all over her and my room seemed to be a safe haven for the feline.

We padded down the back stairs to the kitchen. With each step, the coffee aroma got stronger and stronger.

"What are you doing here so early?" I asked Madison, holding Duchess to one side as I grabbed a cup to pour myself some coffee.

"There's my baby." Bitsy's lips were all squishy and mushed together. She grabbed Duchess and did kissy faces. I rolled my eyes.

"Early," Madison scoffed. "It's eight AM. Early bird gets the worm."

"Good thing, because I hate worms." I dragged myself over to the table and sat down. "Seriously, what's up?"

Bitsy was too busy filling up Duchess's bowl with kibble to have an ear in our conversation, which told me that she'd already questioned Madison and knew why she was here so early.

"I thought we'd get our day started off by grabbing a cup of coffee at Small Talk Café and then head over to a house before we go to the Garden Club meeting." She clapped her hands together. "Chop-chop."

"Listen, I didn't say I was going to be at your beck and call since I'm staying another week." I took a sip of the hot coffee, instantly releasing a happy sigh. It was my very favorite time of the day.

"You are?" Bitsy stopped milling around the kitchen and jerked her attention to us.

"Calm down." I had to put a halt to any nonsense wrangling around in her pretty little head. "I'm going to hang around a few more days to bake Bryce's birthday cake."

"Oh, happy birthday to Brycie." Bitsy always put the "ie" on a child's name in an endearing way. "Can you believe it's been two years since we had your baby shower at the Garden Club?" She eased back down into one of the kitchen chairs.

"I know. I was telling Matthew that I couldn't believe we were parents." Madison pulled a leg up under her and popped her elbows on the top of the table.

Bitsy called her out. "Honey, that's not ladylike." My mouth twitched as I tried to contain my smile. "Sophia, you go on upstairs and get ready. It's not proper to keep your guest waiting."

Who knew what Bitsy and Madison had talked about while it took me a good forty-five minutes to shower, fix my hair, and apply makeup? If I'd been going straight to the RCC to cook, I wouldn't have taken so long to get ready, but I was going to the Garden Club meeting and snooping around. I needed to fit in as much as possible.

I opted to wear a pair of ankle-length khakis paired with a white button-down and a pearl necklace. It was strange looking at my image in the mirror, an image I'd worked so hard to get rid of. Not that I was uncomfortable; it just wasn't the real me. The real me was happy in a pair of scrub pants and chef's jacket. I didn't even mind the hairnet. Today I was sacrificing my comfort to help out Charlotte and Evelyn.

"Ready?" I asked, grabbing my bag.

"Yes." Madison bolted up so fast I knew she'd spent enough time with Bitsy.

"Can you bring the Blueberry Buckles to the Garden Club

meeting?" I checked my watch because I knew they'd be much better refrigerated until the meeting. Who knew what Madison had planned for the next hour.

"Of course." Bitsy's hand slowly rubbed Duchess. "See you girls there."

"What on earth do you have planned this morning?" I asked after I'd gotten in the swaggin' wagon and buckled the seat belt. My bag was nestled on the floor between my feet.

"First, coffee before anything." She jerked the gearshift into drive and zoomed out of driveway. "After two years of no sleep and because my tolerance of caffeine is so high, I need a gallon of coffee before I'm functional." She whipped the car out of the subdivision and headed straight toward town. "Don't get me wrong, I understand Matthew is tired. I'm tired. I'm the one who gets up and goes to work every single morning."

"Doesn't Matthew go to work every morning too?" I hated that I hadn't been a great friend over the past ten years. I didn't even have any social media accounts to keep up. Being in charge of a pastry division of a big restaurant took up enough of my time, and getting lost in social media didn't sound like much fun.

"He's a stay-at-home dad. I mean, it was a joint decision." She said it like she had to defend their reasoning.

"That's very popular nowadays." There were several fathers who came into The Manhattan with their children and friends during the day for a fun dessert after they'd been to the park.

"Honestly, it wasn't by choice." She gripped the wheel and took a left out of the gated community. "He worked at the stock-yard with cattle. It's all he's ever known. But all those jobs got outsourced to cheaper labor and it's really affected Rumford's farming community. So I went back to get my realtor license."

"I'm sure you're really good at it." I wanted to make her feel better.

"Did you even listen to what I said about this car yesterday?" She groaned. "Or are you just being nice? Because I don't need nice. I need a real friend and someone to really vent to."

"By all means, vent. But I'm no expert in marriage or children." It was true. There wasn't a maternal bone in my body. I'd spent so much time working and being the perfect girlfriend to Noah, I'd never thought about children. "It just seems to me that if you're in a financial situation, you'd both go to work."

"Who'd watch my young'uns?" she asked. "That's the problem. Any sort of money he'd make, we'd spend in putting the kids in daycare."

My mind quickly wanted to change the subject. There was a tension in her voice telling me she didn't want advice.

"That's something I wouldn't know about." I looked out the window. The Kentucky post fence zoomed by as the car hugged the curves of the road that led us into town. "But I do know about cakes. You really want a Big Bird cake?"

"Standing, yellow legs, orange claw toes, and all." She smiled.

"What on earth have I gotten myself into," I half-joked so I wouldn't make her mad. "I'm assuming Bryce loves Sesame Street?"

"Loves it. He has to watch it every morning or he's in a bad mood all day until the next day." She let off the gas a little when the speed signs changed from fifty-five to thirty-five outside city limits. "You'll see."

I wasn't sure what she meant by that and didn't respond.

She pulled into the parking space at the curb in front of Small Talk Café. It was just as busy as it had been yesterday morning. I didn't see a Rumford Sheriff's cruiser and my heart sank a bit. It would've been kind of nice to see Carter to start my day, but I wasn't sure how the tension would be between us since we hadn't parted on great terms last night.

Madison put on her pretty smile and grabbed some flyers off the seat. "You ready?" She waved the papers in the air. "Gotta sell something."

Apparently Small Talk was the gathering place to be at in the morning. Madison looked as if she were running for office, greeting everyone with a big hug and asking about their families before slipping them a flyer about one of her houses for sale. Of course, they all said they'd pass along the information.

While she did that, I stood in line to order a couple of cups of coffee. I needed to wake up and get my mind into thinking mode. The same girl from yesterday was at the cash register.

"You were in here yesterday, right?" She asked, snarling from behind her register.

"Yes. Two coffees, please," I simply stated.

Her head tilted. Her eyes drew down my body and flew back up again. She turned around and poured the two coffees.

"Here you go." She pushed them toward me while I dug in my bag to get my wallet.

"How much?" I asked, and unsnapped the snap to retrieve my money.

"Free for you." She seemed irked.

"Excuse me?" I asked, ducking my head forward.

"Sheriff said that if you came in this morning to put it on his tab." She stared at me with a blank stare.

"He did?" I smiled. Instead of pulling money out of my bag, I pulled out his business card. Holding it between my fingers, I used my other hand to put my wallet back in my bag. I slipped his business card into my back pocket and took the coffees. "Please tell him thank you."

"He said you'd say that and that if you wanted to thank him, you should do it yourself." Her eyes glanced over my shoulder. "Next!"

Madison was still giving her sales pitch about how convenient some house was to somewhere, so I headed over to the only empty table in the corner. I set the cups down and took my phone out of my pocket along with Carter's card. I sent him a quick text thanking him for the coffees. No sooner had I tucked my phone and the card back in my purse than my phone rang.

A slight smile crossed my lips when Carter's number scrolled across my phone.

"Good morning." I wasn't sure what to say. It felt really intimate telling him that, but it's something I'd have said to his face if he were standing here.

"Is this really Sophia the baker?" was the first thing out of his mouth.

"Yes." I thought it was weird for him to ask that.

"Wow." There was a joking tone to his voice. "This is a nice side of you. Brett called me last night after he'd gotten Charlotte calmed down, and he was still mad about you accusing him of killing Emile."

"I didn't accuse him of anything. I was simply asking questions that might've been overlooked," I protested.

"Overlooked by me?" He questioned back.

"I'm not saying that." This was definitely not how I had thought this phone conversation was going to go.

"What is it you do for a living?" he asked, as if he didn't already know.

"You know what I do. I'm a pastry chef." I knew what he was about to say and prepared myself for it.

"A fancy term for baker." There he went. "I'm the lead investigator on this case and you are baking the wedding cake for my best friend's wedding. Why don't we keep those lines separated?"

"Fine." I wasn't going to really agree to anything, but I knew he was going to keep using this line of reasoning with me if I did protest. "Anyways, I wanted to thank you and a simple text could've done the trick. You are the one who called me."

"It was the only way I could get your phone number without having to call Bitsy and get into a lengthy conversation with her. You didn't give us your phone number when we were taking your statement at the RCC concerning Emile's death," he stated matter-of-factly. "We need your signature for your statement and your fingerprints. Do you mind heading down to the station sometime within the next couple of days?"

Everything stopped around me. At least I felt like it stopped around me.

"You mean to tell me that you bought me a coffee because you knew I'd call you to thank you?" I was trying to wrap my head around this warped sheriff's mind.

"And it worked." His southern drawl dripped through the phone, smooth as silk in my ears.

"Yes. Bitsy did teach me good manners that I pride myself on. Just like I called Charlotte this morning and thanked her for having me over last night." I made a mental note to shoot

Charlotte a quick text to thank her just in case Officer Know-It-All decided to investigate. At this point I wouldn't put it past him.

"I'll leave it at the front desk so you just need to give the clerk your name." He was all business.

"Yeah. Thanks." I hung up the phone right before Madison walked over. I pushed the cup across the table. "Compliments of Sheriff Carter." I dragged my paper cup up to my mouth and took a sip.

"Really?" she asked with excitement and looked around. "I don't see him."

"He just wanted to be a good sheriff and make sure I come down to the office and sign off on my statement." I lifted my brows and took another drink.

"Speaking of statement." She looked around before leaning over the table. She whispered, "Let's go so we can talk about the case."

We got up and I stopped, looking back at the counter of Small Talk. There were egg sandwiches and the typical southern food but nothing like a muffin or a doughnut, which would really go well with my attitude and I knew I didn't have anything in my bag to munch on.

"What's wrong?" Madison tugged on my sleeve.

"I was looking to see if they had something for me to grab to eat, like a doughnut." I shrugged.

"I told you that with Ford's shut down, the only place to get a doughnut—if you want to call them that—is down at the Piggly Wiggly." She snorted and walked around the car.

Before she unlocked the doors, she stared at me from over the hood. It was long enough for me to notice.

"What?" My eyes narrowed as I wondered what was in her head.

"Nothing," she quipped, and jumped in the driver's side, leaning way over and pulling the lock up to unlock my door.

Madison drove the car in silence on our way down Main Street toward the business district. It looked pretty much the same. There was a medical building where most of Rumford's medical professionals had their offices. I could still remember the smell that hit you as soon as you opened the door. The combination of the dentist, the ophthalmologist, the dermatologist, and the family physician wasn't a smell that I'd ever want to be bottled.

Rumford First National Bank was on one corner of the four-way stoplight. The thrift shop was on the opposite corner. The insurance agent was on another.

When we pulled into the medical building parking lot, I broke the silence.

"Where we going?" I asked, a wee bit nervous.

Childhood memories of Bitsy taking me to the dentist weren't very endearing, and I'd taken great measures to forget them.

"I was going to take you to one of my houses, but I got a different idea when we were at Small Talk, so I wanted to stop by the real estate office and grab a set of keys." She slammed the car into park. "You can hang tight here."

"Where is your office?" My nerves calmed.

"We are in the old medical building." She pointed.

"What happened to the doctors?" I asked.

"They built that annex hospital on the outskirts of town. Instead of traveling to the city for an emergency, they added a hospital annex and a new medical building." With that, she got out of the car and darted up the steps in front of the building.

In no time flat, she jogged back down the steps with the keys dangling from her fingers.

"I've got two places to go." She put the car in gear and we headed out of the parking lot. "We've got a house near Charlotte. It's darling. My target market for that area are people our age. The up-and-coming entrepreneurs. These little redone Cape Cods have been so popular. This is the last one, and I think it hasn't sold because it hasn't found the right buyer."

"You make it sound as if the house makes the decision who its buyer should be." I laughed at the thought.

"And shouldn't it?" she asked.

I looked over at her and she was serious.

"I do believe that a house speaks to the soul of the buyer. The house has the magic that makes the buyer fall in love. This will be one of the houses that you will bake your Crunchies in on Monday. And it won't be on the market for long."

"Funny, because I think the perfect dessert speaks to the intended customer." An image of the guests at Charlotte's wedding enjoying the cakes took over my thoughts. Some of the guests even asked for a business card.

"We are heading back to Charlotte's neighborhood." Madison brought me out of my daydream.

"Speaking of Charlotte, have you heard from her?" I asked.

"Last night after I got home, I decided to call her and feel her out on what she knew about the case, just in case Brett had said something to Carter." That was a smart move, I thought. "Brett told her that it wasn't looking good to have their wedding and reception at the RCC because Carter didn't have any suspects other than Evelyn and Mayor Pickering is breathing down his neck to get it solved. Saying something about the townfolk calling at all hours of the night and how the RCC brings in a lot of revenue for Rumford." She turned the car into the driveway of a house catty-corner to Charlotte's. "Apparently, the members are too scared to come to the club and are looking to see how they can transfer or sell their membership."

"That's awful." It suddenly hit me that it was now more important than ever to get Evelyn off the hook. More than just to make sure Charlotte's wedding went off without a hitch, it was to save the beloved RCC that was so dear to my heart.

"Right?" She jerked the keys out of the ignition. She motioned at the house. "Let's go in."

Both of us grabbed our coffees.

"It just seems so obvious that Evelyn would be the suspect." I had to think out loud. It was how I created my best recipes, and I was hoping it'd do the same for these new-to-me sleuthing skills that I so desperately wanted to have.

"They did have a big blow-up the night before, according to Charlotte, and it wasn't pleasant." She pulled her phone out of her purse and held it up to the big, door-knocker-looking keypad attached to the arm of the front door handle. "New way of doing things. It's like Apple Pay, only for realtors instead of having to get key codes."

"That's neat." I was impressed—not only by the new technology but also by the look and feel of the entryway when we stepped in. "This is a great house." I looked around. "I thought for sure it was going to look like the inside of Charlotte's, which I love, but it's nothing like it."

"That's one really cool thing the architects came up with

when Brett had taken on the neighborhood. Of course, the Beautification Committee about had a fit when he said he wanted to come in and buy up all the run-down houses that were getting ready to be used for government housing. Luckily, he was able to strike a deal and give them a substantial amount up front. And with each sale, the city of Rumford gets a percentage." She shut the front door behind us.

"I love that nook!" I squealed and took a left into a room that we'd used to call a living room. In the south, it was considered to be the room where you'd entertain guests, and no one was allowed in there unless there was a special occasion.

"The architect said that in the original design of the house, there was a window bench. Over the years the owners had it torn out. This particular house was actually stripped down to the bare studs and brought back to the way it was when it was first built." She pointed out the chair railing and the thick crown molding that today's new houses seemed to lack.

"I've always loved how old and charming the houses in Rumford are." I put my hand out. "Not that I don't love my parents' house. It's just a bit too modern for me."

"What about your apartment in New York?" she asked, and sat down on the blue, thick cushion that fit perfectly in the little nook. She patted the space next to her.

I picked up the blue-and-white-striped pillow and hugged it to me when I sat down, easing myself back on the white pillow with the blue diamonds.

"It's industrial. Noah loved it, and I was willing to go wherever he wanted." I hugged the pillow tighter to reel in the hurt feelings that still seemed to linger. They definitely weren't as strong as they'd felt before. Maybe they were even a little different. The fact still remained that there was a part of me that wasn't healed. Maybe spending another week in Rumford wouldn't be so bad. "But this place is really nice and cozy. Something I'd definitely buy if I lived in Rumford."

"I can see you here." She pointed up to the jeweled chandelier over our heads that made the space even more adorable.

"Don't be getting any ideas," I teased her, though I could see myself sitting here.

"Fine. Come on, I'll show you the kitchen where I'm going to have you bake the Crunchies." Her brows did a wiggle dance.

There had been no expense wasted on the house, that was for sure.

"This is really nice." The kitchen had modern gas appliances that any pastry chef would love. There was white subway tile along the backsplash. The white kitchen cabinets were nice and deep. The window over the farm sink was the perfect touch, allowing the natural light to flow into the space.

"These are marble countertops." She continued to make the loop around the kitchen and stopped at the island. "They decided to use butcher block on the island to tie in with the other wood elements of the house."

The open shelving in the kitchen was beautiful. Madison had done a great job staging the house with the wood bowl accents stacked on the white plates. Even the light-blue Kitchen Aid mixer seemed right at home.

"This is really a neat house, but your keen eye really sets it apart," I said as I turned to Madison. "Does the furniture and all the decorating come with it?"

"We have a price sheet that lists all the items." She opened a drawer in the kitchen and pulled out some sales sheets. She pushed one across the island.

I sat down on one of the steel island stools and glanced over the list. There was a sales price for the house, a sales price for the house as is with the furniture, and a breakdown of all the items she'd decorated with along with their prices.

"When I first told my boss what I wanted to do with the houses, he scoffed at me. He said it would never work," she said.

"And?" I asked.

"I don't know. This is the first house I did it to." She cackled. "That's why it's important to get you in here and bake for me. Which brings me to the next stop, which we have just enough time for before the Garden Club meeting."

I followed her out of the house, but not without thinking again how adorable and pretty perfect it was.

"Where to now?" I asked after I got in the car and fastened my seat belt.

She turned the engine over. "Ford's Bakery." She threw the car in gear and zoomed out of the neighborhood. "It's going to be a great space for you to bake Bryce's cake."

"I can't do that." That seemed so illegal to me.

"Why not?" she asked, but didn't let me answer. "I have full control over the kitchen, according to the contract. I have no way of knowing if the appliances and equipment works to even tell potential buyers. I don't have the knowledge that a real baker like you'd have. So you are going to be my expert."

"Really?" It just all sounded too good to be true.

"Really." Her voice rose excitedly. "They even have some stocked pantry items they said were still good to use."

My head bobbed back and forth. The idea of me having a place to escape to for the next few days did sound enticing. It being a real bakery was even better.

"Deal?" she asked.

"Yes. Deal." I wasn't about to look a gift horse in the mouth. "Then we don't have to run by there. We are running thin on time anyway. I don't want to be late to the Garden Club meeting now that you and I are on the case." I rubbed my hands together.

"Don't get too ahead of yourself there, Agatha Christie," she joked.

Chapter Eleven

"That's just hearsay, Dolores. Natalie and Arnold are just fine. So fine that he came down to the jewelry store and bought her a diamond the size of your head," one of the members of the Garden Club was saying as I eavesdropped on their conversation through the fake potted plant separating us. "Besides, what on earth would a strapping young man like Emile want with a wrinkly old woman like Natalie Devin?"

"I'm telling you, I walked in the RCC after a late night of tennis, and the two of them had their heads together," another woman said. "I saw it with my own two eyes through the swinging kitchen window. I was going to get a glass of water because I was so parched. I stood there for about five minutes trying to process what I'd seen. The giggling and the low murmur. There was definitely chemistry."

"Dear"—the other woman's voice dripped with skepticism— "Emile flirted with anyone in a tennis skirt. Trust me." There was a pause. "Look at these old legs." She giggled. "Once he commented on how in shape I was, and he made me feel like a young schoolgirl. I blushed in places I shouldn't've."

131

"There you are." Bitsy nearly scared the bejesus out of me, almost causing me to knock the plant over.

"Mama, stop that sneaking up on me." I held my hand up to my heart and straightened my back.

"I was doing no such thing, Sophia Cummings." She held out the plate of Blueberry Buckles. "I'm sure you want to do something with these before I ruin them."

I took the plate from her and headed over to the table Catherine Fraxman had unfolded for the Garden Club to use for food.

"Hi, Catherine." I greeted my old high school classmate with a smile.

She'd not changed too much since school. Her long black hair was pulled back in a side ponytail and fishtailed into a braid that hung over her shoulder. She'd always been tall and graceful. Her hips tapered into long, straight legs, something I'd always been envious of. She'd been the go-to gal if I ever needed help with history or writing a paper. She was so smart.

"Hi, Sophia. I heard you were back in town." She smiled and pushed her red glasses up on the bridge of her nose.

"It seems that Bitsy has told everyone." I looked around the table at all the food.

Patrice Davis had brought some sort of meatballs in a Crock-Pot. Beverly Scamper had brought some pigs in a blanket, while Crystal Nettles had brought some sort of pimento cheese spread and small squares of bread. The Garden Club wasn't nearly as fancy as Bitsy's Junior League. These women wanted to get their hands dirty, while the women in the Junior League only wanted their hands to be in hot manicure wax.

"I think I heard it down at Peacocks and Pansies." She shrugged, moved around some of the food, and took the Buckles out of my hand, placing the tray in the spot she'd just cleared. "Something about you needing a dress for Charlotte's wedding."

"I met Carol Bauer, and she said she had the perfect dress for me," I said.

"A little secret." Cat smiled and continued to adjust the food containers. "She says that to everyone. And when you get in there, she's going to tell you that so many people have tried on the dress and it didn't look good on anyone but you. That's why it's not been sold yet."

"So she's a good salesperson?" I joked and took one of the paper plates.

"Yes." She nodded. She placed a soft hand on my arm. "It's just so good to see you." Her southern drawl made the *you* sound more like *ewe*.

"Bitsy insisted I come to the meeting to say hi to all her friends." *And I wanted to see if Natalie killed Emile because they were playing bedroom rodeo.* "What are you up to nowadays?"

"I'm the librarian now. Sabrina Wells retired and I'd gotten my degree in library science, so I took over." There was a proud tone in her voice.

I took a step back and she took a step forward to move out of the way of the Buckles so a few members could grab one.

"Catherine, that's great! I'm not surprised. You're the smartest person I know, and it's because you kept your head in a book learning all that stuff." It was so fitting for her.

She drew her slim fingers up to her chest. "Why, thank you, Sophia. That's a compliment coming from you. You have no idea how I wished I could bake like you."

"I'm having a hard time wrapping my head around how much Rumford has changed in just the last ten years," I said.

"We're all grown up. I expect to see you at Friends of the Library. Bitsy is very involved with putting up all those free little libraries around the neighborhoods." Her eyes appeared magnified through the lenses of her glasses as she stared at me. "Don't get me wrong. She's not putting them up. Heavens to Betsy, no. Bitsy Cummings lifting a finger?" She winked. "You know she's much better at pointing."

Friends of the Library was one of Bitsy's clubs that'd started as a book club. When the community had noticed that the library was not being utilized as well as it could be and that literacy programs in the schools were declining, the book club had gotten together with the mayor and the city council to propose a committee that would help bring the library back as the center of our small town.

When I'd been a child, Bitsy had had me at the library almost every single day. She'd checked out books to read while letting me check out books on baking. With the small boxes they were calling free little libraries, they were going to be able to reach people who had a hard time making it to the library. It was a great concept: "Give a book, take a book." If you didn't have a book to give, it was okay; just return the book after reading it so another person could enjoy it. Plus, it kept Bitsy busy, and I liked that.

"I heard Bitsy on the phone last week talking about making the little libraries. I'm glad to see there's a club just to keep the library going," I said.

"I'd be lost without my nose in a book, and the free little library event is going to help us put books all over Rumford and at the fingertips of everyone, not just those coming to the library." She nodded. "Can you imagine the love for reading the program is going to create?"

"Y'all are doing a good thing," I assured her, taking another step away from the table. It seemed that word had gotten around about the Buckles, because everyone was walking up to get one. "I'm leaving sometime early next week, so I'm more than happy to help in any way I can while I'm here."

My Buckles were the only dessert on the table. Thank God I'd made plenty.

"I see." Her face pinched up in a fake smile. "I'm always here." She tapped her fingertips on my forearm before she excused herself and left me standing there.

"I'm telling you, Sophia, these are so much better than Ford's ever made," one of the women gushed after she'd devoured her Buckle.

"Have you ever thought about opening up a bakery here in Rumford since we don't have one now?" another one of Bitsy's friends asked.

I politely told them that I was just visiting. It never failed; they followed up my answer with a nice, sweet *Bless your heart; your Bitsy told us all about you getting dumped, and you are so fortunate that Bitsy is here to help you through. Your Bitsy is a giving soul.*

If we weren't among company, I'd probably have killed her right then and there. Nothing was secret or sacred to Bitsy, not even her own daughter's broken heart. Like always and like Bitsy had taught me, I put a big smile across my lipstick-painted lips and hid my crazy, thanking them for their very kind words about Bitsy while cursing her in my head.

"Have you gotten any information regarding Natalie or Ella?" I asked Madison after she'd finally gotten away from the women who insisted she do something about the dried-up bushes in front of one of her real estate listings.

"I swear, they only invited me to be in this club because they think I can just go in and pretty up everyone's yard once they list it." Madison was none too happy to be at the meeting. "But I did hear that Ella did in fact have an affair with Emile. And from her own mouth."

"Shut up," I gasped. It was our first real piece of evidence of a true motive that we'd discovered.

"Yes. She said that he was every bit the Italian lover we would assume him to be." Madison's brows bounced.

"Did you ask her what happened?" I asked.

"No. That's private, Sophia." Madison acted as if we were in the bedroom with them.

"But that's what we *need* to know. A motive. Did he dump her for another? Did she find him with another member? Natalie, perhaps?" I questioned.

Madison tapped her finger on her chin. "Yeah," she said blankly, "I didn't ask her those questions. I guess I should've."

"Go do it before the meeting starts." I gave her a little shove.

"She left. She's got an appointment at Peacocks and Pansies. She only came by to drop off the tickets that were printed up to sell for the garden show," she said.

Carol Bauer, the president of the Garden Club, got everyone's attention with a two-finger whistle. Something I was never able to do.

"Is that Priscilla Cartwright?" I leaned over to Madison, asking about the girl standing next to Carol.

"Oh, yeah. Crazy as her mama. She goes by the name Prissy now," Madison quipped. "But she does have a green thumb. She opened up Back-en-Thyme Flowers." Madison nodded. "She makes those big grapevine wreaths with all sorts of flowers, seasonal decorations and such." She crossed her arms. "Some people have all the luck. She's one of them."

"Ladies. Ladies!" Prissy yelled above the crowd. "Can everyone please take a seat? Cat was gracious enough to let us use the room for the full hour until it's time for kiddie hour. So we need to get started."

There were a few claps in honor of Cat as Madison and I took our seats in the back. My head bobbled back and forth trying to find Bitsy. I should've known she'd be right up front.

"There's Natalie." Madison nudged me. "She don't look like a grieving lover to me."

"And exactly what is that look?" I asked.

"Honey, look in the mirror," she teased.

"That's not nice. Unfortunately, I'm pretty sure Noah is still breathing." My eyes zeroed in on Natalie.

She wore a sleeveless red dress. The pattern changed from polka dots on the top to a floral design below the waist. The white gloves she wore on her hands stopped a little shy of her wrist. Her brown hair was cut into a very stylish asymmetrical bob, and her lack of wrinkles told me that she'd definitely had some work done. The years, though they'd been kind to her, still showed a little in the weight gain around her midsection. She wore it well.

Prissy talked about the plant exchange they'd scheduled for the next meeting and told them how to properly package the plants to bring in so they wouldn't be ruined. She also talked about the garden show, but my mind went other places.

"I'd like to address the elephant in the room." Prissy Cartwright brought everyone out of their boredom.

There was a blanket of whispers.

"We all heard about the head chef at the RCC. I'm sure Evelyn is working very hard to fill the spot. I've talked to her, and she handed me a nice piece of information that I think we will all love." Prissy's eyes were laser-focused on me. She put her hands out in front of her, and suddenly everyone followed them as if they were shining a spotlight on me. "She's informed me that our very own Sophia Cummings is going to run the kitchen until an adequate replacement is hired."

Prissy turned her attention to Carol, and they nodded at each other.

My mouth opened and nothing came out. With her palm face up, Bitsy gestured for me to shut my mouth. My mouth closed. Bitsy tapped her lips. I smiled.

"Natalie"—Prissy turned her, as well as everyone else's, attention to the woman in question—"I'm sure you and Sophia will find the time over the next few days to go over the menu for the flower show."

"This is great," Madison squealed. "You're staying longer?"

"No." I shook my head.

"Obviously," she snorted. "The flower show is not for another couple of weeks, and first you have to bake Charlotte's cake, then Bryce's, and after *that* is the flower show."

"Evelyn assured me she'd have someone in a couple of days," I mumbled so only Charlotte could hear.

"Sophia, I'd never have recognized you. You've grown up so lovely," Natalie interrupted us from behind. She held a piece of paper between her fingers. "Here's my address. Please stop by tonight so we can talk about the menu." She drew her eyes to Madison. "I'm looking forward to our meeting in a couple of hours."

"Couple of hours?" Madison looked at her watch. "I thought I was going to call you for a time. I can stop by tonight with Sophia."

Natalie looked between us a few times.

"Fine." She twisted around on her heels and sashayed out the door.

"For a woman who was getting a little on the side, she sure is uptight," Madison noted. Both of our heads leaned back as we watched her walk out of the library's room.

"Or she's uptight because she killed her lover." My eyes narrowed.

Chapter Twelve

"Craigslist? *Craigslist!*" Evelyn screamed through the receiver of the phone and motioned for me to come in and sit. She looked up. A sleepless night and a bunch of worry had found a home under her eyes. "Who is it? I want to know."

There was a long pause.

"You need to get ahold of Craig and have him take it down right now," she demanded. "Where is this list?"

Apparently, Evelyn had never heard of Craigslist. I pulled my phone out of my bag and hit my Safari app, typing in Craigslist. I handed her my phone. Her eyes scanned over it, and her mouth dropped when she realized exactly what it was.

"I'll call you back." She slammed down the receiver. "Is this some sort of garage sale site?" She handed me the phone back and took a big inhale as if she were preparing herself for my answer.

"Yes." I'd never thought of it as a big garage sale online, but technically that's what it was. "You can get some really good stuff on there. I got my café table for my apartment there."

"Did you know that a few of our members have put their

membership bonds on there? This is ridiculous." She pushed her chair back from the desk and stood up. She paced back and forth, gnawing on her lip. "Damn Emile," she spat.

I wished I'd not heard that. It wasn't helping to turn off the spotlight that I was desperately trying to get off of her.

"He always said that he'd get me fired. Someone is framing me." She wagged her finger at me. "Someone is trying to get me fired. This Craigslist thingy"—her hand flew into the air—"just might do the trick. Whoever heard of a prestigious bond like the RCC being sold at a garage sale?" Her voice escalated. "A garage sale!"

She flopped back down in her chair.

"Why on earth would someone want to frame you?" I asked.

"This job." She jabbed the desk with her finger. "My contract is coming up and I hear things. You don't work among a bunch of hoity-toity people and not hear things."

"What kind of things?" I asked.

"Arnold Devin, for one. He wants my job," she said.

My ears perked up.

"Arnold Devin, as in Natalie's husband?" I asked, as the idea of Arnold, not Natalie, as the killer started to form.

Was I sniffing up the wrong tree? Had Arnold found out about Natalie and Emile and killed him? After Natalie learned about the murder at lunch at the RCC and sent her food back, had she rushed home and confronted Arnold? Arnold had given her a big ring. According to the women at the Garden Club, the diamond was as big as her head. Too bad her hands had been covered with gloves when she'd handed me her address.

"That's the one," she snarled. "He recently retired. I heard they've gone on a budget. At least *Natalie* was put on a budget, and her tennis lessons have gone down from six days a week to three. And she's canceled all of her appointments with LuAnn Farris."

"Who is LuAnn Farris?" I asked.

"She's our massage therapist here. She's the best around, and it took me a lot, plus a big salary, to get her here." She drummed her fingers on the desk.

"Why would he want your job?" I asked, trying to get a clear picture of why he'd want to make it look as if Evelyn was the suspect.

"If you have my job, you get free services. Do you think Natalie Devin just idly sat by and let her luxuries be taken away?" Her nostrils flared, and it wasn't a good look on her. "I heard he stopped doing the extracurricular activities outside what the membership fee pays once he retired. And it just so happens Natalie cancels her appointments and cuts back on her lessons?" She asked the question as if I could answer her. "Not a coincidence."

She smacked her hand on the desk and dragged the Rolodex from underneath a stack of files. She ran her fingers along the alphabetical tabs and flipped the cards.

"I'm calling the sheriff right now. I'm telling him he needs to be looking at Arnold Devin." She picked up the phone, stuck it between her ear and shoulder, and jabbed at the numbers.

"Maybe you should call my dad instead and let him know this information. He did stop by, right?" I asked.

Her head lifted, and she looked as though she were pondering what I'd said.

"Regardless, I wanted to stop in and make sure you had someone to replace me in a couple of days," I said. "People are getting the wrong idea that I'm staying in town and asking me to do all sorts of events. I don't want to say anything to them, but I do want to make sure you have someone."

"John Cummings, please. Tell him this is Evelyn Moss," she chirped into the phone. She pulled the receiver away from her chin. "Yes. Don't worry. The new chef will be here in the morning, so if you don't mind, please be here bright and early to help with the transition."

"Great." I planted my hands on my thighs and pushed up to standing. "That's perfect. I'll be here."

"Yes. Evelyn Moss," she said again.

"I'll let you get back to your phone call." I took a few steps to the door and turned around. "And Evelyn . . ." When she looked up at me, I continued, "I'm so glad you called my dad. I know you didn't kill Emile. I'll keep my ears open too."

"I appreciate that, Sophia." She offered a wry smile. "Do you mind making your famous cream puffs for tonight's supper?"

"I'd be delighted to." It was the least I could do for her.

"It's so refreshing to have someone in the kitchen who listens to me without a fight." Her words brought me back to the reason she was the number one suspect, making me doubt my scenario of Natalie's husband killing Emile and causing me to wonder if Evelyn really had done it.

My suspect list was growing, and I really needed to work fast to narrow it down.

On my way down the hall to the kitchen to start my shift, I got a text from Madison. She asked if I could bake some Crunchies tonight after we went to Natalie's because she had a late showing. I texted back immediately to say that I'd love too. I was itching to break in those fancy appliances in that cute cottage.

After a few texts back and forth about timing, I put my phone in the pocket of the chef's jacket I'd grabbed off the hook and put on, but not without taking out a pink slip that was stuck in the bottom of the pocket.

It appeared to be a slip from the laundry service that picked up the aprons, towels, and rugs. They picked up the laundry once a week and replaced the items with clean ones. Dirty linens were just as common as food in a kitchen. The slip was signed by Emile and dated a week before the day of his death.

"Good afternoon," Nick greeted me. "What do you have there?"

"It's a receipt from the laundering service. Do you know where Emile kept those?" I questioned so I could see this week's receipt and possibly talk to the person who did the RCC's laundry. Maybe he'd seen Emile or had just seen something.

"I have no clue." Nick grabbed his apron from the hook. "How are things going?"

"Things are going great." I folded the slip back up and put it in the pocket, noticing I'd put on the jacket that had CHEF embroidered on the right side.

"I didn't think they wouldn't be. Thank you so much. I love how you just pitch right on in." I wanted to pay him as many compliments as I could so he'd just consider the job. "And it's exactly how a head chef behaves, and I'm sure the job could be yours," I said over my shoulder on the way to the walk-in refrigerator.

"No." He returned to what looked like mashed potatoes.

"Fine." I sighed and mentally went down the list of ingredients I needed to make the cream puffs.

The creative mood for figuring out exactly what fillings I

wanted wasn't happening. There was no doubt in my mind that once I got my hands in the dough and the smell of the freshly baked puffs was surrounding me, my creative juices would flow.

In the meantime, I grabbed the eggs and the butter. When I grabbed the butter tub, something fell to the ground. I tilted my head to the side and looked past the tub of butter and eggs. It looked like a pack of Juicy Tart gum.

"The strangest thing just happened to me." I made idle conversation with Nick as I put the ingredients down on the island near the electric mixer.

"What was that?" Nick stopped stirring the cream in the pot and looked over at me.

"Evelyn asked me to make my famous Surprise Puffs." I cackled at the name.

I'd made all my pastry names up as a teen, and now they all sounded so silly. After all this time, they'd stuck. These names would never fly at The Manhattan.

"That's the strange thing that happened to you?" He seemed a bit confused but went back to stirring the cream into the potatoes.

"Oh, no." My mind was going from one thing to another, I was so distracted. I grabbed the dry ingredients from the dry shelf. "When I took the butter off the shelf, a pack of gum fell to the ground."

"Pack of gum?" Nick dropped the spoon in the big pot. "Did you say gum?"

"As in chew-chew." I had the flour bag tucked in the crook of my elbow and the salt container in my grip. I set them down next to the mixer.

Nick let out a loud sigh and dragged the paper hat off his

head. He leaned on the island, visibly shaken up by what I'd said.

"Are you okay?" I asked.

"I was afraid I was right." His words were hushed.

"About what?" I wasn't following him. "Right about what?" I asked again to get his attention.

He blinked a few times, shook his head, and sucked in his bottom lip.

"Patrick," he muttered. "I've been thinking about this whole murder thing. Evelyn is too easy to point a finger at since Emile was obviously intimidated by her."

"You're saying *Patrick* killed Emile?" I asked, a bit confused.

"I'm afraid so. He comes in real early to do some of the extra duties Evelyn had him doing, like the table linens, gathering the towels from the tennis court locker rooms, cleaning up the spa's water glasses and plates of food the members have while in their treatment from the day before, things like that. Patrick's parents rely on his income to help pay the bills, with his mom sick and all. Patrick is hoping for a college baseball scholarship, because without it, he'll be the RCC dishwasher the rest of his life." Nick walked over to the refrigerator. He looked down at the pack of gum. "When he has night practice, he comes in early to make up the hours he misses. Emile teased him so much and called him names. Emile was so mad that Evelyn had Patrick come in early because he never did anything right. Emile said that he'd have to come in each morning and have to redo everything Patrick had done. And he let Patrick know it too."

"How does a pack of gum make you think that Patrick did it?" I asked, and made mental notes of everything he was telling me.

"Patrick didn't have refrigerator duties. The refrigerator was one of the first places Emile went, and Patrick knew it. It'd be a perfect place for him to hide until Emile got here." Nick crouched in the corner of the refrigerator toward the door to show me what he was talking about. He lifted his left arm in the air. "When Emile opened the door"—Nick's arm came down as if he were hitting something—"*whack!*"

I jumped. My eyes popped open.

"He must've hit Emile over the head and killed him." He pointed to the pack of gum. "That's proof he was in here. He's always chomping on gum. Another thing Emile hated about Patrick."

I gulped, adding yet another suspect to my mental list. At the rate I was going, everyone was going to be a suspect. It seemed as if Emile hadn't gotten along with anyone.

"Doesn't that make sense?" he asked, and looked around the refrigerator before he bent down and picked up the pack of gum.

"No!" I screamed. "Too late," I groaned.

"Crap." He dropped the gum after he realized he'd just tainted evidence. "Crap, crap, crap. I'll call that cop."

He headed out of the refrigerator and down toward Emile's office. I left the gum on the floor and decided to start on the Surprise Puffs. I'd question Patrick when he came in, or at the very least, Carter would. Everything Nick had said made sense, but every reason someone on my list had to kill off Emile made sense. But whose motive was the real one?

Plus, the thought of the skillet used to whack Emile was still unsettled in my head. Whoever did it, I was sure, had brought in their own skillet to make it look like it was Emile's. I knew in my bones that Emile hadn't used an unseasoned skillet. That would be something a teenager like Patrick probably wouldn't know. I doubt that Natalie ever cooked, so she probably wouldn't know, either. Or her swanky husband. Plus, I still needed to get in front of Ella. My heart thundered in my chest.

The more I thought about the case, the more ingredients I added to the electric mixer. Before I knew it, I'd made enough batter to feed the entire Rumford community.

"How's it going?" Evelyn called after me when she saw me walk by her office door.

"Good." I snapped my head inside the door and looked around, trying to find her.

"Over here." An arm shot up in the corner of the room from behind a few stacked boxes.

"How on earth do you find anything in here?" I asked, and stepped inside.

I could have sworn it was messier today than it had been yesterday.

"It's a chaotic filing system only I understand." She got to her feet and brushed her hands down her shirt. "I'm collecting all the written notices and warnings I'd given Emile over the years. This way Carter will see that he had plenty of warnings and I still managed to work with him."

She held a bunch of papers in her hand and waved them in the air. Right next to her was a box with food inventory printed in black Sharpie marker on the side.

"Anything at this point can only help." I pointed to the box on the floor. "What's in there?"

She lifted the lid and showed me that it was filled with more ledgers that looked like the one I'd found in Emile's office.

"Emile's past ledgers." She put the lid back on. "I don't even know why I keep them. It's not like we deviate too much from what we make each season, but now that he's"—she paused and gulped—"gone . . ." Her voice cracked. "I guess it's good I've got them, so in a pinch, we can see what he did order."

"Do you mind if I take the box and look through them?" I asked.

"Have at it. It might help if I get this junk out of here and into the storage unit." She pushed the boxes toward me.

"I found his current ledger in his office, and there appears to be a different handwriting in a couple of places." It might've been nothing, but it struck me as odd given that Emile was such a stickler about his menus, ordering, and control of the kitchen.

"He was having a bout with carpel tunnel over the past month and had a hard time writing. He even used a computer for a little bit because he said he could hunt and peck with a finger." She laughed as she recalled the memory. "We might've had our differences, but we had a friendship too."

She was the second person to tell me about Emile's carpal tunnel, which would make sense.

"I wanted to ask you about Patrick. The busboy." I picked up the box and gripped it on both sides.

"What about him?" She moved a couple of the boxes out of both of the seats and gestured for me to sit down on one chair while she sat in the other one.

"It's been brought to my attention that he's been doing some extra work around the RCC in the mornings. Was he here the morning Emile was killed?" I asked.

"About that." She hesitated for a second. "I'm sorta paying him under the table. I know it looks bad and all, but he's a really great kid who needs the money."

So she was telling me that she was illegally cooking the books to be able to pay him . . . this didn't look good. It would just prove that she had something to hide, calling her character into question. I'd seen it done a bunch of times on those television crime shows.

"How?" I asked.

"He isn't able to work every day now that he's in practice. To help make up for the lost hours, I let him come in for the morning and do odds and ends." Abruptly she stopped. Her eyes grew; her jaw dropped. She lifted her hand to her mouth.

"What?" I wondered what was going through her head.

"You don't think?" She gasped between the cracks of her fingers. Her hand dropped; she closed her eyes. "They didn't get along at all. Patrick told me that Emile bullied him. Emile told me it was to build character when I approached him about it. I did nothing to stop him."

"I'm not sure what I think, but I know Patrick has a motive, just like you have a motive. Do you keep a record of him being here in the morning?" I asked.

"No. I trust Patrick and know he's doing the extra work in the spa area as well as the tennis courts, because the managers there wouldn't hesitate to let me know if he weren't." She slumped down in her chair. "Are you going to tell Carter?"

"I don't know what else to do. I hate for the kid to go to jail for the rest of his life, but if he did it . . ." I waffled my hand in the other. "On the flip side, I'd hate for you to go to jail for a murder you didn't commit."

"The RCC will find out I've been lying on payroll." Her voice was soft. "I'll still lose my job."

"How were you lying on payroll if he was doing the work?"

"All extra hours of help in the morning have to be approved by the committee. They didn't approve Patrick's new shift in the morning, saying the employees who work those areas the night before should already have the next day set up before they leave to go home. It should be included in their duties." She gnawed her bottom lip. "That's when I didn't change his hours in the evening."

"Did you tell my dad about Patrick and his hours?" I asked.

"Oh, Sophia," she cried out. "I don't think I can. If Arnold Devin found out that I didn't take this to the board, he'll use it against me in a campaign to fire me. Then he'd for sure replace me."

Another character flaw for which Carter would rake her over the coals.

Chapter Thirteen

A late afternoon jog was a perfect way to work off all the Surprise Puffs I'd eaten. Especially since I'd made so many delicious fillings: vanilla cream, custard, coconut cream, lemon cream, chocolate cream, and strawberry cream. There wasn't one that I didn't taste, nor could I stop myself. These were the times I knew something was on my mind and stressing me out. A few weeks ago, it'd been the demise of my relationship, but today I had to blame it on Emile's murder.

The pavement thumped underneath my shoes, thundering in my head, letting me escape from my thoughts—something that was much needed. The fresh country air filled my lungs and breathed new life into me, clearing out any blocks I was feeling. I'd been struggling with how to get Bryce's Big Bird cake to stand up, and it weighed on me just as much as getting Evelyn off of Carter's suspect list.

The keychain with my parents' house key and the key Madison had given me for the old Ford's Bakery jiggled in the small inside pocket of my running shorts. I'd seen on one of those crime shows that a key was a perfect stabbing weapon. Ever since then, I'd kept a key with me on my jogs through the city. New York City was actually very safe, but there were times when I'd get goose bumps rounding one of those big rocks in Central Park when no one was around and I'd take off in a sprint to get to civilization. I wasn't going to sugarcoat it; I did feel a little nervous with a killer on the loose in Rumford, and I still couldn't get Carter's words out of my head when he'd told me to watch my own back.

It was funny how I knew what time it was by the position of the sun. That was something kids in Rumford instinctively knew. It had to be around four thirty, and Madison was going to pick me up around five to head on over to Natalie's house. After that, we were going to the house listed in Charlotte's neighborhood so I could bake the Crunchies for her late showing.

By the time I realized I needed to start running back, I was standing in front of the old bakery's display window. The old red lettering that read FORD'S BAKERY in an arc across the window was mainly scraped off. There was an empty cake stand and a decorative tablecloth around it. Loving memories of standing there as a child salivating over the amazing pastries they'd made fresh that day flooded my memory, making me miss the simpler times in my life.

I took the keys out of my pocket and let myself in. The sun poured into the big room. The two-person café tables that dotted the café were still there. The two glass, dome-shaped display cases were empty, but the memories remained. There was even a hint of the sugar smell that I was sure was baked into the walls.

My eyes closed as I sucked in a deep breath. I walked over to the left side of the room and opened the door that had a cheap peel-and-stick OFFICE sticker on it. Excitement bubbled up in me. Many times I'd wanted to open the door and see if there were little bakery elves back there. Now was my chance.

A little bit of me really did want to see little people baking delicious treats, but when I opened the door, it was just a regular office with a desk, a few filing cabinets, and some dust.

"Silly girl," I whispered, and smiled.

It was strange being in the bakery as an adult and not hearing the sounds of the laughter it brought to so many people. Sadness washed over me as I walked through the rest of the building and into the kitchen. The hum of the walk-in freezer and the walk-in fridge filled the space as I walked around and noticed the two ovens, two stoves, three sinks, and one big long workstation in the middle.

I ran my hand along the island and silently took in the magnitude of all the wonderful things that had been made in that very spot. My phone chirped, bringing out of my nostalgia. I dragged it out of the waist of my jogging shorts.

Madison: ON MY WAY.
Me: PICK ME UP AT FORD'S BAKERY. ON A JOG AND NOT
    ENOUGH TIME TO RUN BACK.
Madison: OKAY. BE THERE SHORTLY.

I bent down and looked into the door of the stove. My reflection stared back at me. The ponytail was still in place, and though I didn't look fit to be seen in public, there was nothing I was going to be able to do about it now. Besides, I was on a mission to find out about Natalie and Emile's secret love affair and which one of the Devins had killed him. Not to mention I was going to be baking after that. Nothing a good handwashing couldn't fix.

While I waited for Madison to pick me up, I headed out of the kitchen, through the front of the store, and into the office, not without noticing the sun was going down. I flipped the lights on and sat down in the chair behind the desk. It was a good time to give the laundry service from the RCC a call to see what I could find out.

"Hello, this is Sophia Cummings. I'm the new chef at the Rumford Country Club, and I'm trying to get my schedule straight. I know that you service the RCC, but can you tell me what day and time?" I wasn't lying; if only for a couple of days, I was in charge of the kitchen.

"Let me look at the calendar," the lady on the other end of the phone said. There was some shuffling of papers. "The RCC is every Monday morning at seven AM."

"Can you give me the name of the person who does the pickup and delivery? I need to put them on a list to get into the RCC." I was surprising myself at how good I was at this sleuthing stuff.

"Danny Mischler. Is there a problem with the service that you've seen since you've been there?" she asked with a concerned voice.

"Oh, no. In fact, he's done a great job and I'd like to tell him myself. Do you happen to know his phone number?" I asked and opened the top drawer of the desk.

I found a piece of paper and pencil.

She spouted off a number and we said our good-byes.

Immediately I dialed Danny, but when the answering machine picked up, I left a message.

I tapped the piece of paper with the pen. At the top I made two columns and wrote SUSPECT in one and MOTIVE in the other. One by one I began to list anyone I could think of who would've killed Emile.

It was sorta like looking at a recipe and seeing what ingredients fit and which ones to take out.

Evelyn was first on the list. The only motive I could think of was killing Emile over the fight they'd had, which didn't seem like much of a reason, but I wrote it anyways.

Patrick was next. Not only had he been bullied, but he liked to cook, and was Emile bullying him about that and not being man enough to follow his dream? It'd be enough to send a young kid over the edge.

Had Emile told Patrick's dad, and had Patrick's dad killed Emile for poisoning his son's mind, potentially hurting his baseball career?

I sucked in a deep breath and gnawed on the end of the pen before writing down Brett's name. Charlotte sure would be mad if she saw me writing this one. Regardless, Brett was definitely upset about the thought of serving French food, which seemed to be Emile's passion, at the wedding, not only because Brett couldn't pronounce the names but because the cost was outrageous. It was enough to keep him on the list even though he did have an alibi. Yes! You never know. Besides, it was a silly list made by me. A baker, as Carter so liked to remind me.

"Hello, Natalie Devin," I said out loud as I wrote her name.

If she had had an affair with Emile, how was I really going to find out? She was also the one with a husband who could have been jealous of the flirting between his wife and Emile. Arnold Devin was going on the list. Had Natalie caught Emile with another member and gotten jealous? These were all questions I needed to look into.

Last but certainly not least and the person I couldn't wait to talk to tonight, there was Ella Chapshaw. I used the pen to circle her name. Since she was single, had she killed Emile because he wanted to end it? Had she caught him with another member?

I glanced over at my phone to make sure it was on. Not that I'd turned it off, but I sure did want to hear from Danny Mischler, the delivery guy from the cleaners. I wondered how Emile was the morning of his death.

"Who's in here?" The voice caused me to jump in my seat.

I could feel my panic rising when I knew that deep voice wasn't Madison's. I grabbed my keys off the desk and tiptoed over to the door. The heavy footsteps were getting closer and closer. Taking very small breaths in and out my nose, I positioned the key between my forefinger and middle finger with the jagged edge sticking out, making a plan to swipe and run.

"Come out!" the voice demanded. "I know someone is in here."

The door to the office swung open and the shadow of a figure lay out across the floor with the shadow of a gun sticking out from the hand.

"Don't shoot." I dropped the keys and lifted my hands in the air.

"Sophia?" Carter let out a sigh of relief. "What on God's green earth are you doing in here? I almost shot you. Why didn't you answer me when I called out?"

"Oh, I don't know." Panic and fear were still racing through my veins. "Maybe something to do with your words that I'd better watch out for my own safety."

"Your own safety isn't trespassing in a building that you do not own." He snapped his gun back into his holster. "Why are you here?"

"I have a key." I put my hands down and pointed to the set of keys on the floor. I fumbled over my words. "I . . . um . . . Madison gave me the keys so I could bake her son's birthday cake to make sure the ovens and stoves work before she officially puts it on the market. How did you know I was here?"

"I didn't know it was you." He walked around the room. He stopped at the desk and looked down. He dragged my list of suspects to the edge. "Someone radioed in that they'd seen someone creeping around inside the abandoned bakery. I never figured it'd be you I'd run into, and with a list for me to use in my investigation."

He picked up the paper.

"Give me that." I tried snatching it out of his hands, but he lifted his arm so high, I couldn't get a grasp of it.

He stared at me with a half smile on his face.

"I was just doodling until Madison came to pick me up." I folded my arms across my body. "And I'm just trying to figure out how to make sure Charlotte has her wedding."

He took a better look at the paper.

"It'd take me longer than a twenty-four-hour period to look into all these people." He held the paper out, facing me. "So if you're wanting me to check out all these leads, three of these people have to do with Charlotte's wedding and would set the wedding back." He held up fingers as he counted them off. "Brett, groom. Patrick, busboy working the wedding. Ella Capshaw is host . . ."

". . . of the shower." I finished his sentence. "What about the skillet?"

His face went grim. "The skillet came back with only Emile's handprints on it."

"And the note he had next to him?"

"It was a list of the menu items that correlated with his inventory list." His lips thinned into a smile. "It appears he was looking at his list with his head down when he got hit by the skillet."

"He didn't see it coming." The sadness of the situation hung in the air between us for a few silent minutes.

His eyes focused on my Operation Wedding list of suspects.

"But I see on your list that you name more than just Evelyn. Is all that hearsay and gossip, or is there more you can tell me with substance?"

"Working with Emile's staff, I've learned that Emile wasn't the nicest of people. Not only did he have a beef with Evelyn, but also with the busboy." I unfolded the paper and pointed to Patrick.

"Is this the whole gum-pack-in-the-fridge theory?" he asked. I nodded. "I got the call from the RCC sous chef. Patrick is off tonight, but I'm going to make a visit tomorrow afternoon when he comes to work."

"According to the staff, Patrick comes in early in the morning too." I'd forgotten to write that down, so I rushed over to the desk and scribbled more notes next to his name. "They said his family needs his paycheck to help with the bills. Since he's got ball practice at night, Evelyn lets him come early in the morning to do other odd jobs around the RCC."

Carter transferred his gaze from the paper to me. He took a step closer to me. "Sophia, I need you to stop looking into this. This is a real murder. There is a killer out there and it's dangerous. I'm not only worried about your safety, but mine too."

"Your safety?" I asked.

"From your mama." He let out an audible long breath and took another step closer. He was close enough for me to get a whiff of his aftershave, and it sure did tickle my insides.

"Bitsy. *Pfft*." I waved him off. "I can deal with Bitsy."

"Then for me." His words stuck in my throat. "I can't have you going around Rumford playing Columbo with no credentials and questioning people."

"Can you promise me that you won't arrest Evelyn at least until after the weekend and our friends get married?" I wanted him to promise me, even if he did cross his fingers behind his back.

"Sophia! Let's go!" Madison walked into the office. Her mouth opened into a wide grin. "Did I interrupt something?"

Ahem. Carter cleared his throat and took a step back. "From now on, if you decide to give someone keys to a property, can you please call dispatch so we aren't called to a burglary in progress?"

"Sophia? A burglar?" She busted out laughing. "The only thing Sophia has ever stolen was a bunch of boys' hearts when she lived in Rumford."

"Is that right?" He turned back to me with a blank stare.

"Oh, hush up." I shook my head and walked past them.

"See you later, Carter. We are on our way over to Natalie Devin's to—"

I jerked Madison's arm.

Carter's expression grew still and serious.

"To talk to her about the menu for the Garden Club's flower show." I'd yet to promise him I'd stop snooping, and I wasn't about to. He didn't need to know that I was going to question Natalie about her relationship with Emile, nor did he need to know that I was going to make a detour around her house to snoop while I looked for a bathroom. "I'm going to help her plan the menu."

"The menu? It's not for a few weeks." His brow cocked. "I thought you were just visiting. Going back after the wedding, or you keep telling everyone that." He smiled.

"Just pull the door shut behind you when you leave. It's already locked." I wasn't going to argue with him. Not when he was acting like Mr. Know-It-All.

I dragged Madison out of there as quickly as I could.

"What was that all about?" she asked once we got into the station wagon.

"While I was waiting for you, I made a list of suspects and motives," I said.

Out of the corner of my eye, I could see Carter through the back window standing behind us with his hands on his hips.

"Just drive and I'll tell you." I snagged the paper back.

"You sure are touchy." She put the key in the ignition and threw it in drive. "Did I interrupt something? It felt like I interrupted something."

"He almost shot me." I turned and looked over my shoulder, where Carter was still standing watching us drive off.

"Shot you?" she asked nervously.

"Yeah. He thought I was a burglar like he said. I didn't respond when he called out." I chewed on my lip. In hindsight, that hadn't been the smartest idea, but how was I to know he wasn't the killer?

"Sophia, that man is smitten with you." A satisfied sigh escaped her. "I can't wait to see how this turns out."

"There's nothing turning out." I turned my head to look out the window to disguise my smile.

"I think you are just as smitten." She took her eyes off the road for a quick look at me under her furrowed brows.

"Road." I pointed. I'd decided to change the subject, because no matter how many times I'd told her that I wasn't staying in Rumford, she just didn't get it. "Anyway, as I said, I made a list of suspects."

I opened the paper and read down the list, giving a quick rundown.

"Natalie Devin is an obvious suspect just because it's rumored she's been having an affair with Emile. There are two things I'm thinking." I held up my two fingers. "One, she found out he was having an affair with other RCC members and got jealous. Two, Emile was going to come clean about the affair since she and Arnold were already on shaky ground. She wasn't about to leave her cushy life for the kind of life Emile could give her."

"This is so interesting. You're like a little investigator," Madison squealed. "So much more fun than my boring life."

"Which reminds me, I need to find out where Emile lived. Maybe there are some clues as to who killed him there, not that the police haven't been there. I'd just like to see things for myself." I stared out the window.

"Let me look around. I have a way of finding out real estate stuff. What did you think about the bakery? Did you see all the baking ingredients left in there?"

"Yes, and most of them are still good. When did they close?" I asked.

"A couple of weeks ago," she answered.

"Gosh." I chuckled. "Everyone in town, Bitsy, and you made it sound like it's been years."

"It does seem like years. Especially since I went every day for a sanity sweet break." She pulled up to an old Victorian house with a pond that curled around it like a kidney bean. "We're here. What's the plan?" She changed the subject back to my suspicions about Emile and Natalie.

She pulled the keys out of the ignition and reached around the seat. She grabbed her satchel and dragged it over the front seat.

"I'll go over the menu with her so she gets comfortable with us there. After we've done that, I'll excuse myself to go to the bathroom, and you keep her busy with whatever work you've got."

We nodded at each other. I almost felt like we should put our hands in a huddle and yell "Break!"

"This place will sell in a heartbeat." Madison was practically salivating over the massive house with the beautiful backdrop. "Look at the reflection of the sunset on the pond."

Both of us stopped before we walked up to the front porch and took a nice long gander around the property. There was a small bridge that led to a small island in the center of the pond. The island had a gazebo with twinkly lights strung all around it. The orange sun reflected off the water and created a halo around it. If I had owned this place, I'd never have sold it.

"Right on time." Natalie stood at the front door. "Come on in, girls."

Madison and I walked up the steps and greeted Natalie.

"Sophia, I'm so glad you're home. Bitsy has a joy in her that

I've not seen in a long time." She exaggerated. Bitsy got joy from walking into her fancy designer closet on a daily basis, but I liked her kind words. "I'm beyond thrilled to have you making the pastries for the flower show. The designs of the treats are just as important as the flowers themselves."

"I do love a good design." I realized I should've brought my bag, which had some great designs in it, but I hadn't known I was going to be jogging so long and not going to be able to make it back to my parents' house. "No matter what we come up with, I'm sure all the women of the Garden Club will be pleased."

There was no way I was committing to make the pastries for the event. I was going to be long gone by then and she'd probably be someone's girlfriend in jail. The idea made me giggle inside as I looked at her standing there.

She had on her cardigan sweater and pearls around her neck. The woman at the Garden Club had been right. The ring on Natalie's finger *was* as big as her head.

"Gorgeous ring," I blurted out.

"Thank you." She dragged her hand up to her chest as well as dragged out the vowels in her words. "My Arnie gave it to me for our wedding anniversary."

"Congratulations," Madison and I said in unison.

She swung the door wide open and we stepped inside.

The entry had a marvelous, dark wooden staircase, with an Oriental red carpet tacked to the center of each step. "I'm anxious to talk to you about selling the property."

"I'm sure we'll get asking, if not a bidding war." Madison was practically foaming at the mouth.

"For that area?" Natalie smirked. "We figured fifty thousand for both."

"Excuse me?" Madison's eyes narrowed, her chin jutting forward.

"Now that Emile is—you know . . ." Her voice cracked. ". . . dead, we don't feel like trying to find another renter."

"Renter?" Madison asked.

"Emile rented our little house in town." Her head leaned to the side and there was a blank stare on her face. "Did you think I wanted to list this house? My house?"

"I guess I didn't hear you correctly. Sure, I'd love to talk to you about the house Emile rented." Madison did a good job of covering up because we needed to know where Emile had lived. It would be much better to have a key to get in to look around instead of breaking and entering.

* * *

"Great. Come on in and we can discuss that and the menu." Natalie offered a smile as we walked into her home. "You two can have a seat in there while I go grab us some tea."

"Are you okay?" I asked Madison when we sat down on opposite sides of the couch.

"No. I'm about to have a nervous breakdown." Madison buried her head in her hands. "I can't believe I honestly thought they were going to sell this house."

"But we also learned that she has yet another connection to Emile. He rented from them. Arnold caught Emile and Natalie in a compromising position, so he killed Emile." It was a perfect motive.

"You've got to be kidding me!" Natalie had come into the room with a tray. The glasses clinked because of her shaking hands. Was she shaking because she was mad about me accusing her husband of killing Emile or mad that I had put it together? "I'd never cheat on my husband, and I'd be ashamed if I were you," she scolded me.

"Oh, no," I groaned, wondering why Madison hadn't warned me that Natalie had walked in behind me. I turned around to face her and the music. Her face was fire red and the olives in the martini glasses she had in both hands shook back and forth as her anger erupted inside her.

"My husband didn't kill anyone. Especially Emile. Nor did Emile and I have any sort of affair." The anger spewed from her eyes. "Your mother will be so embarrassed by your behavior. I invited you into my home. I trusted you to cater the food for the flower show, and you treat me like a common whore? Get out," she spat. "Get out before my husband gets home and hears your lies and gossip."

"I'm sorry. I'm just trying to . . ." I apologized, but she wouldn't let me finish.

"Get out," she said through gritted teeth and tight lips.

"Let's go." Madison shoved past me and out the front door.

"Really, I'm sorry," I said as I walked past her. She wouldn't look at me. I had to get it out of me. "It's just that . . ."

"Out!" she shouted, before turning her back to me.

"Can I get that key to Emile's rental so I can take a look at it?" Madison asked meekly.

"Out!" The door slammed in our faces.

Chapter Fourteen

"That didn't go so well." I broke the silence after five minutes in the car. "For either of us. I guess you're going to have to come up with the flower show menu on your own." I sighed.

"I don't think so. You agreed to it just as much as me." She was good at reminding me what I'd agreed to.

"I'll come up with some ideas and put them on paper so you can have them when the time comes." It was my way of actually being present to bake the items. Surely Madison could bake a few simple things. "At any rate, I'm sorry she didn't give you the listing tonight."

"Well, I'm hoping it'll turn around with my showing tonight. Can we get all the ingredients from the Piggly Wiggly?" she asked, steering us back toward Rumford.

The poor pig snout and hat were the only two working bulbs on the sign for the only grocery store in town.

"Yes." I pointed ahead. "You can pull up and I'll run in."

Madison pulled up in the no-parking zone in front of the store to let me out.

"I'll be right back," I called out over my shoulder as I jumped out.

The store was exactly the way I remembered it. The automatic front door slid open. The carts were pushed into each other on the right and the coin-operated horse and cow rides were on the left. It felt like yesterday that my dad had brought me here just to ride the toys. It'd become a weekly treat after my friends would talk about the fun they'd have if they'd been good while their mamas were grocery shopping. Bitsy never went to the grocery, and I'd begged her to go so I too could be good and get to ride the cow. Weeks of begging went by until my dad finally gave in. After that, we went every week. He'd enjoy a candy bar—which Bitsy would've thrown a hissy fit if she'd seen—while I enjoyed a few coin trips on the cow or the horse.

Aisle three was always the baking aisle. I'd spent many of my paychecks in that very aisle. I was happy to see it was still there. It looked like they'd added a wine section, which deserved a little perusal before I left. Madison and I definitely needed a little swig.

I gathered up all the ingredients to make chocolate chip cookies and a little red food dye and I was ready to go check out the wine selection. That was a big step forward in Rumford. It hadn't been until I was well into my teens that Rumford had become a wet city. Most of the counties in Kentucky were still dry. It'd really boosted the economy. My dad had been the lawyer on the side of the people who'd wanted it wet, and he'd gotten it done.

"Lawyer." I let out a little gasp and took out my phone. I wanted to find out what Evelyn had told my dad. "I need to talk to my dad," I whispered to myself.

Scrolling through my contacts, I'd walked a little past the wine aisle. I took a couple of steps back and saw someone checking out the selection from the corner of my eye. Without hitting the call button, I looked down the aisle, where Carter had two bottles of wine in his hands. He was looking between the two. There was a pretty intense look on his face. He wasn't dressed in his uniform. He had on a pair of khakis along with a very nice pair of brown loafers and a blue button-down that showed off his dark features. His hair was even gelled.

I would have known that look from anywhere. Men who came to The Manhattan dressed like that, and those who took extra time to look at the wine bottles were there to impress a woman.

My excitement for baking suddenly took a quick spiral down. Not that I'd thought he was interested in me, but the flirting sure had been nice. Why did I care? I brushed it off and made a beeline to the refrigerated section and grabbed a premade roll of chocolate chip cookie dough. Luckily the Piggly Wiggly had put in a U-Scan line, and since no one but me, the one lady working the lane, and Carter were in the store, I quickly made my purchases and got out of there as fast as I could. With my head down.

Madison was exactly where she'd dropped me off, fiddling with her lipstick and the mirror in the visor.

"Go." I hurried her up. "I don't think we're going to have time to bake a batch from scratch, so I grabbed a premade roll and some food coloring."

"But I wanted your recipe." There was a sad tone to her voice. "I'd love to watch you in your process."

"Then you'll have to come visit me when I bake Bryce's

cake." I slumped down in the seat as she drove past the sliding doors of the store just in case Carter was walking out.

"Wow. Your mood just went south."

"I'm sorry," I apologized, knowing I was taking my annoyed and unchartered feelings I seemed to have developed for Carter out on her. "I'm tired and I really want to make sure Charlotte's wedding is a go."

"I'm helping you. Remember?" She was good at reminding me.

"Yes. And that's why I'm going to bake Bryce's cake. So after we get these baked, do you mind dropping me back off at the bakery so I can look around at the ingredients to see what I need?" The Big Bird cake was going to take more than what I'd seen on the shelf. "That way, when I'm done, I can jog back to my parents' to finish the run I started."

It was a solid plan.

"Sounds good." She sped toward Charlotte's neighborhood.

We didn't say a word to each other until we pulled into the driveway.

"This sure is a cute house." I stood next to the car waiting for Madison.

She was busy fumbling around in the car, grabbing some papers, a briefcase, her phone, and whatever else she could fit in her hands. While she took her sweet time, I took a good look at the house. The pale-yellow house was the smallest in the neighborhood. There were two windows on each side of the front door with wooden window boxes under both of them filled with an assortment of wildflowers. There were some pink and white wild cosmos, teal blue forget-me-nots, purple coneflowers, a few red poppies, and some black-eyed Susans.

A few butterflies fluttered around the boxes. It was beautiful.

Underneath the window box on the right side of the door was a small fountain set in a bed of river rocks. The gurgling water flowed from the top and spilled into a pool of water at the base of the fountain where the water circulated.

On the left side of the house, there were a couple of small bushes to even out the landscape.

"Adorable, right?" An exhausted Madison stood next to me with her hands full.

I strapped the grocery bags on my wrists and took a few of her things from her.

"When I was a kid, I always thought this house was a shed or some sort of garage," I recalled.

It was true. As I said, it was the smallest house on the street and the paint on the clapboards had been peeling, faded, and practically falling off.

"Years ago it was the carriage house to the mansion that was right over there. Then some developer bought the land to build all of the Cape Cods after doing the business dealings with Brett. They tore down the mansion because it was out-of-date and old, but they kept the carriage house for a tool shed while they built the houses around it." She tilted her chin left to right. "Brett took interest in the carriage house and saw potential. He was right. Plus, the only lake in the entire neighborhood is right behind it, so that'll help sell it too."

"I didn't even notice a lake." My brows furrowed.

"It was so overgrown back when we were kids that we had no idea it was back there until Charlotte's fiancé decided to revitalize the neighborhood." She jerked her head to the side. "We better hurry up and get in there."

It just so happened to be forty-five minutes until her client was supposed to be there. I'd be able to get the food coloring mixed really well into the premade dough, ball it up, and stick it in the oven with a few minutes to spare. The house was going to smell amazing.

"This is really a great kitchen." I looked around.

I was amazed at all the baking supplies she'd used to stage the place. It was every dream appliance I'd have loved to have in my own house when I had a big enough kitchen.

Madison simply smiled. "I'm pretty good at staging when a house really speaks to me. This is a kitchen that needs a lot of fun baking in it." She pointed down the hall. "Could you imagine a little kitty in the window seat? Oh my God, adorable," she gushed.

"Actually"—I nodded my head—"I can."

The image of me baking new ideas in the kitchen had occupied my mind the entire time we'd been there. I'd even pictured Duchess on the window seat. If it hadn't been for that image, I'd almost have fooled myself into thinking this house was meant for me. Bitsy would never get rid of Duchess.

Madison walked around the house while I finished up the final baking. For good measure, I added a few chocolate chips on top. It made the perfect-looking cookie, as if they'd been baked like that. It was those little details that had helped me stand out from the others in my culinary class.

The door to the pantry was the cutest repurposed screen door. The screen had been replaced by a chalkboard with the word PANTRY painted in white at the top. I picked up the piece of chalk and wrote WELCOME HOME.

"There's even an adorable milk glass cake platter in here!" I yelled into the kitchen from the walk-in pantry.

All the shiplap walls were exactly the right touch to make this house cozy and sweet. I actually envied the person who bought it. For a second I thought about burning the last batch of cookies to ruin the smell.

I pushed the idea aside because I'd never have the guts to burn delicious cookies. I grabbed a potholder from the drawer and carried the sheet of cookies over to the platter, tripping on a small rug in the middle of the floor.

Luckily, I didn't drop the cookies. I put them on the counter, bent down to straighten the rug back, and noticed a small door.

"What on earth is this?" I asked about the strange discovery when Madison came in with a look of "What in the world was that noise?" on her face.

"That's the door to the cold cellar." She tapped the toe of her shoe on the opening. "It's pretty neat. It's still cold to this day, since it's underground. There's some shelving down there, with nothing on it, of course."

"Is there electric?" I questioned, thinking it would be a great refrigerator for baking ingredients that needed to be kept cold. It was perfect so they wouldn't take up space in the cabinet and refrigerator or even the pantry.

"Oh, no. Just a cold cellar." She shrugged and eyed my cookies.

There was about five minutes until her client's appointment. There was no time to let them cool on the cooling rack. Quickly I swiped the spatula under each baked cookie and placed it on the milk glass cake platter. It was too pretty not to use.

After I filled the platter, I took a step back and looked at it. The cookies had turned out a lot better than I'd thought they would since I'd used the cut-and-slice dough.

"Please come in." I heard Madison's voice and quickly grabbed up the dirty baking tray and utensils, shoving them in the oven for hiding before the potential clients walked into the kitchen.

"Oh, who cares. If they are going to live here, it's going to be dirty sometimes," I said to myself and took the tray and spatula out of the oven, sticking them on the stove.

I even left the soap suds in the sink.

"This is the kitchen." Madison smiled before her eyes focused on the mess and the clumps of cookie dough on the counter I'd yet to wipe up.

Her jaw dropped and her eyes widened before she closed her mouth and gulped.

"Umm . . ." she didn't really know what to say when the couple stepped in.

They couldn't've been more than my age. I knew that a kitchen would sell the house to the wife. Right now this particular kitchen wasn't spotless.

"My friend is a baker and she . . ." Madison was at a loss for words.

"Cookie?" I picked up the platter. "Freshly baked." I stuffed one in my mouth.

I glared at the couple and felt a twinge of jealousy, not only for their happiness but for the fact that this woman might be the one baking in my . . . I meant, this . . . kitchen.

The man and woman looked between each other. Their eyes were shifty and a fake smile curled on their lips.

"Where is the master bedroom?" The wife asked Madison.

"Cookie?" I asked again, and practically shoved the dish in the woman's face.

She shook her head and followed Madison's finger as Madison pointed down the hall.

After the man and women stepped out of eyesight, Madison jerked around.

"What happened in here? It's a mess." There was a deep-set worry on her face. Her eyes searched mine for any explanation.

"You told me to bake, so I baked." I shrugged, and when she darted down the hall toward the master bedroom, I leaned on the counter with a smile on my face. I reached for a warm cookie and enjoyed every single bite.

After the couple were through with the tour, Madison showed them the outside while I cleaned up my mess and tried to reason with myself. Why was I so upset about the potential buyers? Yes, if I'd had a house, this would have been the exact kitchen I'd have wanted, but I didn't own this house. Now I felt bad because I could've just ruined it for Madison.

"Damn." Madison walked in. "They aren't going to buy." She snarled her nose and made pouty lips.

"Are you kidding?" I asked. She shook her head. "This kitchen is enough to sell the house."

"You mean the kitchen they saw before you cleaned it up. The one where it seemed like it was your kitchen?" She looked at me. Her eyes narrowed as though she were studying some sort of idea in her head.

"No. Forget it." She sat down on one of the bar stools and shoved a cookie in her mouth.

"Forget what?" I asked.

"Say." She lifted her head and her eyebrows rose. "You really like it and it's perfect for one person. Why don't you just buy it and save us all the trouble?" She smiled.

"You're crazier than a bedbug." I shook my head, but I wasn't convinced that I meant it.

For a brief second, I'd already made the kitchen mine. I looked out the window over the sink and noticed the sun had almost set. My heart dropped at the amazing sight of the last of the day's rays spread across the still and calm water of the lake Madison had told me about earlier.

There was a small porch off the back of the house and a small café table and chairs with a black-and-white-striped umbrella. I pictured myself sitting there in the wee hours of the morning sipping coffee and watching the geese on the lake.

"Did you write WELCOME HOME on the chalk board?" she asked through a mouthful of cookie, bringing me out of the pretend life I'd conjured up in my head.

"Yeah," I muttered.

I took a cookie and broke it in half before I took a bite, hoping it would help get the ridiculous idea out of my head. I had a great job. I had a great life outside Noah's cheating. I was happy. At least I thought I was happy.

"It was supposed to be a subliminal message to the clients," I said, leaving off the part that maybe my message had sunk into my own head.

"You are a good friend." She took another cookie. "And I've got other property to show, so why don't you live here for the next week or so? That way Bitsy gets her house back. You can come and go as you please."

She picked up the key and dangled it in front of me.

"It's perfect for you while you're here. Kinda like one of those fancy Airbnb's I've seen on the Travel Channel." She jiggled the key more.

It was like a worm and I was like a fish, dying to take the bite.

"It's late. There's towels in there and an empty comfy bed. And for staging purposes I even have some extra running clothes and some jeans and tees that are probably your size hanging in the bedroom closet." Her brows rose. "Tomorrow I can take you to get a loaner car from Poochie's Garage." All of her words were so enticing. No wonder she was good at sells. "You can bake here, bake at Ford's and the RCC. And also do that make-believe sleuthing stuff you've been up to without hiding it."

"Really? The owners won't care if I live here for the next week?" It sounded exactly what I needed and too good to be true.

"Nope, and it's a shame we didn't run into each other quicker than the Junior League meeting." She tossed the keys my way and I caught them. "You could've been staying here this whole time."

The keys felt like home when I gripped them and let the feeling sink deep into my soul.

"I have to pay rent or something," I suggested.

"You're making Bryce's cake. Consider your stay here paid in full." Her smile reached her eyes.

"Then what are we waiting for?" I asked, and walked over to the chalkboard. "We've got a murder to solve."

On the very top, I wrote OPERATION WEDDING, and underneath I wrote down everything I'd written on the piece of paper at the old Ford's Bakery waiting for Madison to come pick me up.

"You are a little CSI baker," Madison joked after I stepped away from the chalkboard and looked at my list of suspects and their motives.

Her eyes scanned down it. Her lips muttered every word I'd written.

"We really can't cross Natalie off our list." I jabbed Natalie's name with the piece of chalk. "She said she didn't have an affair. Who wouldn't say that if they were caught? But if Arnold did catch them together and he killed him, she'd for sure cover up her husband's big mistake. She'd never make it on her own." I looked down my list. "I need to go see Ella."

"You know." Madison's mouth dropped. "Ella loves to shop. Particularly at Peacocks and Pansies. So much so that she works there half a day on Friday."

"And I do need to go look at that dress Carol said would fit me like a glove for the wedding." It sounded like a plan was coming together to question Ella about her relationship with Emile.

"Yes, you do." Madison winked and took another cookie.

I ripped a paper towel off the holder that was shaped as a spoon and walked over to the chalkboard to erase what I'd written.

"Don't!" Madison's yell stopped me. "Leave it. Maybe for the next few days I can come over for a glass of wine and girl time until you go back to your awful life."

"Awful life?" I giggled. "Wine and girl time sounds great. Spy girl and wine time."

"Spy girls. Southern spy girls," she added.

Chapter Fifteen

After Madison left me alone in the house, I couldn't help but walk around and imagine myself in every single room. It was as if the house had been built and decorated just for me. Bitsy took the news about me living in the house much better than I'd anticipated, though she did make me promise that I'd come by in the morning to help her put together the free little libraries for the Friends of the Library Club. That afternoon, she wanted me to help her put them up around Rumford, which was code for me doing it by myself without her help or with her just pointing, giving directions.

The next morning, I woke up thinking about Ella and what I was going to say to her, someone I'd never met. There wasn't a better time for me to clear my head and put on my thinking cap than a quick morning jog before Madison got here to pick me up to take me to get a rental car. It'd do me good to clear my confused thoughts and emotions I seemed to be having about Carter and Rumford.

The fresh morning air was perfect for a run.

I tucked the house keys back into my pocket and put feet to

pavement. The light breeze felt good on my sweaty neck as I headed out of town on a country road.

As soon as I jogged past the city limit sign, the air was a bit nippier. The trees made a bridge over the old road, shielding me from any sort of warmth the morning sun had intended. Crickets and cicadas were in harmonious sync as they sang the dawn away into the day. My feet beating on the pavement were the bass to their song. The problem with running was that I could get lost for hours in the sounds of nature and feel it in my soul. This morning was just a quick run, so I turned around and headed back.

The sound of a car came from behind me. My tennis shoes hugged the pavement's edge. As the car got closer, I turned around and saw it was barreling right at me, even swerving toward me. My phone fell out of my pocket and landed on the road. There was no time to get it or I'd be road kill.

The gravel spit up under my tennis shoes as I stumbled over myself to get off the blacktop and into the grass. I tucked my head and did a few frontward rolls. The truck tires spit up the grass and dirt from underneath them as they came to a halt. A rock flew out of the window and hit me in the side. As soon as I reached for it, the tires dug into the earth and the truck sped off.

My adrenaline was rushing through my veins, and I jumped to my feet trying to get a look at the truck that'd clearly tried to kill me. My chest heaved up and down as I tried to take deep breaths to calm myself. My hands shook and my knees wobbled as I bent down to get the rock that had been thrown at me. There was a piece of paper wrapped around it with a rubber band. I could see the entrance to my new neighborhood, and if I could just get there, I was sure I'd be fine.

I chose the no-road way just in case that truck came back to finish off the job, but not without grabbing my run-over phone. I gimped through some tall dead grass and a couple of fields that had yet to be bush hogged for the first spring cut.

In the distance, I could see Charlotte's kitchen light on. Gratefully, I made it through the fields and limped up to her back door. With the rock in my grip, I beat on the door with my flat palms. When Brett opened the door, I pushed through. "Sophia?" he asked.

"Sophia?" Charlotte pushed past him and grabbed me. "What on earth happened to you?" she cried out and pulled a twig from my hair.

"Someone tried to run me over." I was in so much shock, I wasn't sure if I was going to cry or laugh.

"Is that blood? Oh my God! You're bleeding! Brett!" Charlotte rushed me to her kitchen table and sat me down. "Sophia is hurt. Call Carter!"

"No." I waved her off. "I'm fine."

"No, you aren't. Someone has tried to kill you." Her head twisted over her shoulder. "Call Carter now."

While Charlotte ran off to get me a washcloth, I eased back in the chair, extending my legs forward. There was blood dripping down my shin from a scratched-up knee. I licked my lips, and a coppery taste filled my mouth. I put my hand up to my lip and pulled it back to look at. There was blood.

Suddenly I felt a little woozy, and I was getting woozier by the second. Charlotte dabbed at me, cleaned me up, and asked all sorts of questions I couldn't answer before Carter showed up.

"What happened?" Carter stood in Charlotte's kitchen. "Sophia." He crouched down between my legs. He grabbed the washcloth from Charlotte and used the edge of it to blot my lip. "Are you okay?"

I looked between Charlotte and Carter.

"I think she needs to lay down," Carter said, and stood up.

"I'm fine." I waved them off. "Just a little light-headed, that's all."

"What happened to you?" Carter's voice was steady and strong.

Charlotte was shivering in Brett's arms. Both of them were staring at me.

"I was jogging and someone didn't see me and nearly hit me." I tried to whisper low enough not to alarm anyone.

"Did you hear her?" Charlotte questioned. "Someone tried to run her over?" She cried out, "Brett, you've got to do something. Right now."

"What do you expect me to do, Charlotte?" he asked. "Carter is right here and he's the law."

"Nearly hit you?" Carter dabbed the scrape. "It looks like you did some sort of dive because they were coming at you."

"Coming at me, didn't see me," I nonchalantly said, and bit the edges of my lips.

"What is that?" Carter asked about the rock in my hand. I'd completely forgotten about it. Maybe I was in a little bit of shock.

"A clue." My eyes shot open. "They threw this rock at me."

Carter took it from me and took the rubber band off, releasing the piece of paper. I watched as his eyes scanned the paper.

"This was no accident." He held the paper out. "Someone is trying to send you a message to stay away from Emile's murder investigation."

"Sophia Cummings," Charlotte gasped. She rushed over to the cabinet under the sink and grabbed the first-aid kit. "You have to stop putting your nose in this investigation. Someone thinks you are putting your nose in others' business. I want you at my wedding. Not dead like Emile."

She took a couple of Band-Aids out of the red box and placed a couple on my shin.

"Do you two mind if I have a word alone with Sophia?" Carter asked Charlotte and Brett.

"Actually"—I stood up on wobbly legs—"if you can get me across the street, we can talk in private all you want."

"Across the street?" all three said in unison.

I nodded toward the front of the house. "I'm renting that house from Madison while I'm in town." I started to stumble forward, but Carter grabbed my elbow to steady me. "I'll explain all that later. Right now I just want to get a cup of coffee and a shower."

Carter put one arm around my waist to steady me a little more.

"Oh, hell." He gave up, probably because I almost took both of us down, and hoisted me up in his arms.

This would've made me feel all sorts of romantic if I didn't have the ache of my shin and the worry that someone was after me hanging over my head.

"I'll call you," Charlotte called from the front door as Carter trotted through her lawn, across the street, and onto my porch.

Gently he put me down and kept on arm around my waist as he wrestled with the key I'd given him.

"Let's get you inside." He shoved the door open and, once he had me in, slammed it shut with his foot.

He carried me all the way into the family room, sat me on the couch, and fluffed a pillow behind my back.

"I'll be right back." He walked into the kitchen.

There was the sound of cabinet doors opening and closing before I finally heard the suction break of the refrigerator's door and the clinking of ice cubes.

*   *   *

"Take a drink. You'll feel a little better." He returned with the glass of water. His voice was gentle and soothing. He sounded like he knew what he was talking about.

My hands shook when I took the glass.

"You are a little more shaken up than you want me to know." Carter sat down and scooted closer to me. He rested his arms on his thighs.

"I'm sorry." Tears burned my eyelids.

"For what?" he asked.

"For a lot of things. Mainly for snooping." I lifted the glass and took a drink.

"You're only saying that because you're probably in shock. It's too dangerous." He pointed to the glass. "Take some more sips."

He stood up and looked around.

"This is a pretty nice place. Looks like you." He walked over to the family room doors that led out to the backyard. "That's beautiful."

"I'm lucky to still have good friends after all these years." I was beginning to feel better. My hands weren't shaking as much and I was aware of the pain. "Please help yourself to a cookie. I made them last night."

"Before or after you went to see Natalie Devin?" he asked.

"I told you I was going to see her." I used my fist to push myself back up to more of a sitting position.

"You didn't tell me you were going to harass her." He sucked in a deep breath. "She said you were over at her house harassing her and saying all sorts of untrue things about her and Emile. She even implied you accused her of killing him." He stopped in the kitchen. I looked at him. His hands were crossed over his chest and he looked at the chalkboard, slightly shaking his head.

"See, that makes me think she did do it, because I obviously struck a nerve," I said.

He turned around and narrowed his eyes at me. He didn't look very happy.

"While I was there, I simply asked a few questions about rumors I'd heard." I shrugged, dragging the glass up to my lips to avoid his stare. He made me even more nervous, so I kept talking. "You should be looking at her. She and her husband are valid suspects. Not Evelyn. I'd heard Emile was a ladies' man and she was one of his rumored ladies. They own the two-family that Emile lived in. Her husband caught them in an intimate situation there. He killed him because of the affair and then bought her that big diamond ring as hush money." My voice faded off.

"She told you all of that?" Carter glanced up at me underneath his brows.

"Not in so many words. But it all makes sense." I tried to redeem myself.

He walked back over and held the piece of paper the person who had tried to run me over had left for me to take.

"Clearly, someone knows that you're snooping." He sat down next to me and eased back into the cushion.

I read the note. Stop snooping or you'll join Emile.

The words sat in my throat like a lumpy piece of uncooked dough. "How did they know where I was?"

"Do you think you can answer a few questions for me?" Carter asked, and pulled out a notebook from his khakis' pocket.

"Wine." I smacked my head, remembering that I'd seen him in the wine aisle.

"I don't think having a glass of wine right now would be good for your state of shock." He shook his head. "And it's a little early. Why don't you start with some strong coffee?"

"No. I mean yes." I shook my hands in front of me. "Yes to coffee, but last night I saw you in the wine aisle of the Piggly Wiggly. Did you have a date?" I asked.

"You saw me and didn't say hello?" he asked. "I sure could've used your help. After all, I was trying to figure out a wine you might enjoy."

"Me?" I asked.

"I don't know a lot about wine. I was going to give you a call and see if you wanted to go over the statement you were supposed to give at the department."

* * *

"I forgot about that." I'd been so busy trying to get other suspects in the murder than just Evelyn. "You didn't stop by."

"No. After I bought the wine, I decided not to. Besides, you weren't even at your parents' house. That would've been awkward. Have you heard anything while working at the RCC?" His brows rose.

"So your plan was to get me tipsy and spill my guts about all the dirty little secrets between the staff and members?" I asked in a joking manner. "Because there's a lot of dirt around that place, and I don't mean the ground soil."

"I only care about Emile." He pushed himself off the couch and squatted down to get another look at my leg. "Do you think you're going to be all right?"

"Yes." I held my hands out in front of me. "Not shaking anymore, so I'm good. Tough as nails."

"Stay out of trouble." He pushed himself up to stand. "Nice chalkboard, by the way."

It wasn't like him not to press me on the things I'd written on the Operation Wedding chalkboard. The only reason, I figured, was that he felt sorry for me and didn't want to press it. For now, anyway.

"Stop snooping. I'll call and check on you later. When you feel up to it, I want you to come file a report about this," he said.

"Aye, aye." I saluted him, which he didn't seem to find funny.

File a report, my hiney. I was going to find out who had tried to run me over. Better yet, who had tried to silence me because they killed Emile.

Chapter Sixteen

"You what?" Madison was shocked when she saw my leg. Thankfully, she knew there wasn't any coffee in the house I was renting from her, so she'd come prepared with two large to-go cups from Small Talk Café.

"I'm not sure who it was." I eased up out of the kitchen chair and walked over to the Operation Wedding chalkboard. I took a sip of the coffee and looked at the lists of suspects. "Now it's personal," I whispered before I took another drink. "Who on this list knew I was here?"

"I wouldn't think anyone, since we just decided it on the fly last night." She walked over and stood next to me. Both of us focused on the chalkboard. "Not that I think Brett did it, but could he've seen you run out this morning?"

"It's worth putting him on here, but he sure seemed surprised when I told him I was living here." I picked up a piece of the chalk and under his name wrote HIT AND RUN with a big question mark. "Then there was Natalie." I wrote the same thing under her name. "She might've followed us after she thought we were on to her, just so she could see our next move."

"But it was a truck." I wrote down that information on the board. "Does Brett or Natalie have access to a truck?"

"Brett would from his job." Madison let out a deep sigh. "Do you think?" Her brows furrowed as she asked with little confidence in her voice.

"Anything is possible." I put the chalk down and stepped back. "There's a lot of speculation up there and I'm hoping to get some of these people cleared today."

When we walked out of the house, I couldn't help but shuffle my eyes around the neighborhood to see if there were any lurking trucks, because someone had to be watching me. "But they left that note and Carter took it." My mind was still on the near-death experience.

"You called Carter?" She smiled really big.

"No. Charlotte and Brett did after I'd made it back to their house." I clicked the seat belt. "Anyways, Natalie called him and told him I'd been snooping. He has questions about that and wants me to file a real complaint about the person sending me a very clear message to stop investigating Emile's murder."

"You didn't tell me that." Her jaw dropped and she shook her head. "And you're going to stop, right?" she asked.

"They can't scare me." I lifted the cup and took a drink.

"I don't think that's a good idea, and I'm not going to try and talk you out of it because you had me up all night thinking about it." She tapped the steering wheel with her finger as we waited for one of the lights on Main Street to turn green. The rental car place was at the only gas station on Main Street. It was like an all-in-one-service deal.

"You do know that Ella Chapshaw is hosting Charlotte's shower tonight?" Madison asked and pulled into Poochie's Garage.

"She is?" I asked, and gathered my stuff from the car floor, careful not to spill my coffee.

"Mm-hmm." Madison nodded. "Of course, I'm invited because I'm in the wedding, but by all rights you should be invited since you're baking the cakes for the wedding."

"That's not really a reason to be invited. I'm going to go to Peacocks and Pansies to see if she's there first." She should be there for her weekly shift, but if for some reason she wasn't, showing up at the shower was another option. "I wonder who's doing her desserts for the shower?"

"I can only think it'd be the Piggly Wiggly, since we don't have someone around here. Though you could show up with something fabulous." She cocked a brow with a delicious idea.

"You just might see me there." I nodded. "Thanks for the ride and the place to stay."

"You're welcome. And you can buy the place, since I want you to stay in town!" she hollered as I shut the door.

I pretended not to hear her but noticed a school bus butted up to the front of the garage bay door. The side of the bus read RUMFORD SCHOOL DISTRICT.

"We better win." Poochie Honeycutt's voice drifted out of the service center office.

There was the garage on one side, the gas station pumps in the front, and a service center office connected to the garage. On the other side of the office was a small blacktopped area where the cars were kept.

"Now with that chef gone, Patrick's father will be happy," an unfamiliar voice followed up.

My ears perked up. Instead of taking a step closer to see which cars were for rental, I walked to the office.

The old red speckle tile I remember from my childhood had faded to a dull, almost salmon, color. The heavy steel desk was still in place, and though the chair had probably been replaced, the duct tape holding the fake leather together told me it'd seen better days.

There were a couple of filing cabinets along the back wall near the open door of the garage. The buzz of drills, the release of air from an air compressor, and the voices led me to look inside.

Poochie and another man stood with their backs to the door. I probably should've let them know I was there. I didn't. I wanted to hear what they were saying about Patrick and Emile.

"That will give Patrick more time to practice instead of worrying about getting up and working those crazy hours before school just to help his family out," Poochie said.

I stood a ways back from the door so as not to make a sound.

"If you ask me, I think the boy likes being around all that food," the other man noted. "On away games, he sits right up front with me on the bus. The cheerleaders are busy hootin' and hollerin' getting the rest of the team pumped up in the back, while the main star of the team is asking me about the ingredients my wife put in the homemade snacks she makes the team each week."

"Huh?" Poochie pulled back, his nose snarled.

"Yeah." The bus driver laughed. "He said that baseball was his career choice but he'd picked up a lot of tips from that Emile."

"I don't know what tips. Not that me and Darlene could afford to breathe the air in that place, but we was once there for a wedding." He shook his head. "Weeee-dog, we didn't know what any of that fancy stuff was. It looked too scary to try. We drove to the Hardee's right after that and loaded up on food."

"We ain't ever been there either. We did get an invitation to the Harrington wedding this weekend because my wife is on one of them committees with the girl's mama, but we heard there was some ruckus going on about the menu. Something about expensive food that no one will eat." He smacked Poochie on the back. "Buddy, I've got to get out of here. If you can get 'er gassed up and ready to go for the game, I'm mighty appreciative."

The two men shook hands and turned around before I could scatter myself gone.

"Can I help you?" Poochie's head peeked around the corner of the door.

My hands clasped behind my back, I swayed back and forth, looking around.

"Poochie." I smiled real big. "It's me, Sophia Cummings."

"Little Sophia." His smile reached his soft blue eyes. He'd aged, but I could tell he was still as kind as ever. "You're home."

"I'm outta here." The bus driver nodded and excused himself from the office.

"Yeah, man. I'll get that done." Poochie watched as the man left. "What on earth are you doing back here?"

"I'm baking Charlotte's cake for the big day this weekend." Instead of telling him the real truth of what'd brought me home, I figured it best to see the future instead of the past. "And I'm in need of a rental for the next week."

"Just a week?" He *tsk*ed. "Darn shame. I bet Bitsy and Daddy are just over the moon with their little girl home. They keep braggin' on your fancy job."

"That's so sweet. I've enjoyed being home and reconnecting with everyone." Somehow I needed to slip in the questions milling around in my head about Patrick and the bus driver. "Who just left?"

"That's Ducky Hemphill. You remember old Ducky. His family owns that pharmacy on Main Street." He spurred a faint memory. "Anyways, he retired and then decided to become a bus driver. You know, most men my age are doing that." He took a greasy towel from the back pocket of his garage overalls and wiped his forehead. "I'd never want to deal with youngins."

"I heard him saying something about the baseball game." I led slowly into the questions. "I probably should catch a game while I'm home to support my old school."

"Honey, they're away. Ducky is the team's bus driver. He loves it." He jammed the oily rag back in his pocket.

"He mentioned Patrick. I work with Patrick at the RCC right now." I explained quickly how I was helping Evelyn Moss out in the kitchen.

"Poor kid can't cut a break." Poochie ran his fingers along a pegboard that held a few keys with yellow sales tags and grabbed a couple.

"What do you mean? He is a good worker, from what I've seen." I followed him out the door and next to the office, where he pointed out a few cars.

"He's got a sad home life. Mother took ill and sister has to stay home with the other kids. I don't know all the particulars, but I bet Bitsy would know." He cackled and opened the door of a four-door Corolla. "Now this car here is probably the one I'd let you rent. I remember how hard you were on cars."

Driving slow hadn't been part of my vocabulary when I'd gotten my license. It was probably a good thing I didn't have a car in the city even though I did keep insurance. Poochie had always been working on my car for my parents when I was in high school.

"Get on in and sit down." He turned his face to the rusty truck next to us. "Or you can drive that. It's a tank."

"I'll take this one." I tapped the wheel once I got in.

"Here you go." He gave me the keys. "I'll settle up with the paperwork later. I've got a bus to get ready before school lets out." He shut the door. I rolled down the manual window. "You be careful and stop in a couple times to see me while you're here."

"I will." I put the keys in the ignition and it started right up. "Thanks, Poochie."

I'd had plans to head on over to see Bitsy, but that had all changed when I heard the bus driver talking about Patrick. If Patrick did have another motive to kill Emile, what could it be?

If Patrick enjoyed cooking as much as the bus driver said, there had to be more to his relationship with Emile than the bullying. Something was fishy.

It was as if I'd lost myself in my thoughts and questions concerning Patrick, because when I looked up, I had mindlessly driven to Rumford High School and already parked in a visitor's parking space.

A knock on the window made me jump.

"Sophia Cummings, is that you?" Claire Edmond, the school's librarian, stood next to the car.

I gave a slight wave, turned off the car, and got out.

"Hi, Mrs. Edmond. How are you?" I asked.

"Fair to middlin'." She rubbed the small of her back. "Gettin' too old for this job. Up and down, carrying them books to the shelf, is startin' to wear on my back. Instead of quitting or retiring, I figure them ebooks'll run me out of my job."

"You aren't old enough to retire." Heck, she was past it. I'd thought she was one hundred when I went to school there.

"You always were my favorite student." She pinched my cheek and I took it like a champ.

"Are you here for career day?" She nodded toward a sign stuck in the schoolyard. "You're probably the most famous person to come out of Rumford. Bitsy's always a-braggin' about you at the Friends of the Library meetings."

"She's one of a kind. Yes, I'm here for career day." I rubbed my hands together. "I better get in there, because I'm late."

"It's like an act of Congress to get into the school nowadays." She took a few steps and called over her shoulder. "Come on. I'll let you in the library door so you don't have to worry about going through the rigmarole they put you through just to get into the office."

"Are you sure?" I didn't waste any time to let her change her mind. I hurried alongside her.

"Sure as Shinola." She and I walked to the side door, and she unlocked it with her key. "I guess you know where you're going."

"I sure do." I gave her a quick hug. "It was so good to see you. Will you be at the little library event?"

"Yes." Her chin lifted up and down. "Even though Catherine Fraxman is the new librarian of the city's library, I'm helping in any way I can." She leaned in. "You know, she's still a little young to run such a big job, if you were to ask me. Even though you didn't ask. I still took off work here just in case this old shelf up here needs to be dusted off." She slapped her knee and laughed. "I just might get fired after all," she said in delight.

"Don't count on it. This school couldn't function without you." I waved bye and headed out the double doors that spilled into the hallway.

I stood there for a second to let my mind warp all the way back to my high school days. To the right was the cafeteria, and if I could remember correctly, the gym was to the left. I was on the hunt for the athletic offices, where I knew they kept the players' information. If I could get my hands on Patrick's address, I'd stop by and talk to his parents. I wasn't sure what I'd say to them or what I was looking for. I guessed I'd figure that part out when I got there.

First, I had to get the information. As I'd assumed, the baseball coach's name and gym teacher's name were the same. Rumford liked to save money by having the gym teacher coach a few different teams. This made things much easier on me, since gym class was in session and there was no coach in the office.

I had to be very vigilant because I knew that any minute the class bell could ring and the hall between the office and the gym doors would be filled with wandering teenage eyeballs. I didn't want anyone to see me.

Before just waltzing into the gym office, I walked by and casually looked through the door's window. A few feet after the door, I turned around and looked up and down the hall before I turned the knob and let myself in.

The light was already on. There were several helmets, baseball uniforms of all sizes, and stinky gym bags stacked next to a couple of those big orange barrel coolers, no doubt ready to get put on the bus once Poochie got it there for them.

Another thing I knew from high school was that if a public school bus was used, it was a liability for someone under the age of eighteen to ride without parental consent. Not only that, but there was a file that had to be carried on the bus with those signatures. The forms always had the parents' names, insurance information, and medications to be dispensed along with the student's address.

I looked around the top of the desk to see if the file was sitting there among the millions of files stacked on top. Nothing stood out. I opened the desk drawers. They were filled with mouthpieces, baseball bats, baseballs, paper clips, rubber bands, pencils—things that weren't what I was looking for.

"The stack of stuff." I smacked my hands together and turned to eye the bags and equipment in the corner. I hurried over there and started to go through the items. Just as I thought, there was a bag with the playbooks and headsets for the coaches to communicate during the game along with the permission slips from all the players.

I squatted down and put the file on the floor, quickly thumbing through it. When I found Patrick's information, I took my phone from my back pocket and snapped a couple of photos. I threw the file back in the bag, zipped it up, and tossed it on top of the other bags just before the bell to switch classes rang.

I scurried out the door and tried to blend in with the high schoolers as best I could, until a pair of eyes caught mine. Patrick stared at me with a blank expression on his face.

Chin tucked to my chest, I kept my head down until I felt a heavy hand on my shoulder.

"Excuse me." I jerked around to see a man with a Rumford logo cap on his head and a whistle around his neck. "Did you need something?"

"I'm sorry?" I asked, as if I didn't know what he was asking.

"I just saw you come out of my office. Was there something you needed?" he asked.

"You're the coach," I snapped, nodding and trying to come up with a good explanation for why I was there. Over his shoulder, I saw Patrick walking past us. "Patrick"—I grabbed the boy—"I wanted to know why you weren't at work, but I see why."

"Hey, Chef. Yep. I've got baseball. I told y'all that." Patrick took a tone I wasn't accustomed to from him. Like a big-billy badass tone. "Baseball is more important, and if you can't understand that . . ."

Out of the corner of my eye, I saw the coach roll his shoulders back, furrow his brows, and nod in complete agreement. Patrick was saying everything the coach wanted to hear.

"I'm sorry." I stopped him from saying anything else. "I just realized I was looking at an old calendar. That's all. See you at work." I hurried off into the crowd of students before they could stop me again.

Patrick's eyes and his hard words haunted me the entire way to his family's house. He'd looked like a deer in headlights. If I'd not heard the bus driver say something about Patrick's love for cooking, I'd never have believed it from his attitude.

My phone's GPS led me straight to the poorer side of Rumford. I'm sure that in its heyday, the area had been somewhat desirable.

My heart hurt when I pulled up and parked the Corolla in front of Patrick's home. No wonder he had tried to stay at work or school more. The front porch had caved in; some of the dingy siding boards had rotted and not been replaced. The roof was partially covered with a blue tarp—"partially" only because the other part of the tarp had blown off and hung down the front of the house.

I got out and looked down the street to see if anyone else was out. It was silent. Eerily silent.

"Can I help you?" A woman with a cigarette dangling from her lips and a diapered baby stuck on her hip had walked around the corner of the house.

"I'm looking for Sherri, Patrick's mom." I stepped a bit closer.

"Who's asking?" She was one talented woman. She was able to take a drag and blow it out without taking her hands off the baby.

"Sophia Cummings. I'm from the RCC and wanted to talk to him about his work hours coming up."

"He ain't gonna be working there much longer," she snarled.

"You are his mother?" I asked.

"Hell, no. Mama's sick. I'm his sister and this here is our little sister." She held the baby out for me to get a gander at.

"Sweet." It was my standard reply when I saw a baby that wasn't necessarily super cute, but was awfully sweet.

"Mm-hmm," she hummed, and stuck the baby on her hip again. She let the cig drop from her lips and snuffed it out with the toe of her ripped-up shoe. "I reckon you got what you came for."

"Wait." I stopped her when she turned to disappear around the house. "Why is he quitting? He loves his job."

At least that's what I'd gathered from what the bus driver had told Poochie.

"Daddy said that even though times are tough, we'll get by, because Brother"—she was referring to Patrick—"needs to focus on getting a big-time contract for baseball instead of being a sissy in a kitchen."

"Sissy?" My jaw dropped.

"Yeah. You know, like a girl. A boy acting like a girl."

"I know what a sissy is, but why does working at the country club make him a sissy?" I asked.

"Because he started talking all sorts of nonsense about becoming a cook or something like that. Daddy gets mad and says Brother's lost his mind. Sometimes he hits Brother, sayin' he's knocking some sense back into him." She gave a bit of a shrug and transferred the baby to the other hip. "I reckon he's right. Kitchen work is a woman's job."

I gulped. When was the last time Patrick's father had hit him? Had Emile put all sorts of ideas in Patrick's head? Had Patrick's father killed Emile?

"What's wrong? You're all white and stuff." Her eyes swirled around my face.

"Where's your dad?" I asked, and took a deep breath.

"He's working a double down at the factory. Between his double shifts and Patrick's money, we barely have enough to pay for gas to get my mom back and forth to her chemo treatments and stick any sort of meat on the table." She lifted her chin in the air. "Well, you better get back to your fancy job."

I took a couple of steps backward toward the car.

I had thought I was going to leave here with answers. Unfortunately, I left with more questions that needed to be answered.

The drive back into town made me think about the case and what I'd uncovered that would make someone want to threaten me. They could've killed me if they'd really wanted to, but they hadn't. The reason, I thought, was that they wanted to scare me.

Downtown was the heartbeat of Rumford, and it was beating today. Peacocks and Pansies was located next door to Small

Talk Café. The cobblestone street of downtown added that cozy, small-town feel Rumford was known for. I scored a parking spot in front of Small Talk.

The inside of Peacocks and Pansies was adorable. The walls were wooden shiplap and the ceiling was tin. A few comfy and fluffy-looking cream couches were spread out over the boutique. The pillows had cute southern sayings on them and a price tag dangling off. Even the rugs on the floor had a price tag. Not only did Carol Bauer sell clothes; she also sold the furniture and accessories you'd need to make the cozy French country look that had gotten so popular.

I picked up a couple of pieces of the leather cuff jewelry and smiled at some tried-and-true quotes stamped on them. There were several long brown wood bead necklaces with tassels hanging off the bottom of them. Small leather pouches meant for small items rested on a round table along with some fancy soaps.

"Sophia, is that you?" Carol asked from the other side of the boutique. "I'm worn plumb out and I don't know why. I got to bed with the chickens." She winked. "Let me get that dress I was telling you about."

"Thanks." I grinned as I put the piece of jewelry down and walked over to the dressing room.

"You go on in that dressing room right over there behind that curtain." She pointed to the hanging drape.

I'd seen dressing rooms like these in boutiques in New York. Carol had done a great job with the place.

"What's your name?" the young girl asked, coming closer.

"Sophia Cummings." I put my hand out and could see that she wasn't as young as she'd looked a few feet away. She just had really beautiful pale skin. Her coal-black hair lay in long loose curls over her shoulders. "Did we go to school together? I've been gone so long, people look so different."

"I don't think we did. I work for Carol a couple of hours a week. You know . . ." She leaned over me and grabbed the small chalkboard hanging from a hook. She wrote my name in pink chalk and hung the board back up. "I like the discount."

"Are you Ella?" I asked.

"Heavens, no." She laughed. "I'm Lori. Ella usually works today, but she's off because she's hosting a big wedding shower tonight."

"Charlotte's?" I asked.

"Yes." She nodded with a big smile. "You're going?"

"I'm a longtime friend of Charlotte's." Now I knew I had to go to the shower as Madison had suggested. I had to get one of these suspects crossed off my list.

"Longtime friend, nothing." Carol came up from behind and rested her hands on my shoulder. "Sophia is baking the best part of the wedding. The cake." She shifted her weight to the right and looked at me. I twisted my head to the side and agreed.

She dropped her hands from my shoulders and grabbed a hanger from the rack next to us. She handed me the dress.

"You let me see that on you, now, ya hear?" Carol basked in her assertion that the dress was meant for me.

"I will." I walked into the dressing room and Carol pulled the curtain closed.

I held the dress up to get a good look and knew that it'd need a lot of work to look better on me than it did on the hanger. It was a red strappy dress with a low cowl back and a flirty skirt that hung to my calf. Something I'd never pick. I normally stuck with the standard black or white. I was a little partial to both since I wore a lot of those colors in the kitchen.

"Well? We're waiting," Carol chirped from across the curtain.

Without looking in the mirror once I'd changed, I pulled the curtain open. Both Carol and Lori stood on the other side. Both of their jaws dropped.

"Yeah, red isn't my color." I wanted to let Carol off the hook easy. "It's okay. I'm sure there's something else in the boutique."

"Oh," Lori gasped. "You look great!"

"I'll be," I muttered, looking at myself. "Carol, you're right." I twirled to look at the backside. The dress fit me like a glove. "This dress was meant for me."

"Honey, if you wear that dress to Charlotte's wedding, you won't be single for long." Carol spoke to me, but her gaze was on the dress.

"I'll take it." I looked at myself one more time. There was no way in hell I wasn't going to wear this dress. If only Noah could see me now. I'd knock his socks off in this dress. Too bad he wouldn't see me. One day, I'd get back at him. I didn't know when; I just knew my day would come.

Like Bitsy always said, heaven help the man who did a southern woman wrong.

Chapter Seventeen

Charlotte's wedding was fast approaching and I was no closer to getting Evelyn off the hook; the cakes had to be layered, iced, and decorated. At least I could cross off Peacocks and Pansies to get the dress. Not that I cared about the dress too much, but I wanted to talk to Ella, which didn't pan out. All my new questions along with the old ones were going to have to wait until I got something done for the wedding.

I parked in the RCC's employee parking. The only cars there were Evelyn's and another small car with rental barcode stickers on the back passenger window.

The back entrance was open and Evelyn's door was shut when I walked past it down the long hall to the kitchen. I dipped my head into the ballroom to see if Charlotte was in there meeting the new chef, but it was empty. The kitchen was empty too.

I put my bag on the island and pulled my phone out of my back pocket, quickly texting Nick to see where he was since he wasn't even here. The place was deserted, which was a prime opportunity for me to get some quiet time to decorate a couple of layers of Charlotte's cake.

"A little pat of this and a little dash of that." I sang a snappy tune when I walked into the refrigerator to get a couple layers of cake.

When I walked out, Charlotte was standing next to my workstations.

"The new chef is here," Charlotte whispered, pointing to the swinging kitchen door.

About that time, Evelyn pushed through the door.

"I'm sorry for interrupting," I apologized.

Charlotte had a big smile on her face and Evelyn looked as pleased as a dead pig.

"Sophia." Evelyn stepped out of the way and gestured to the new chef coming into the kitchen behind her. "This is . . ."

"Noah?" Disgust laced my voice. My stomach clenched. "What are you doing here?" Anxiety, anger, and sickness coursed through my veins.

"Noah?" Charlotte's smile turned into a scowl. "Your Noah?"

"I'm going to be sick." I ran out of the room down the hall to the bathroom.

My hand gripped the porcelain sink as I tried to steady myself from the spinning room. My chest heaved up and down as I tried to get air. Panic jumped inside of me.

"No, no, no," I said after I looked up when I saw Charlotte walking in. "He can't be the new chef." Tears stung my eyes. I shook my head. I tried to gulp back the lump in my throat.

"I had no idea." Charlotte took a few paper towels and got them wet, placing them on the back of my neck. "When he introduced himself, I didn't even catch his name. I was taken aback by the food he'd prepared. It's gorgeous."

"Why? How?" I started to ask all sorts of questions that I knew Charlotte couldn't answer. "How did Evelyn find him?"

"I don't know, sweetie." The tears ran down my face as all the memories of the hurt came crashing into my heart.

"I won't use him," Charlotte offered some kind words. But it was only that. Words. "I'll tell you one thing." She nodded. "He's slicker than owl shit. He was wining and dining me like we were on a date. For a second, I'd forgotten I was getting married in a couple of days."

"That's his M.O." I remembered that charm well. "I'm not going to let you not get married. There's a way around me running into him." I brushed my hand across my face to dry my tears. "I'm not going to give him the satisfaction of seeing me like this."

"But he did you dirty." Charlotte scowled.

The knock on the door jerked both Charlotte and me out of our conversation.

"Sophia, please, open the door," Noah said, and jiggled the handle. "Please talk to me."

"Go away!" Charlotte yelled at the door.

"Shh." I hushed her and took a step toward the door.

"He cheated on you and had the nerve to show up here. That dirty, low-down, good-for-nothing dog," she spat, and stepped between me and the door. "Go back to New York. We don't want you here."

I reached around Charlotte and turned the handle of the door, popping the lock out. The door cracked opened.

"Sophia?" Noah's strong northern accent flowed through the opening before his head peeked in.

Our eyes met. The trusting eyes that I'd loved for so long were dull. Or at least they looked muted to me. It was the first time I'd stared into his green eyes and felt nothing but disgust.

"You knew I lived here." My voice was flat, with no emotion. Though I didn't want him here, I wanted to know exactly why he was here. "You had no right to come to Kentucky."

"I had no idea you were here. I'm here to do a favor for Ritchie." He was referring to the owner of The Manhattan. "He said his friend had died and the restaurant he worked for needed a chef in a pinch and it was in Lexington. He suggested in light of things that I take a much-needed vacation because my head hasn't been on straight since you left." His voice cracked. "I didn't know that he meant Rumford. You have to trust me."

"Trust you?" I laughed, throwing back my head. "You were the only person in this world I trusted until I caught you in the arms of another woman."

"You're lower than a snake's belly in a wagon rut," Charlotte continued to give Noah the business.

"Come on, Charlotte." I waved her to follow me down the hall. "I'm going to find Evelyn."

"It's not going to do you any good." Noah stalked after us. "I've signed a temporary contract that keeps me here until after the wedding. Then I get to sign a permanent one if it works out well on both ends."

With each step, I got madder and madder. Some might say I was mad as a wet hen, but I was madder than a wet cat. I wanted to claw his eyes out.

"Did you hear me? I signed a contract." He continued to bait me.

"Oh, I heard you." The words came seething out of my mouth. "I heard you telling her how good she felt and how much you loved sneaking around with her. I heard everything." My eyes narrowed.

"Stop it, you two." Evelyn appeared in the hallway. "This is a business. A very reputable country club. The finest in all of central Kentucky. I won't have this type of behavior."

"Evelyn." My mouth flew open. "I talked my father into representing you, and this is how you repay me?"

"I had no idea he was the one Ritchie was sending. He called to find out what happened to Emile. They'd been friends and one conversation led to another. The next thing I knew, he said he had a guy that needed a vacation. Here he is." She pointed to Noah.

"Then you can fire him. Rip the contract in half," I demanded.

"You and I both want what's best for Charlotte." Evelyn grabbed me by the elbow and dragged me into her office, shutting the door behind us. "He is our only hope. He has the experience and know-how to pull off her wedding."

"What about Nick? He runs that kitchen exactly like Emile. He might even be better." I couldn't let her off the hook that quickly.

"Nick can run a restaurant where people stream in and out all day. He's never catered an event for over two hundred people, and if Charlotte's wedding doesn't go flawlessly, I might as well go on to jail for a crime I didn't commit because they will fire me here. I don't know which is worse." Her voice trailed off and her eyes looked down.

"I can't work with Noah." My words were simple. There

wasn't a need for an explanation. I just knew I couldn't do it. "But I don't need to work with him. Madison has given me the keys to Ford's Bakery. I can transfer the cakes I've made for Charlotte's wedding there and finish them. I can even bake the RCC's desserts down there and bring them a couple of times a day for the next few days." It was the only way I was going to work around her not firing Noah. "I'll be leaving in a week, so you're going to have to find a replacement for me because Noah can't even make an ice cream sundae, much less make a dessert from scratch."

"You can't just work today and tomorrow here to make it easier on everyone? The wedding is tomorrow. I'm not saying he isn't a jerk, but I'm saying that he's going to help save our beloved RCC. You know that you love this place just as much as I do or you wouldn't have stuck your neck out to not only get your dad to help me but put all your needs aside and work here over the last couple of days."

She was right. I did love this place.

"Besides, I did give you your first baking job." She gave me a sly smile.

"You got me there." I hesitated and quickly thought about working next to Noah. "Fine. I'll finish the cake here and the desserts for the day. That's it."

"That's all I'm asking you to do." She pulled me into a big hug. "Thank you, Sophia. Now you can go back to your old job without Noah there and be much happier."

"That's something I didn't think of." My brows shot up.

In a week when I left Rumford, Noah was going to be Evelyn's and the RCC's problem, not mine or The Manhattan's. Suddenly,

I hated him more. He was the one getting the reward, staying in Rumford with good and loving people. People I loved. So why was I going back to The Manhattan?

I gulped back a lump in my throat. I couldn't believe it had taken seeing Noah in Rumford to realize how much I loved being home and making simple desserts that my family and friends loved.

Chapter Eighteen

A good, old-fashioned, wealthy Rumford party was one not to be missed. Since I hadn't gotten to visit with Ella Capshaw at Peacocks and Pansies, I'd decided to throw on one of my old party dresses. While I snatched the dress from my parents' house, I also grabbed the frozen skillet apple pie along with the box of Emile's ledgers Evelyn had said I could take. My heart broke when I was leaving their house, and Duchess was crying. When I picked her up, she purred and snuggled close to me.

"Are you missing me?" I rubbed down her soft fur. "Want to have a sleepover?" I asked her.

She let out a soft meow and that was my cue to take her with me, but not before I gathered her some food and left Bitsy a note to say that Duchess was going to go home with me.

While I got dressed, I questioned several times whether I would just show up or if I should call Ella to let her know I was coming. What was one more guest? I twirled in front of the mirror and couldn't help but smile at Duchess lying on the bed behind me. She was purring deeply.

"We are southerners," I said to Duchess. She lifted her head and gave a simple meow. "You're right. We have an open-door policy around here." I tickled the top of her head and made sure she had some kitty kibble before I left for Charlotte's shower.

"Good evening." A young and vibrant woman answered the door. She had on an LBD with high heels, a strand of pearls, and matching earrings. Her black hair was cut in an angled bob and parted neatly down the middle. "I'm Ella Capshaw, and you are?"

"Sophia Cummings." I smiled while she busied herself looking at a clip board.

"You won't find her on the guest list." Carter trotted up to the door. "She's with me."

"Hi, Carter. Welcome to my home." She took a step back, and it didn't go unnoticed that she kept an eye on me after we walked in.

"What are you doing here?" Carter asked as he dragged me into the hallway.

"What are you doing here?" I asked back.

"I'm in the wedding. It's a rehearsal dinner."

"Rehearsal dinner, *pfft*." I laughed, and when he didn't laugh back, I realized he wasn't joking. "Are you kidding me?" My blood started to boil. "Madison told me it was a shower."

"Brett has to work tomorrow night on a big development coming to town, and he didn't want to have to wait until he got back from the honeymoon to seal the deal. So the rehearsal is here tonight." There was a spark in his eye.

"You're enjoying this." I shook my finger at him.

"Now I think it's funny that your friend told you it was a shower and you showed up." He laughed at his own words. "If it were a shower and you still weren't invited, then why are you here?" He stuck his hand out. His body shifted to the right and his eyes lowered. "Wait. I know why you're here."

"For Charlotte." I stiffened.

"You're here because Ella Capshaw is giving this shower and she's on your little chalkboard list of suspects. You're here to snoop." He shook an all-knowing finger at me.

"Am I that transparent?" I asked just as a loud squeal came from behind us.

"Are you two together?" Charlotte's pointer finger gestured back and forth between me and Carter. "Oh my gawd," she gasped. "Carter." She playfully smacked his bicep underneath the baby-blue suit coat that made his eyes pop and softened his skin tone. That I did notice. "Did you ask Sophia to be your date?"

"Yes, I did." Carter agreed with a big grin on his face. "And you should've seen her jump at the chance."

"Mm-hmm," I hummed, and grabbed a flute of champagne from the waiter's tray as he walked past me. "Nearly clobbered him when he asked." I took a nice long drink.

"After all this time." Charlotte's shoulders lifted to her ears and fell back down with a happy sigh before she got dragged off by her mother.

After all this time? What was she talking about? I'd just met him this week. I brushed it off as her being nervous about getting married in forty-eight hours.

"I can't believe you are here to snoop and use Charlotte as a cover-up." Carter didn't miss a beat.

As soon as he could jump on me, he did.

"Emile's death wasn't just some joke. Or some run-of-the

mill murder. Someone is going to great lengths to cover it up." He told me as if I didn't already know that.

"When they tried to run me over, it got real personal." I took another drink, nearly emptying the glass.

"Make it unpersonal." He darted off down the hall.

"Unpersonal?" I asked. "Is that a word?" I hollered down the hall, only to get a glare back from over his shoulder. "Unpersonal. Who ever heard alike?"

"You made it." Madison and Matt looked so nice all dressed up.

"You didn't tell me it was a rehearsal dinner." I noodled the idea that she knew she was setting me up with Carter. "Were you trying to fix me up?"

Madison smiled and tucked her arm in the crook of Matt's, leading him down the hall.

After another glass of champagne, I'd gotten the liquid courage to finally do what I came for: figure out if Ella had had an affair with Emile.

With everyone greeting the happy bride and groom, I made my way around Ella's home and found her in the kitchen barking orders to the staff she'd assembled for the occasion.

"I've got a niggling suspicion that you aren't really here as Carter's date, are you?" Ella looked over the trays some waitress had before she gave the okay to serve them. "I'd heard you'd been running around town playing detective about Emile's death."

"Is it that obvious we aren't a couple?" I asked. It really popped my bubble too. I'd thought we looked good standing in the hallway snickering back and forth.

"There's definitely a little chemistry there, though." Ella wasn't seeing through my cover-up.

"Honestly, I wanted to talk to you about Emile." By her silence, I could tell she wasn't going to just tell me all about him. "It's my understanding that you and Emile had an affair."

"Affair?" She scoffed. "The last time I checked, I was an adult that was single and he was a single adult. So I have a hard time calling it an affair."

"Bad choice of words." It was my way of apologizing. "Were the two of you an item?"

She stuck a piece of the fancy cheese square in her mouth. "I ain't gonna lie. We did have a fling. But a week ago"—she did a little happy shimmy-shake with her shoulders and rolled her eyes with a great big smile on her face—"I met Grant Livingsworth."

She wiggled her brows while I narrowed mine.

"*The* Grant Livingsworth?" she asked, as if I should've known the name.

"Who is that?" I asked.

"His family only owns the biggest franchised store in town." She winked. "The Piggly Wiggly." Pride dripped out of her mouth.

"You want to be the Queen Sow?" I joked, scooting out of the waitress's way.

"Oh, Sophia Cummings." She playfully swatted at me. "I heard you have a wicked sense of humor. You'd have to in order to really want to stick your nose in a murder investigation. Though I don't blame you. Carter is a fine, fine specimen of a man." This time she gave me a long, theatrical wink.

"Back to Emile." I hurried her back to the subject before

Carter noticed I wasn't with the rest of the guests and came looking for me.

"Anyway, I broke up with him over a week ago." She brought her finger up to her temple and tapped it. "Or was it just a week ago? What day is it?"

"Thursday."

"That's right." Her mouth oozed with sophistication. She leaned on one hip and rested her hands on her waist. "You'll get to meet Grant at Charlotte's wedding." A happy sigh escaped her. "I will tell you a little secret." She jutted her right shoulder and got a little closer to me. "Emile's a lot more fun than Grant in the sack. He was a fun fling. But Grant." She brought her hand out in front of her and wiggled her ring finger. "He'll be able to put a big fat diamond right around my ring finger. Emile couldn't afford a bread tie. Besides, I was on an airplane coming back into town when Emile was killed. I have the ticket stub and Grant as my alibi."

She wasn't the killer, but she did have my curiosity up.

"How did Emile take the big breakup?" I asked.

"He sorta saw me and Grant at the RCC having a little lunch that involved some kissing. He went into a jealous rage." She smiled. "It only made Grant realize I was a hot commodity and it sealed our relationship. I'm gonna own the Piggly Wiggly one day."

I'm going to own my own bakery one day. The thought made me pause, which gave Ella the opportunity to walk back out to her guests.

After dinner was served and everyone was waiting on the dessert, I bid farewell with the excuse that I had to get back to the wedding cake. Besides, I wasn't about to waste my taste buds on a Piggly Wiggly dessert. Though a dessert did sound good.

As soon as I got back to the little cottage, I slipped off my heels and walked into the kitchen. Duchess was on my heels. I picked her up and took her back to the kitchen with me.

The chalkboard was the first thing I set my eyes on. I could either make myself a dessert and forget about the investigation, as Carter had warned, or I could write down what I'd learned about Ella. So I did both. I put the skillet apple pie in the oven and looked over the chalkboard while I waited for it to heat up.

"Duchess, Ella has an alibi." I talked to her as if she were going to talk back to me.

Under Ella's name, I wrote down what she had told me about her and Grant using the words AIRPLANE and OUT OF TOWN WITH GRANT. This would be easy to find out, and why would she lie? She'd admitted to having the affair, which I also wrote down, but Emile was the one who'd had the anger, not her.

"Then there was the little matter of Patrick. Was Nick right? Did Patrick hide out in the fridge and whack Emile over being bullied? There were so many more layers to Patrick's life. What would killing Emile do for him?" I looked over at Duchess. She'd curled up in a ball on the kitchen chair cushion.

"What if it was Patrick's father?" I questioned, drawing an arrow from Patrick's name. "His dad didn't want him to work there because he told Patrick he was a sissy. Maybe Emile was putting ideas of becoming a chef in his head, so Patrick's dad wanted to silence him?" I wrote down all my thoughts. "He wouldn't know what a seasoned skillet was if it hit him in the head," I joked. "But Patrick probably would, since he had an interest in cooking."

My eyes drew over to the pantry door, where I'd set down the box of Emile's past ledgers Evelyn had said I could take.

"Maybe something is in here." I talked to Duchess, but she didn't look at me.

The bottom of the box dragged across the floor as I pushed it with my foot. I popped open the lid and took out some of the journals and a few of the inventory receipts, spreading them across the kitchen table. I was happy to see Emile had kept notes about events at the RCC and even some little details like food allergies. For someone who fought with everyone, he sure had kept the needs of the members in his mind when he'd made his food and even done the preparation.

My stomach gurgled as the subtle hint of cinnamon and hot apples blanketed the kitchen in a warm hug.

There was a knock at the door. My eyes shifted to the clock on the microwave. It was a little too late to be having visitors, and if it was anyone, it'd be Charlotte. But there was no way she'd be back so quickly after I'd gotten back. Besides, she would have texted first.

I grabbed the wooden rolling pin out of the crock sitting on the counter and drew it over my head as I walked toward the front door. The massive figure was distorted from the frosted glass in the front door.

"Who's there?" I demanded to know in a very deep, disguised voice.

"Sophia?" Carter called from the other side. "Are you sick?"

"Carter." I swung the door open and let the rolling pin dangle at my side. "You scared me."

"You were going to—what did you say at the rehearsal dinner?—clobber me." His eyes drew down to the weapon. "With a rolling pin?" His right brow cocked as he looked at me with an amused grin. He lifted up his hand, which gripped a bottle of wine. "I came with a gift."

"Piggly Wiggly wine aisle?" I asked with a giggle.

"The most expensive. Five dollars." He flashed that grin that made my breath quicken.

"What gives?" I asked.

"I know you talked to Ella. I know you saw Patrick. I'm guessing you're about to pop like a full-blooded tick to tell me what you know." Slowly he waved the bottle in front of me.

"I'm not above a good bribe." I opened the door and walked away, allowing him to let himself in. "I guess we can have wine while we discuss the clues." I got a little excited.

"We?" He tried to hide the upper lip curl.

"I've got clues that you need. But first, I need you to promise me you won't arrest Evelyn." I opened a drawer, pulled out a corkscrew, and handed it to him.

"And this just so happens to be red, which goes great with apple pie." I took the bottle and found a corkscrew to open it.

I took the pie out of the oven and set it on the stove. The light golden crust was flaky, delicate, and perfectly sealed to the edges of the skillet. "You just so happen to have apple pie?" Carter walked over and looked at the pie. He took a deep breath, closed his eyes, smiled, and let out a sigh. "Smells so good."

A way to a man's heart was through food, and I could see in his eyes that his heart was thumping for a piece of my pie.

"Actually, it's skillet apple pie. My version of the apple pie." The knife slid through the crust. I plated two perfectly formed pieces of pie and was filled with joy when I noticed that the apples were evenly distributed, a delicious complement to the crust.

"If you are ever on a date and want to pick a dessert to go with wine, you need to remember that the wine should be at least as sweet as the dessert. Red pairs nicely with cheesecake and with berries, tarts, carrot cake, and some dark chocolates." I pushed a couple of the ledgers away from a spot on the table and set the plates down while Carter poured a couple of glasses of wine.

"I think I'm going to have to take you to dinner just to make sure I remember this." He eyed me under his brows. He held my glass out to me. After I took it, we clinked the glasses together.

He was flirting with me. Not like earlier, when I'd dismissed it. Not that I was a great sleuth—clearly not; the facts were the only clues I could go on. He'd bought me coffee. He'd bought wine with me in mind. Regardless, now he was asking me to go to dinner with him? My inner amateur sleuth would have said that he was definitely flirting.

We sat down. He picked up a ledger and glanced at it.

"What are these?" he asked, taking a bite of his pie.

"I'm sure you noticed Evelyn's messy office." Who wouldn't? "She had this box in there, and I asked if I could take it home to look through because I know there's some clues in there about Emile."

"Here we go," Carter groaned. He leaned back in the chair.

"Hear me out." I knew I was stepping over his bounds again, but I had to tell him. "Emile supposedly had carpal tunnel over the past few months, but only a couple of weeks ago his hand-writing changed in his detailed ledgers. If he'd been having trouble writing, why would he write fine up until a couple weeks ago and then last week while doing Charlotte's wedding be fine?"

"Carpal tunnel comes and goes. I'm not sure it would hurt your handwriting that much." His finger outlined the bottom of the glass.

"Now you're a doctor?" I shook my head and stood back up. The wine glass dangled in my hand while I looked the chalkboard over. "You can compare the handwriting. All of it is the same until the last couple of weeks. Even the signatures on the inventory delivery slips."

"So tell me what you heard at the RCC." He quickly changed the subject but continued to look through the ledgers.

"I know that it's rumored Emile has had a few affairs. Ella has an alibi I'm sure it'd be easy for you to check on."

"Now you want me to use my investigation skills?" he asked with a sarcastic tone.

I ignored him and continued my train of thought.

"Natalie, who I still think you need to look at, owns that house he rented. How do you know her husband didn't catch them together."

"We already went through his house and cleared it. There's nothing there. He had a bed, a few pieces of clothing, and that's about it. No personal items. He didn't even have a cell phone, and all the records on his landline were clean. From all the interviews I've done, Emile was a big flirt and that was it. It seems he lived for the RCC, married to his job, which makes me believe that Evelyn had more of a motive than most."

"What about Patrick? Did you look into that?" I refused to talk about Evelyn and her motives. Granted, there really weren't a whole lot of solid clues, now that I thought about it. Most of it was speculation that I needed to mark off my list as I went.

Carter nodded. "So you're saying Patrick killed Emile over his love of cooking?" he asked.

"I'm saying that maybe Emile teased Patrick about not being true to himself, or even Patrick's dad killed Emile thinking Emile had brainwashed his son into cooking." I shrugged. "I don't know."

"Patrick's dad?" He was even more confused.

"I sorta stopped by Patrick's parents' house after I went to the school to look through the coach's files for his address." I bit my bottom lip and watched Carter rake his hand through his hair with an exhausted "I can't believe you keep doing this" sigh. "I know. I know you said to stop looking into things, but that's like taking a hunting dog to the farm and telling it not to hunt."

"It's not just for the compromise of the investigation." He stopped pacing and put his hands out in front of him, shaking them toward me. "It's for your own safety. This is a murder."

"Fine. Don't use my leads. Use what I've already given you. I've made Natalie mad, so see if she is the one who tried to kill me and sent the note."

Something must've struck him in what I'd told him about the whole Patrick thing, because he started writing on that little notepad again. I squinted to see if I could make out what he was jotting down, but when he looked up, he covered the pad with his large hand.

"I hit a nerve with Natalie when she overheard me talking about Emile, and she followed me and Madison back to town after we left her," I said. "I told Madison to drop me off at the bakery so I could work and Natalie overheard us. She even asked me about it before she kicked me out." I smacked my hands together. "That's it!" I jumped up and headed to the pantry. I loaded up my arms with ingredients. When I baked, my head cleared and I processed things better. "Maybe she was going to leave the note at the bakery, but when she saw me jogging off, she decided to run me down and make it even more dramatic. Believe me, it worked." I pointed to the oven. "Hit PREHEAT 350 for me."

"You saw her following you?" he asked, walking over to the stove.

"No. I'm talking out the clues." I walked into the pantry.

While Carter tried to figure out the fancy oven (which took him a few minutes), I grabbed the dry ingredients to make the basic vanilla cupcake I use as the base. It was the pudding filling that made it banana pudding cupcakes.

"What are you making now?" He asked.

"Banana pudding. Baking helps me think, plus I need a kid dessert for Charlotte's wedding." I set all the ingredients on the counter.

Every restaurant in the South pretty much had banana pudding on its menu. As a kid, I'd liked the taste, but there was just too much of the pudding. We'd gone to one of those smorgasbords-type restaurants. I remembered taking a cupcake and a plate of banana pudding from the dessert section. I wasn't sure which one I wanted to eat, and Bitsy was beside herself that I'd taken two desserts when people on the other side of the world just wanted one dessert. She'd been good then about making me feel guilty. Anyway, I'd done my teenage job of ignoring her and scraped the icing off the cupcake. I scooped some of the banana pudding up with a piece of banana and frosted the top of the vanilla cupcake with it. My dad watched from across the table with a look of disgust on his face. Of course I had to try it, and no matter how bad it was, I had to pretend it was good. I took a deep breath and bit into my creation. It was an experience unlike one I'd ever had. Unfortunately, the term *food porn* hadn't been created then, but it was for sure food porn.

I guess the look on my face spoke so loudly to my dad that he reached over with his fork and, upon my agreeable nod, took a bite. The next day, there was a twenty-dollar bill and a note from my dad that said to head to the grocery store and buy the ingredients I needed to create a real banana pudding cupcake.

"Is there anything else I can help you with?" Carter leaned against the counter and looked at all the ingredients.

If I stopped focusing on my batter, his nearness made my hands shake. It didn't help matters that he looked very comfortable and fit in so well with the small cottage, almost like he was meant to go with the house.

"Take the cupcake liners and line the cupcake pan." I measured and mixed the ingredients while spouting out directions to Carter.

It was strange working in the kitchen with Carter watching me, and I was shocked that it didn't bother me. I'd always preferred to work on my pastries and baked goods alone. When Noah had come along, he'd been different. He'd always been too busy making the food to even notice what I was doing.

"I'm keeping my ears open at the RCC because there's a lot of talk around that place." I let the mixer hum while I got started on the filling.

"That's a lot of speculation about Natalie being the one who tried to run you over. I'll check into it." Carter didn't ask to help with anything else. He went back to eating his pie. "And I don't see her driving a truck."

"It could've been one of her many handymen that she uses for that fancy house of hers." It sounded like a pretty good suggestion.

"I'm going to check out Patrick's family too." Carter looked at me. My hands were wrist deep in dough. I shrugged. My insides jumped for joy. Maybe I'd just helped get Evelyn off as the number one suspect on his short list.

Chapter Nineteen

Baking was better than taking melatonin. The heat of the oven along with the hum of the mixer and the smells that filled the air were more relaxing then a warm bath and warm glass of milk. Having a cute sheriff by my side didn't hurt either.

It'd been the best sleep I'd gotten since I'd been back in Rumford.

"Rise and shine," Bitsy singsonged through the front door of the cottage. She walked into my house with a carafe. "I've got your favorite thing—a cup of hot coffee."

"Thanks." I pushed my bed head back and eyed Duchess, who was sleeping soundly on the couch pillow. "Are you mad I took Duchess?"

"No. She started missing you the night you started staying here." Bitsy looked around. "This house is adorable."

The bright morning rays spread across the open floor plan of the cottage, and specks of gold danced on my ceiling. Duchess stretched her arms out in front of her and spread her paws apart, pushing herself up to stand and arching her back to finish off the yawn.

"I'm not completely happy that you're still staying here"—she paused—"alone." She rolled her eyes and shook her head ear-to-shoulder and side-to-side. "Duchess will be a good roommate."

Bitsy pulled out little baggie of kibble out of her purse. She dangled it in front of her and helped herself into the kitchen, where she found a small bowl and put Duchess's food in it.

"See." Bitsy pointed when Duchess scurried over to the bowl and started to eat. "She thinks she's at home. Maybe I'll cry when you come over and you'll bring me here to live."

"You just miss my cooking," I joked, giving Bitsy a hug. "Thank you for the coffee."

I took out two cups and poured the contents of the carafe in them. I handed her one and we sat down at the small table.

"Is it true?" Bitsy drummed her fingers on the table.

"Is what true?" I asked. I ate a piece of bacon.

Duchess finished eating and rubbed herself between our legs. Bitsy dragged Duchess into her lap. If Duchess could have talked, I swear she would have called Bitsy annoying. Bitsy held the feisty feline tight to her chest and rubbed down her fur, ignoring Duchess's attempt to claw her way out of her grip.

"You were baking in the old Ford's Bakery?" she asked.

"Yes. Why? Who told you?" I asked.

"As you know—" She tilted her chin in the air and looked toward the window, which was a surefire sign she'd been on the phone gossiping. "Everyone knows about your near-death experience and that you ran away from the killer."

"Mama," I gasped, but it didn't stop me from eating. "I didn't run away from a killer. Trust me, if they had wanted me dead, they'd have rolled a few more feet with their truck and run me over."

"Still, you almost died," she whined. "And I needed to talk to Nora, Carter's mama, because we are on the committee for the Friends of the Library little library project." Bitsy nodded. "And she asked how you were doing because, like a good son, he's close to his mama and tells her things. She doesn't have to hear it over the phone from her friends."

"Mama, there's nothing to tell." Bringing over the coffee had been a nice touch.

"You didn't tell me anything about last night and how Carter took you to the rehearsal dinner." She batted her eyes at me.

"Fine," I said. "He asked me to go." I lied to keep it simple and not let her worry by letting her know that I really went there to question Ella. "Or is it the bakery you're interested in, or me getting run off the road?" I wondered.

"All of it, so I can tell people the right story." She seemed pleased.

"First off, the Fords have a really nice bakery. I'm actually excited Madison asked me to try out all the equipment so she can sell it. Plus, all that room to make the Big Bird cake for her son is really going to be much nicer than trying to have all my stuff here." There was an excitement growing in my stomach.

"As for getting run over, Carter said there's no leads in that yet." I took another sip of the coffee and let the warmth warm my soul along with the memories of last night. "The rehearsal dinner was nice. Carter even came over and we baked some banana pudding for Dad."

"He will be so pleased." She looked happy that I'd given her some insider information. She'd gnaw on that for a few days, which would keep her out of my hair. "He said he had a nice chat with Evelyn Moss."

"He did?" I questioned, though I knew he wouldn't tell Bitsy anything that I was looking for. "Is he working at the office or at home today?"

"He's at home. I have to have him help me build the free little libraries this morning." She drank her coffee while more ideas circulated in my head.

"Why don't I get showered and pack up some of the banana pudding for him, and I can help you build them so he can work?" This way I could take him the pudding, bribe him for some information, and make Bitsy happy.

It seemed like a great plan.

"That's wonderful." She kissed Duchess and put her down. "Duchess, you be a good girl."

"Are you sure I can keep her while I'm in town?" I asked, giving Bitsy the opportunity to back out.

"You two need each other. She will be a good guard cat. She doesn't like much company, so if anyone tries to come over, she'll let you know." Bitsy emptied the contents of the carafe in my cup and headed to the door. "I'll see you in a little bit."

* * *

A little bit was more like an hour. I wasn't sure what to wear, since I'd told Bitsy I'd help her build the free libraries. I'd decided on a pair of jeans and a light-blue long-sleeved sweater that was perfect for the day.

"What are you doing here so early?" I asked Carter. He was sitting on my parents' back porch with Bitsy. I set the homemade pudding on the table. "And without your fancy cop uniform on."

Bitsy dismissed herself by giving the excuse that she was going to make a fresh pot of coffee and took the batch of banana pudding from me.

"My mom asked me to come over to show Bitsy how to build a little library." He nodded toward the pieces of wood and a box sitting on the deck.

"Oh, Carter, Bitsy has played you." I laughed and glanced toward the kitchen window, where Bitsy was looking out at us. She jerked back when saw me looking at her.

"I figured that out when I got here and I was about to open one of the boxes to build one of the free libraries. She told me that she couldn't possibly help out, but you were coming to help me." He smiled back.

"Bitsy and her matchmaking." Both of us laughed.

Bitsy had done good today.

"I was off this morning anyways. Plus, I was hoping to talk to your dad about Evelyn." The real truth as to why he'd offered to help Bitsy came out. "Bitsy said he wasn't here."

"Darn. I was hoping to talk to him this morning about seeing Evelyn." I said, but quickly realized who I'd said it to. "Not that I'm interfering or anything."

"Of course not." Carter's brows rose. "You know that if you hear anything, I'm going to assume you're going to tell me."

"You mean you want my help with the investigation?" I drew my hand up and exaggerated my facial expressions with a high brow.

"I don't think I can stop you," he said. "No way am I saying to go out of your way and put yourself in danger."

"Aha." I lifted my chin. "I see. You need me to help you."

"I didn't say that." He tried to save himself, but I knew better. "It sure does seem like you've got a knack for getting things out of people."

"You'd be surprised how comfortable desserts make people

feel, and that's why meeting up for dessert is so popular. Food brings people together." I loved to make people happy with my pastries.

"Here are your coffees and I thought you'd like one of Sophia's treats." Bitsy was good at the whole way to a man's heart idea. "Don't you think she should stay here in Rumford and open the Ford's Bakery back up?"

"If that what she wants to do." His aloofness showed on his face. He took one of the assortments of baked goods that I'd put in the freezer.

I picked up the creamer and gently stirred some in my coffee, ignoring Bitsy.

"For goodness' sakes, Carter. You're no help." Bitsy *tsked*.

"Why don't you show me how to do these little libraries, since Bitsy already knows and seems too busy to help us and I'm the one who's going to build them anyways?" I suggested and walked over to the box.

The directions were taped on the front and, at first glance, they didn't seem that hard. There were magnets, wood glue, hinges, natural wood, and nails.

"It's like building a cake." Carter used the analogy that I could understand. "Like a cake, you have to have a base." He pointed to the directions and the wood. "If you follow the directions, like you would on one of your recipes, then at the end you'll have a finished little box."

"Like a cake brings happiness to some, books do the same to others." I thought I was pretty witty, finishing off his analogy.

"Yes." His smile reached his eyes. We locked stares.

No matter how much I wanted to deny there was something going on inside of me when I was near him, I couldn't. Clearly, he intrigued me. Instead of being excited, sadness washed over me. There was no way I could let my heart get involved since I wasn't going to be here much longer.

"Well, I'm sure I can do this. If I have questions, I will text you." I glanced over his shoulder out into the green field to break the stare and dragged the cup of coffee up to my lips. "Why don't I walk you out?"

"Sure." He nodded.

In silence, we headed inside and through the kitchen.

"Patrick works at the RCC this afternoon. I guess I'll see you there?" he asked once we reached the front door.

"I won't need to be there since Evelyn hired the new chef." I held the doorknob and leaned my weight on the door. "I'd like to finish up Charlotte's cake at Ford's, and I have to get started on Bryce's cake."

"Okay." He put his hands in the front pockets of his jeans. "You need to give your statement, so I'll give you a call to set that up."

"Fine." My lips formed a thin line.

"Did you check into anyone on my list?" I asked. I dragged the toe of my shoe on the floor. "You know, the ones we talked about last night?"

"We are going over everything with a fine-toothed comb." He wasn't going to give me any answers. "Maybe a few of your ideas, too. Don't be going and getting a big head. Let me do the work."

I was happy to know that he at least was open to some of my suggested suspects. Maybe I was good at this sleuthing thing. But was I good enough to get Emile's killer behind bars for tomorrow's big day?

Chapter Twenty

"I can use you at the Friends of the Library meeting this afternoon and go around Rumford to put up the little libraries" was the last thing Bitsy said when I walked out the door. There was a lot to do today and little time to do it.

And maybe helping her for the day was a good idea, since the news about Noah being hired as the RCC head chef spread like honey on a warm biscuit.

Nick and Jane watched me like a hawk when I got there to get Charlotte's cakes that I'd already baked. Anytime I walked near the chef's stove or oven, I could feel their beady little eyes boring into me. I made sure I stayed out of Noah's line of vision.

"Why don't you just leave them here to decorate?" Noah asked. "I'm not going to bother you. I know this is important to you, and anything I've got to say will wait." He leaned his body up against the counter. "I'll wait as long as it takes."

As much as I hated to admit it, he was right about the cakes. The less I moved them, the better they'd be. The last move would be here to the RCC for the wedding anyway. So I plugged my earphones in my ear and clicked on the radio app to play some romantic music to get me in the mood to give Charlotte the cake she so deserved.

The first layer was going to be a nice chocolate mousse in the middle. With my bag of buttercream icing, I ran a thick circle around the edges of the bottom layer. When I walked into the refrigerator to grab the chocolate mousse, I could see Noah staring at me. I quickly grabbed the premade bag and headed on over to the makeshift workspace I'd created near Patrick's dishwashing station. He had an entire stainless steel top that ran along the side wall he didn't use. It was perfect for assembling the layers and being out of Noah's sight. I took the notebook out of my bag and opened it up to the sketches I'd shown Charlotte. The same feeling I'd felt when I was drawing it flooded over me. The excitement of seeing one of my designs come to life was a gift. My gift. My purpose in life and gift to the world was to create amazing desserts that allowed everyone, no matter their race, socioeconomics, or age, to escape into a treat that'd give them a wonderful feeling. I loved to make people happy, and when I saw their faces light up like Charlotte's had, I knew I was doing my life's work.

I happily snipped the corner of the mousse bag and filled the center of the first layer to evenly match the height of the ring of icing I'd made around the layer. I lined up the second layer and made sure it was going to sit perfectly on the bottom layer before I placed it on top, making the mousse a little secret until someone sliced into it. The other layers were assembled the same way, only I used a raspberry filling and alternated the layers with mousse. It'd take about two hours for all the layers to settle. Once I stacked all the layers on top of each other, they would take another couple of hours to settle before I could begin icing and decorating. Settling was very important with this particular design because the fondant and decorating would be heavy. There couldn't be any air bubbles in the filling in any layer.

There was no way around the first two hours. I had to get the layers stacked today. The icing was the fun part and the decorating came naturally. If I was in a pinch, I'd be able to get that done in the morning. Right now, the less time I had to spend in this kitchen, the better.

Though Evelyn was looking for me to make something spectacular for the dinner dessert, I just wasn't feeling it. That was not to say I was going to disappoint her. I was going to make a dessert for the entire RCC. My tasty Kentucky Butter Cake, only in cupcake form.

Each batch of batter made about twenty-four cupcakes, and in a kitchen the size of the RCC, I could easily triple the batter. By the time they baked up and I'd iced them, I'd be ready to head on over to the library.

"Only you could pull off a design like that." Noah's voice dropped in volume as it drifted over my shoulder.

I bit my lip and closed my eyes before taking a deep breath and turning around. The nearness of him coursed anxiety, excitement, and anger through me.

"I still love working around you." His gaze lowered.

I tried to steady my shaking hands by gripping the spatula with one and fisting my other.

The long lashes of his liquid brown eyes were the first characteristics I'd noticed about him during the governor's son's wedding. And it was the first thing I noticed now. It was a deadly combination, those lashes and eyes. A man as pretty as Noah should be outlawed.

His brown hair was longer on top than usual. It was a little mussed. This was a sure sign that he was a bit stressed and had swiped his hands through it a few times throughout the morning. On those days, I would give him a gentle kiss and pat it back down, giving him encouraging words. Not today.

"How's what's-her-name?" I wanted to say something mean and evil. I wanted to hurt him like he'd hurt me.

"I don't even know her name." He shook his head and reached out, curling his hand around the side of my neck like he used to. "I've missed this spot. I've missed you. Us. The way we worked together. You kept everything going smoothly. We can do that here. Me and you."

"That spot is no longer yours." I tried to keep my emotions flat, hard and painless. I put my hand up to his to jerk it away.

"Oh. I'm sorry. I guess I walked in on something." Carter had rounded the corner to find my hand on Noah's in what looked to be a very romantic position.

"Carter." I gasped his name and my heart fell. It took me off guard for a second that my feelings about him seeing me with Noah were stronger than they should be. He was the Rumford police chief and I was just a native visiting my parents. Sure, there was the little murder thing that tied us together, but my feelings far exceeded that.

I smacked Noah's hand away as Carter backed out of the kitchen.

"Jerk," I muttered. "I've got to get these cupcakes baked."

"Who's Carter?" Noah questioned as I walked around the corner and into the kitchen.

The swinging door between the kitchen and the ballroom was still moving.

"He took off that way. Lickety-split." Nick pointed with his serrated knife toward the ballroom. "What'd he walk in on?"

"Nothing." Noah appeared. "Get back to work," Noah demanded.

Nick looked at me. His brows rose. I snarled.

It was times like these back at The Manhattan that had made us a good team. He'd get cranky and I'd be the one to clean up his angry words and soothe them over. The kitchen crew would listen to him but take it with a grain of salt as I made the atmosphere fun with music, singing, and crazy delicious treats for us to sample. He was on his own at the RCC. He knew it.

The quicker I got the Kentucky Butter Cupcakes in the oven, the faster I could get out of here. Nick would take care of getting them out and sprinkling a little powdered sugar on them. Later that night, when everyone else was asleep and dreaming of the big day, I'd come in and get the cakes iced just in time.

After I wrote down a few instructions about the dessert for Nick—though I was sure he didn't need them—I turned off the oven.

"Simple. Easy. Perfect," I whispered at my cupcake trays as I slid them out of the oven.

"Just like you." Noah stared at me.

My nostrils flared. I jerked the tie of the apron from around my waist and threw the apron in the dirty laundry bin. With my bag in my hand, I shoved the door open and disappeared into the hallway with only one thought in mind—getting the hell out of there.

The wedding planner was busy placing lace doilies under each blue-and-white large china plate that was the base of the three-tiered place settings Charlotte had wanted. The next plate was a bit smaller and had a nice pale pink ring around it with some gold-lined blue flowers. It was going to look perfect with the wedding cake. On the small top plate, the planner had placed a menu card along with a tented place holder with the name of the person who was going to sit there. The blue cloth napkin was tucked in a gold ceramic napkin holder. On the sides of the plate were silverware, a water glass, and a champagne glass.

The florist had already put the finishing touches on the birdcages in the center of each table. They'd even added real votive candles that hung off the outside of the birdcages. It was something I'd never seen, and it was going to look gorgeous once all of them were lit.

Charlotte glanced up from the front of the ballroom and gave me a thumbs-up. I returned the gesture. I knew she wanted to take a look at the wedding cake. That wasn't going to happen. I hurried out of the ballroom and out the front door.

Chapter
Twenty-One

The Rumford Library was on the south side of downtown. It was a pretty big library for a small town. Most of the town's meetings were held in the conference rooms there and the town made sure the library was well funded.

The parking lot was full when I pulled in, so I found a spot on the street. It looked as if there was going to be a new addition to the back. There was caution tape, stacks, and a backhoe ready to go.

The library was only one floor but very big. When you first walked into the double sliding doors, the reference desk was on the left. On the right was a big children's library with tiny shelves for little hands as well as a children's stage, computer stations, and some very comfortable-looking beanbag chairs.

The children's library had its own reference and checkout desks in the middle of their room.

The rest of the library was typical. Different shelves were clustered together by genre and alphabetized. Along the windows were large leather chairs that replaced the boring hard table and chairs that had been there the last time I'd visited.

The cackle of Bitsy's laughter breezed through the quiet library from one of the conference rooms in the back. I followed the sound and found her showing off her little library that she'd made. It was painted pink and had fake pearls hot-glued along the border. Bɪᴛsʏ's Booᴋs was painted in white along the top.

"There she is." Bitsy pointed to me when she saw me walk into the conference room.

The three friends she was talking to turned around and smiled.

"Sophia, these are a few friends who are on the Friends of the Library and here to help put up the free little libraries." Bitsy gave some quick introductions, but it was Nora Kincaid, Carter's mother, who caught my attention.

I could see where Carter had gotten his dark looks. Nora's black hair was straight, with a side part that fell past her shoulders. She had on a pair of white capris with a black scalloped top and a nice set of pearls around her neck.

"Aren't you every bit as lovely as I pictured." She gave me a hug, which wasn't unusual with southern folks. "Carter didn't mention that you have such lovely dark brown hair."

"Carter mentioned me?" I asked.

"Oh, yes. He said that you are ruining his investigation. Of course, I reminded him that you are Bitsy's daughter." She laughed and walked over to greet the other women walking in with their finished little libraries.

I wasn't sure if that was a compliment Nora had given me or a dig. It sure seemed like Carter wasn't talking very favorably about me either.

"Are you ladies ready?" Carter's voice echoed above the chatter.

I turned around to find him staring at me. His lips turned up into a smile. As much as I tried not to return one, my lips had a mind of their own.

As the women gathered their belongings and their little library kits, Carter took the moment to walk over to me.

"Who was the guy?" he asked.

"My ex-boyfriend."

"You forgave him for cheating on you?" The words came out of his mouth and stung me, reminding me of the hurt.

Carter Kincaid was jealous. Maybe the chemistry I'd been feeling from him wasn't my imagination.

"No. I didn't, and we most certainly are *not* getting back together. Far from it." I watched as his body relaxed. "He's the chef Evelyn replaced Emile with. He claims that he didn't know it was Rumford until he got off the plane."

"You believe him?" Carter was very interested.

"I don't know. It doesn't matter." I peered over his shoulders where Cat, the head librarian, was standing at the door. Her head was bobbing over the group of women as if she were looking for someone. When our eyes caught, she saw I was with Carter and stalked toward us. "I'm leaving next week and he's going to be your problem then," I joked.

"Are you ready? They are disturbing the library. All those women talk, talk, talk." Cat used her hands in a talking gesture. "Don't get me wrong. The library is grateful for them, but there is a short time period before the construction workers start. People are using this time wisely by getting in their reading and research."

"Do you have the map?" Carter asked Cat.

"Map?" I asked.

"Yes. The town council strategically placed each little library in Rumford. The map will tell them where to put their little library. You can grab it from the reference desk on your way out." She turned to me. "I hear your ex is in town."

"News travels fast," I chuckled.

"I also heard you were run over." Her head tilted to the side. "Are you okay?"

"I'm fine." I looked down at my shin. "Just a few cuts."

"Do you know who did it?" she asked, and looked between Carter and me.

"Yes. The killer," I blurted out.

"The killer?" she asked. Her eyes popped.

"No, no." Carter tried to damp down the urgency in Cat's voice. "We don't know who did it. We are still investigating."

"Seems funny that I've been trying to get Evelyn off the hook and had a few suspects. After I did a little digging, I stepped on someone's toes."

"You've been investigating?" Cat seemed interested. "That's so fascinating. Kinda like the cozy mystery genre we have here at the library."

"Cozy mystery?" I laughed at the name.

"Yeah. They are popular mysteries where the amateur sleuth has a job and happens upon a murder. Kinda like what you did. Then she takes the investigation into her own hands. Sorta like what you're doing," Cat's voice rose. "I don't know much about sleuthing, but I can point you in the right direction for good cozy mystery books."

"What. Stop. Stop." Carter pushed between us. "Sophia is going to stick with baking Charlotte's cake."

Cat and I smiled at each other and then looked at him.

In unison, we both nodded.

"Before you head out to put up the libraries, can I steal a second of your time?" Cat asked.

"Sure," I agreed. I walked to the reference desk with her.

"We are having our big grand opening for the new addition. Rumford Library Association and Friends of the Library are hosting a huge celebration with some local bluegrass bands, locally made crafts, and food vendors." She took a brochure out of one of those acrylic holders on the counter of the reference desk and handed it to me.

The front of it had a mock image of what the library was going to look like.

"We are doing all sorts of neat things." She forced open the brochure in my hands, showing me the new green rooftop. "The large community room is going to benefit Rumford so much. The Quilter Club can come in and work on their quilts. We will have computer stations and those fancy interactive whiteboards for businesses to use and hold seminars and meetings. We want to have a little reception up there for the big donors—that's where you come in."

"Me? I didn't donate anything. I mean, I didn't even know about the addition until I got here today." I would be more than happy to donate a few bucks, but I was in no shape to just throw away my money when I had to go find a new apartment. "I'm not asking you to donate anything, silly." Cat giggled. "We want to hire you to cater the desserts for the event. We are going to be hosting the big donors on the green roof before the ribbon cutting. I was interested in desserts that would go great with Kentucky bourbons, wine, and craft beers local to the area. Of course, soft drinks, tea, and water will be provided, but you have that special knack. In high school, I made it a point to sit next to you in our home economics class because, when we'd do the baking homework, I knew if I was next to you that Mrs. Fain would have me taste your stuff. I loved baking days."

"I'm flattered. I really am. And I love that you put that much thought into our homework," I said, starting to decline her invitation.

"I hear a 'but' coming," she interrupted, eyeballing me.

"But," I said, drawing my head down for emphasis. "I'm going back to the city next week after Madison's son's birthday."

"You aren't staying in town?" she asked with a perplexed look on her face. "I'd heard you were going to reopen Ford's Bakery."

"Excuse me?" My head jutted forward. "Who on earth did you hear that from? Because that's not true."

"That stinks to high heaven." Her face contorted. "I was looking forward to getting to know you better and enjoying more of your amazing desserts."

"When is it?" The guilt was setting in. Cat had always been so nice and kind to me. I'd hate to let her down. "I might be able to fly in and do the event."

"You will?" her voice went up. She drew her hands up to her face and bounced on her toes.

"You will what?" Carter just so happened to be walking by with the Friends of the Library group with his mother next to him.

"She's going to cater the donor event for the grand opening." The excitement exuded from her.

"That's wonderful, Sophia," Mrs. Kincaid said.

"Yes, ma'am. It sure is." Cat looked between us with a big smile on her face.

"Nora, honey. Call me Nora," Nora corrected her, only Cat and I knew better. No matter your age, "Yes, ma'am" was standard southern manners, and if Bitsy heard me call Mrs. Kincaid Nora, she'd fly off the handle.

"Yes, ma'am." *Ahem.* Cat cleared her throat. "Nora."

Nora and Cat carried on about the addition. Carter looked fully into my eyes.

"So you're staying in town?" he asked with a low voice.

"No. No." I shook my head. "Cat and I went to high school together. She was always so kind, and I don't want to let her down. I'd like to fly back in and do the event."

"I know you and Cat went to school together." His eyes narrowed. "You don't remember me at all, do you?"

Oh, I'd remember if I met you, I thought. There weren't too many men I'd met with dark eyes like his.

"Huh?" I was confused.

"*We* went to high school together." He totally knocked me for a loop. "You don't remember me because I wasn't in your circle of friends."

"You're pulling my leg." I laughed. "You didn't go to Rumford High."

"Yes. We graduated together." His face had a blank stare. "I even asked you out once."

"What? Trust me, I'd remember if you asked me out," I said. "You've got me mistaken with someone else."

"No. You, me, and Cat had home economics together. You came in late one day because your flan didn't have enough time to rise or something, so you had to sit next to me. You tasted my chocolate chip cookies." The more he talked, the more I began to remember that day. "They were awful, but you were so kind and told me it was good after you took a bite. You didn't want to hurt my feelings. I thought you were interested in me . . ."

The memory of the scrawny kid with greasy long hair flooded over me.

"Trey?" I remembered the boy, but he wasn't the man with pretty teeth, thick dark hair, chocolate dream eyes, and a filled-out physique who stood before me.

"My middle name is Trey. When I went to the academy, they called me by my first name, so now I go by Carter." He continued to stare at me.

"Oh my God." I started laughing.

"I'm glad you seem to think it's funny, because at the time it was traumatizing." He didn't find the humor in it.

"It's just that you're so . . . so . . . different." I wanted to blurt out words like *good-looking*, *hot*, *real hot*, but contained myself.

"I like that excuse. Not many women can say that." He turned when someone called his name. It was one of the women from the Friends of the Library. She waved him to come on.

"Are you coming to help put up the libraries?" he asked.

I nodded.

"Here is my number. Text me yours and I'll be in touch about the grand opening event." Cat wrote down her number on a piece of paper and handed it to me. "I truly appreciate it."

"Did I go out with Carter in high school?" I asked Cat in confidence. She'd know. She'd always had her hand on the pulse of romances when we were younger.

"He asked you to prom, but no, you turned him down. I went with him." She squinted with amusement. "You were too busy being crowned prom queen to even notice."

"I sound terrible." I shook my head and felt really embarrassed.

"You weren't. Everyone liked you. You were always nice. I can't say that about all your friends. But we're older and wiser, right?" She graciously let me off the hook and I was grateful for that. "You better go grab the bus before they leave you."

Chapter
Twenty-Two

There were a total of ten little libraries the town council had agreed to let the Friends of the Library distribute throughout the small town. Of course, Bitsy had already mapped out where every one of them would go and even went as far as renting a small bus to drive everyone around to help put them up. Poor Carter was the one who did all the digging with all the women fawning all over him. Cat was going to go around later tonight after the cement had hardened and start filling them with donated books.

When we got back to the library, I had a little extra time before I had to be at the RCC, so I stopped by the Piggly Wiggly to get some ingredients to bake more Crunchies and get started on some ideas for the Big Bird cake. I didn't want to be caught off guard next week when I went to get the stuff I needed for Bryce's cake and have it not be in stock.

I quickly texted Carter to let him know that I was at Ford's Bakery just in case someone called in a burglar. All he texted back was the okay-fingers emoji. My stomach sank. I'd kind of been hoping he'd send a text asking what I was doing tonight.

Then it would've opened the door to let him know that Madison and I were meeting for a drink in hopes he'd just show up.

"What is wrong with you?" I asked myself and turned off the car. The more time I spent in Rumford, the more I was getting involved, and I was coming to the realization that it was going to be hard to leave.

The empty bakery was so sad looking. The bare windows with the lights out was not how Ford's had used to look. Madison, Cat, and Ella were right. Rumford needed another bakery. But it was silly to even think I could just drop everything in New York and open a bakery. I didn't know the first thing about business. But I knew what pastries the Rumford residents loved. They were simple and delicious, which was all this bakery needed to be successful.

I got out of the car with the plastic grocery bags hanging from elbow to wrists on both of my arms and gazed at the display window. My shadow from the late afternoon sun stared back at me in the glass. Images of twinkly lights around the window, freshly baked goods on stands, and pretty platters with Tiffany blue-colored accents made a perfect picture in my head.

"You're ridiculous." I shook the image from my head and started toward the door.

"Let me help you." Nick appeared out of nowhere and took a couple of the grocery bags from me.

"What are you doing here?" I asked. "You should be cooking for the RCC dinner rush."

"Your ex sent me out to get coconut oil. When I was driving by, I saw you, so I stopped. I figure I have a couple of minutes since everything I had to prep for is ready to go for tonight." He turned the knob of the bakery door after I'd turned the key. He held the door open for me. "What are you doing here?"

"Madison is the listing agent for the bakery and I'm testing out the ovens for future owners while I bake her son's birthday cake." I laughed while I set down the bags on one of the café tables and flipped on the lights. "I had a silly thought."

"What's that?" Nick asked, seeming very interested.

"I can totally picture myself moving home and opening up a bakery." I rolled my eyes so hard I made myself dizzy.

"That's not silly. I think you'd rock it." He helped unpack the bags, putting the ingredients behind the counter.

"Yeah, but I have a real nice-paying job in New York. I thought it was my dream job. Being back home has me questioning my true heart's calling. I don't know," I muttered under my breath and took a look around. It did feel so much like home here, but it was probably because I'd spent so much time in here as a kid. "I think I've let everyone get into my head while I've been here, and this time next week, I'll be back in my comfort zone."

"You've got to do what you've got to do. Life's too short. Take Emile, for instance." He shrugged. "Is that cop any closer to solving his murder?"

"I don't think so. I checked out Natalie Devin and Ella Capshaw." I grabbed a few bowls to start mixing the dry ingredients for the Crunchies.

"I saw your dad and that cop in Evelyn's office today." Nick handed me items as I pointed to them. "It sounds like she's the one who did it."

I pushed the measured mixture to him with a spoon to stir while I worked on the wet ingredients.

"I don't believe it. I told you I think the whole unseasoned skillet thing is wrong. Evelyn knows how to cook. Ella has an alibi. She's got a new rich guy who owns the Piggly Wiggly."

"Grant. Yep. I saw them together after Emile went nuts on him." He smirked at the memory.

"She dumped Emile, saying he was a fun fling, but Grant could offer her the future she wanted." I shrugged. "Then there's Natalie and her husband, who both have motives. Though when I asked her about it, she got all offended and called the cops."

"You asked her?" Nick laughed out loud. "You've got some spunk."

"When it comes to my friends, I'm passionate." I stirred the wet ingredients together and took the bowl of dry ingredients. "Can you grab a few cookie sheets and line them with paper?"

"That ex of yours, he's pretty much a jerk," Nick said as we got the cookie dough on the cookie sheets.

"He was never one to talk to the staff at The Manhattan. That was my job. He was a bit like Emile, I guess. Focused on the quality of the food."

"That's why I think Evelyn did it," Nick said, cleaning his hands off under the warm water coming from the sink faucet.

"I thought you thought it was Patrick," I said, putting the trays in the ovens.

"I told the cop about that. Patrick hasn't been to work since." Nick's words caught me off guard. I could've sworn Carter had said Patrick was supposed to be at work today.

"Really?" I asked. "Did you know that he loved cooking?"

"Patrick?" Nick looked at me as if I'd lost my mind. "The boy couldn't start a microwave."

"Apparently, that's not true." I gave him a quick rundown about what I'd learned about Patrick's secret desire to cook. "I wonder if his dad killed Emile."

"Wow." Nick's jaw dropped. "I never would've thought that.

Maybe you need to stop baking and become a detective," he joked.

"Let me know if he does come back to work." I'd jump in the car and run over there to ask my own questions.

He looked at his watch. "Speaking of work, I've got to get out of here before I get canned."

"Tell the jerk to kiss my grits." I winked and followed him out to the door. There wasn't any way I was going to take a chance on anyone coming in here, mainly the killer, and catching me off guard. "And don't forget I made all the desserts for tonight. They're in the freezer."

"I guess I'll see you there in the morning? Before the big day?" he asked.

"Yes, you will." I sighed. The surreal thought that I couldn't get Evelyn off the hook weighed heavily on me.

We said our good-byes. In the next hour, I made three more trays of cookies and the bakery smelled of cinnamon and sugar with a hint of honey like I remembered it. Only, the glass displays weren't filled with the golden, sweet pastries. I imagined rows and rows of my puffs with all different fillings lined along the top. Croissants, tarts, mini-pies, Derby pies, pecan pies, banana pudding cupcakes, Dutch letters, and éclairs, to name a few.

My imagination filled domed glass cake platters and pastel doilies with decorated petit fours displayed along the tops of the glass cabinets. I could practically smell the freshly brewed coffee that I'd get contracted from Small Talk Café. All the ingredients would be bought from local vendors and I'd cater every event this side of Kentucky.

The warm smell of the chocolate chips melting in the baking Crunchies brought me back to the present. The reality was that

I wasn't a sleuth. The wedding appeared to be going off with Evelyn still as the number one suspect. If there was anything I'd done to help save the day, it was that I'd practically begged my father into representing her.

The timer dinged. The Crunchies were cooked to perfection. Quickly I used the spatula to take them off the cookie sheet and put them on a cooling rack. I topped each one with a few more chocolate chips just for eye candy.

My phone chirped a text. It was Mama. She said supper was going to be ready in ten minutes and she'd made me a chuck roast with all the fixings and asked me to come over. My favorite meal and she knew it. Like a good daughter, I texted her back to let her know I was on my way.

With a few cookies packed in a borrowed container from the old bakery, I pulled into my parents' driveway. I could smell the yummy dish from outside and could almost taste the fat, juicy carrots and soft round potatoes. Delicious. My stomach gurgled. In the wake of the murder, I'd practically forgotten to eat anything that wasn't made from pure sugar.

"I'm home," I called through the house when I walked into the front door.

"In here," Bitsy called from the kitchen. "You're just in time."

"That's what I like to hear," I said when I walked in. "I've had a . . ." I stopped shy of the kitchen counter as I was getting ready to place the bag of fresh-baked cookies on the counter. "Carter, what are you doing here?" I asked, still embarrassed because I hadn't remembered him from school.

The kitchen table was set in Bitsy's good china for two.

"Where's Dad?" I asked, my eyes narrowed.

What was Bitsy up to?

"I thought it would be nice to cook you two a nice supper for helping out the Friends of the Library today. Since we can't pay you, I cooked your favorite." Bitsy walked up behind me and ran her hand along my hair, subtly trying to spruce me up. "You've got flour in your hair, dear," she whispered.

* * *

"I'm a baker. Flour is part of my makeup routine," I joked, trying to lighten the mood.

"I should really go." Carter stood up. "Clearly you didn't know I was going to be here."

"For goodness' sakes, I won't hear of it." Bitsy gave him the wonky eye and pointed for him to sit right back down. Which he did.

The sheriff had nothing on Mama.

She placed both hands on my shoulders and pushed me over to the table. The pot roast was displayed on one of her blue-and-white platters with all the trimmings around it. There were even homemade biscuits and gravy made from the juices of the finished roast.

"I'm not going to tell you I attempted to make dessert, because I didn't." Bitsy folded her hands in front of her, smiling like the dickens. "I'll leave you two alone."

"This is uncomfortable." Carter eased up in his chair. "When she called me, she said that you suggested I come for dinner as a thank you. When I got here, I could tell she'd lied. Again."

"Isn't there a law against lying or manipulating that you can arrest Bitsy on and put her in jail?" Not that I was serious.

"Bisty? In jail?" He eased back in the chair. "No way can I imagine that."

"Welcome to the world of Bitsy Cummings." I grabbed the glass of wine and held it up in the air. He took his and we did a cheer. "You've only seen one side of her."

"I'm afraid there's many more I haven't seen." His smile was warm and easy.

There was something so natural between the two of us that it really wasn't as uncomfortable as it should've been.

"Well, I'm hungry." I reached for the platter. "I'm truly sorry I didn't realize who you were. My mind hasn't exactly been on high school since Emile's death."

"It's no big deal." He grabbed the edges of the platter while I filled my plate. "We can just pretend that the stress of seeing a dead body played a role."

"Thanks." I returned the favor and held the platter for him. "I appreciate that, Carter."

"What made you want to become a cop?" I asked.

"The usual. I wanted to put the bad guys behind bars. All those nights while you and your friends were hanging out in high school, I was watching cop shows with my dad," he said. "Nothing else really appealed to me when I graduated, so I decided to go into the academy to see if I'd like it."

"Here you are today," I said between bites.

"What about you? I mean," he looked up at me with those big brown eyes that reminded me of chocolate chips.

I knew if I stared at them too long, they'd be gooey and yummy from showing his warm soul, just like the effect the fresh-baked cookie had on the chocolate chips.

"I've always known you loved baking, but it's different when it turns into a job that you do day in and out." He did have a point.

"It's not so much about baking as it is the people." By the confused look on his face, I could tell he didn't follow. "It's the faces of enjoyment that make the job still a hobby for me. Of course"—I picked up the glass of wine and took a sip—"I have those who complain and I can never make happy, but the majority are customers who really enjoy the taste of a good dessert."

I looked up from my plate. His eyes had softened. His jaws had relaxed and there was an easy look on his face that made my heart flip-flop. My mouth dried.

"Enough about that." I grabbed the glass again, this time taking a swig.

"You really want to go back to New York?" He asked the question so suddenly it hurt me to answer.

"You know . . ." I set the glass down and scooted the chair back from the table, giving me more distance between us. I needed space and air from the feelings that were making my heart beat rapidly. "I love being home, and if I didn't have my dream job, I might move back."

"Dream job?" He eased back in the chair. Lightly he drummed his fingers on the table. "Working for others, creating all sorts of designs, because that's really what you do, is a dream for you?"

I answered with silence.

"Everyone around here talks about all the basic desserts you make with the funny names and the twist only you can add. That's job appreciation." He dragged the wine glass across the table, closer to him and the edge. He fiddled with the stem. "I'm just saying that there's some sort of gratification that comes with being able to create and sell, not create and hope your manager wants you to make it and not the same humdrum desserts that most fancy restaurants make."

"You have a point. But as the head pastry chef, I do get most of my creations approved." I didn't tell him the real truth. Fifty percent of the time, the owner of The Manhattan wanted me to make a go-to favorite that was a guaranteed sell for the after-dinner dessert diner.

"From what I could see, you looked very comfortable working in Ford's." He dug the dagger deeper into my heart.

"I'm always comfortable when I'm baking, no matter where I'm at." I tried to cover up any notions that told him he was spot on.

While I'd been at at Ford's, my heart was singing, my thoughts were clear, and I was happy.

My phone chirped a text.

"Excuse me." I was happy for the distraction. I was tired of talking about me. I was already confused and he only made it worse.

The text was from Madison letting me know that she and Charlotte were going to the Blue Line Bar since it was the night before her wedding and Brett had to work, Madison figured we'd better spend it with Charlotte.

"It looks like that's important." Carter stood up. "I'm going to get out of your hair."

"Nah. It's just Madison. I didn't mean to run you off," I said. "It's just that I want to visit with my friends as much as possible while I'm in town. I guess it's like a relaxing girl's night before the wedding."

"I get it." He headed to the front door. "It was nice to get to talk to you even if your Bitsy set it up for us."

"Thanks, Carter, for understanding. She can be a bit much." It was nice that he didn't make it any more difficult than it already was for me.

* * *

"I understand." The twinkle in his eyes extended and softened his face.

I opened the door. He stepped outside.

The full moon hung like a shiny globe in the dark night sky above his head. The stars blinked in a soft dance.

"We'll have to make a rain check." His voice was a whisper just before he leaned in a little closer.

Our eyes met. I leaned in a little closer. My lips quivered as his lips descended to meet mine with a sweet, tender kiss. With my eyes still closed, I felt his lips brush my brows. It sent shivers down my spine and into my toes.

I took a big inhale and opened my eyes.

"We'll definitely do a rain check." Though I knew I was needed elsewhere, I sure didn't want to be. "Or you can just go with me. To the bar, I mean."

"Are you sure I wouldn't be intruding?" He asked.

"Absolutely not." And if he was, oh well. They'd have to get over it.

After we got into the car, we casually talked about things we remembered from being in high school while he helped me clean up the kitchen. We even ate a couple of cookies. I made sure to text Madison to let her know I'd invited Carter. She was beyond excited and hired a sitter for the kids so her husband could join us.

"It's a miracle I'm not a million pounds," I said to Carter before I stuffed my face with another cookie.

There he was, sitting in front of me, enjoying the fruits of my labor, so to speak. My heart that'd been so empty and sad was full for the first time in a long time. I loved baking. It was the look on Carter's face that told me I was doing my purpose in life. Even here in Rumford. I was doing what I loved. But was I doing what I loved where I loved?

"There were so many stars out that I know it's going to be a beautiful day for Charlotte tomorrow." I stared out the car window and enjoyed the ride to the Blue Line with Carter at the wheel.

The old country tale was that if there were stars out, there wouldn't be rain the next day. It always held true. My thoughts turned back to the empty bakery. My heart sank as I thought about what on earth it could be other than a bakery. I wasn't sure I'd ever forgive myself if someone put a clothing shop or, worse, a thrift shop in, where an old musty smell would replace cinnamon, sugar, and fresh yeast that warmed everyone's soul.

A few daydreams later, we were in the gravel parking lot looking up at the Blue Line Bar. It had once been a run-down barn that someone had seen the beauty in and restored. Many times I'd driven by the joint, but I'd never been old enough to go in. That was before I'd moved away from Rumford.

The place was packed. They'd used the old tobacco loft and turned it into a pool table area with all the wooden beams exposed. The bar ran along the entire right side of the barn. In the front was a stage with a bluegrass band belting out some old George Jones. The sounds of laughter and singing meshed together as people celebrated the end of a work week.

"Sophia! Carter!" I turned when I heard our names. Matthew was wildly waving in my direction. I lifted my hand and gave a slight nod.

"I'll grab us a drink and meet you over there." The warmth of Carter's palm on my lower back was very comforting.

Weaving my way in and out of the crowd, I made my way over to the table, smack dab into the middle of Charlotte's conversation about Noah and how his creations were like tasting gold. It took a lot of restraint to not roll my eyes and say something awful about him. It would've been a personal dig because, in reality, he was the best damn chef I knew. His food was flawless, but his relationship skills sucked.

"I'm sorry. I guess I shouldn't talk about him." Charlotte curled her bottom lip under her front teeth and gave me a hug, then Carter.

"No." I waved her off. "His food is really good. I'm sure you're going to have an amazing supper for your wedding."

"How are you?" Matthew handed me my drink. "I know about the affair and all, but at least you aren't married."

"Very true, Matthew. I'm fine, though." I turned the questioning off me and onto him. "So, two little ones." My eyes danced around his face. Matthew of all people having little kids was something I wouldn't have imagined just a couple of weeks ago.

Carter walked up with the two drinks and handed me one.

"Yep. Stay-at-home dad, too." He held his glass up, tipping it slightly for us to say cheers and take a drink. "My wife tells me that you're trying to figure out who killed the chef at the RCC. If you ask me, he was a jerk. I tried to send my food back once, and he came storming out of the kitchen saying something about hillbillies liking their steak burnt and not the true way it was supposed to be." Matthew said,. "I told him, 'Listen, buddy, when you start paying for my bill, then you can have a say about how I eat my steak.'"

"No, you didn't!" I laughed.

"You bet your britches, I did." He nodded and let out a *yeehaw* when the band started playing some Johnny Cash. He grabbed Madison by the hand and dragged her out to the dance floor along with Charlotte and Brett, who'd just showed up after his long day at work.

The dance floor had all sorts of white lights draped overhead going this way and that. I moseyed up to the front and leaned against one of the empty bourbon barrels the Blue Line used as circular bar tables and watched my friends take a twirl around the dance floor.

They all looked so happy and content with the life they were leading. A bit of jealousy stung my heart. They were all living the life they'd always wanted, and so was I, but why was I feeling so disconnected to the past ten years I'd been living?

Carter leaned over the small table. "I was going to fuss at you at supper, but Bitsy had gone to such great lengths to make it nice, I decided to wait until we were on equal ground."

"What did I do?" I asked, a bit surprised to see him.

"Yep." He patted his stomach. "I have to keep in shape for my job. I got on the scale today and I've gained six pounds." There was a bright pleasure in his eyes. "I'm blaming you and those cookies you keep feeding me."

We shared a smile. Somehow it breathed life back into me. It was as if he was a fresh breath of air in the musty old confused brain of mine.

"I'm more than happy to take the blame, since you seem to enjoy them so much." I leaned a little closer than I should have. His cologne tickled me down to my toes, something I'd not expected. I gripped the edges of the barrel with my hands to steady myself. "I thought you were going to say that I somehow wrecked your investigation."

"You're doing a bang-up job at that too. The way I figure, you somehow make an impression everywhere you go and everything you touch," he said with a glint of wonder in his eyes. "Supper was really nice."

That kiss was really nice.

The tempo in the music had slowed to a Dolly Parton love song. Carter put his hand out for me to take.

"Would you like to dance?" he asked, breaking the tension between us.

My eyes darted back and forth between his before I caught someone out of the corner of my eye. My gaze slid over Carter's shoulder. Noah was on the other side of the dance floor looking around. He'd yet to spot me.

"I'd love to." I grabbed Carter's hand and dragged him out to the floor in the perfect line of sight for Noah to see.

I snuggled up to Carter a little more than I should've and enjoyed not only the warmth from his arm around me but the smell too. Making Noah a bit jealous didn't hurt either. We swayed back and forth as Dolly belted out her love in the song. With Carter's arm around my waist and the other holding my hand between our hearts, I could feel his beating. Surprisingly, he was a very good slow dancer. He led with his hips and swayed me along with him. The feel of his body up against mine made me forget the real reason I'd taken him up on his offer.

I closed my eyes as my forehead rested again his cheek and listened to him hum low along with the music. My face tilted slightly to the right as he dragged his coarse cheek along my face, sweeping his warm lips up to my ear.

"Let's really give him a show."

My eyes popped open, and the feeling of getting lost in the song immediately went away. I pulled back. Both of our bodies stopped. The music and the people around us continued to dance. It was as if I couldn't hear the music anymore.

"What?' I asked, looking into his eyes.

"I said let's give your boyfriend something to really be jealous about." The twinkle in his eyes faded. "I mean, it's why you decided to take me up on dancing."

"I'm sorry." It was time to apologize. "I'm that transparent?"

"Maybe I know you better than you think." He gave a wry smile. "Or I'm just good at my job of reading people. Like tonight, when we were at your mom's table—I know you loved baking in Ford's."

"Yes. I do like Ford's." The confession felt so good to hear out loud.

He tugged me a little closer. His feet started to move again. "Why not finish our dance and not try to impress anyone? Just enjoy a dance?"

"I'd love that." I sucked in a deep breath. Even though I tried to get back to the feeling I'd had before he'd caught on to my game, it wasn't happening.

When the song was over, Carter and I walked over to my friends.

"You two looked awfully cozy." Charlotte nudged me when we all made it back to our table. Noah had already scouted us out and made room for himself at our table. He stood directly in front of Carter.

"He's just being nice." I picked up my drink and took a sip to avoid any uncomfortable conversation. There wasn't any way

I was going to bring up Bitsy's attempt to play matchmaker or the kiss.

"I'm so excited about my cake." Her voice took an upswing.

"Me too. It's going to be gorgeous. I'm just sorry I couldn't figure out who killed Emile before the big day." It was still unsettling to me, even though I'd come to the realization I wasn't a sleuth.

"It's okay." She looked between Madison and me. "Y'all tried. At least your dad has been giving Carter the runaround. The only bad thing is that some people RSVP'd saying they didn't know if they were coming because they didn't want to come to the RCC where a killer was on the loose."

"Really?" My brows furrowed.

"I tried to tell them that the police thought it was a lone incident, but then they bring up the fact that someone tried to kill you." There was an odd twinge of disappointment in her eyes.

I couldn't help but feel like it was my fault that it seemed like there was a killer on the loose. I pulled my phone out of my pocket and noticed it was already ten o'clock. The wedding wasn't until tomorrow night, and if I could make it back to the RCC tonight and catch Patrick before he left, I could still see if he was a suspect. Since I'd marked Ella off my list, Patrick would be the next logical step, even though I still had my suspicions about Natalie and Arnold. Come to think of it, Patrick had had all the opportunity to do it.

"Hello." Madison waved her hand in front of my face. "Earth to Sophia."

I blinked a few times.

"I'm sorry. I was thinking." I snapped out of my thoughts.

Carter and Noah were staring at me. "I've got to get going. Carter"—I looked at him—"are you ready?"

"Sure." He nodded.

I quickly gave my two friends a hug.

"I'll see you tomorrow," I assured Charlotte, then made my way out of the bar.

The wind whipped around my ankles. The air sent goose bumps along my legs and across my arms. The moon hung high overhead and the dark night wrapped around me. I hurried to Carter's car. He clicked the key fob. The red tail lights blinked along with the beep to let me know he'd unlocked the doors.

"Let me get the door for you," I heard him say, but it was too late. I'd already opened my door.

"Sophia!" The voice trailed the sound of footprints running in the gravel.

Before I could look up, a big hand planted itself on the passenger's side window, slamming the door shut.

"You've got to talk to me." Noah's strength held the door shut as I jerked on the handle.

"Not now, Noah." I pulled the handle again. He didn't budge.

"Hey, man." Carter walked up to Noah. "She said not now. Just respect that."

"I can't keep working around you and not figure something out. It's killing me." His voice was low and intense as he danced around, trying to see over Carter's shoulders. "I don't know how to make it up to you. I was wrong."

"Yes. You were." My words were matter-of-fact.

When Noah stepped forward, Carter put a flat palm on his chest.

"Not a bit closer." Carter spoke with cool authority.

"So wrong that it'll never be right." I wasn't letting Noah off the hook. We were done. I was done.

"We"—he flung his finger between us—"are so good together. We are unstoppable. We have plans to open our own restaurant."

"Had plans. We *had* plans, but you ruined it." I glared at him. "I don't know what your big grand plan was of coming here and all of the sudden becoming buddies with my high school friends, but it'll never work. You'll never fit in here." My angry words echoed into the darkness.

"It's time to go home," Carter warned.

"Oh, go on, Barney Fife," Noah snarled. He stared at Carter with a blaze of anger in his eyes. "You've caused enough problems."

"I'm pretty sure I've not caused any problems. Maybe you should look in the mirror." Carter was calm and super cool, which angered Noah more.

"Listen, buddy." Noah twisted his body toward Carter. "I'm sure you're a good old boy and all, but this is between me and Sophia. You should just mosey on back to your life." Noah did his best southern accent as if he were mocking Carter.

Carter nodded his head up and down. He took a step back, and before I knew it, he swung at Noah. Noah ducked. The two men danced back and forth on their feet.

"Stop it!" I screamed. "This is ridiculous. Act your age!"

"What's going on?" Brett and Charlotte ran out of the bar and hurried over once they saw us.

"These two yahoos are about to kill each other." I struggled to find the words to really describe what was going on because I couldn't. I'd no clue what'd just happened.

"He can't protect Sophia like I can." Noah didn't move a muscle.

"I've got a badge and a gun. I think I can protect her and the rest of Rumford better than you." Carter had a point.

"I'm leaving. This is so stupid. I can protect myself." I opened the car door and slammed it shut before I said something I was going to regret.

Charlotte's wedding had already been damaged enough. The last thing she needed was a chef with a bloody lip and a best man with a black eye.

Chapter
Twenty-Three

It was an intense ride home. I fumed about Noah and Carter. It dawned on me that I should feel flattered, but I didn't. As much as I wanted to hate Noah, he was right; we'd shared some great ideas and some fun times together.

Carter was right too. He could protect me and there was no denying the chemistry we had. Right now, what mattered was putting the final touches on Charlotte's cake.

When Carter let me off at home, I didn't ask him to come in. I headed into the cottage and fed Duchess some kibble.

"You love it here, right?" I sat down cross-legged on the kitchen floor and talked to Duchess. "Rumford isn't a bad place, is it?"

Her pretty eyes glanced up at me and blinked softly before she went right back to her bowl.

"Enjoy, sweet girl. I've got a cake to decorate." I got up, grabbed the Corolla keys, and headed to the RCC.

Though the kitchen closed at nine o'clock in the evening, the last reservation was seated at eight. Many times the late-night tables stayed around and had a few cocktails. Most of those took the evening to other parts of the RCC grounds, like the bar in the courtyard. It was open until midnight for members.

After nine, the chef usually went home, which made sense because Noah had shown up about that time at the Blue Line Bar. It would take Patrick a good couple of hours to get the ballroom cleaned, the kitchen cleaned, and the dishes ready for tomorrow's big day.

I ended up parking in the front lot, where the valets were still waiting on those late-night members to leave. I signed in like all employees were supposed to do and noticed Patrick's car was still in the lot. It was good to see he'd not missed work again, and hopefully I'd get to ask him a few questions.

I took my time in the kitchen getting the items I needed to start decorating Charlotte's layers. When I opened the walk-in refrigerator, I made sure to make all sorts of noise. The dishwasher was going and the sound of clinking dishes came from Patrick's workstation.

Carefully, I took each double layer out of the tinfoil. Using a little bit of the buttercream icing, I slapped some in the middle of each layer as glue and positioned each layer perfectly.

"What are you doing?" Patrick asked when he caught me bent over, eyeballing the layers.

"I'm making sure the levels are even." I stood up and brushed my hands down the apron. "Glad to see you showed up to work. Busy night?"

"Not too bad. I guess some people are still upset about Emile. We even had a few new members who said they'd gotten the membership off someone on Craigslist." He laughed. "Evelyn lost her mind."

"Oh, no," I grunted. "That's the last thing she needs to do, since she's the number one suspect."

"That sucks," he said in true teenager lingo. "She's still running the joint like she's got no care in the world."

"Maybe she doesn't because she's got a clean conscience." I shrugged and took out the buttercream fondant that Nick had dyed blue for me. It had turned out much more vibrant than I'd anticipated, and I loved it. It was a rich blue that would go very well against the gold fondant accents. "I heard that Emile had been a real jerk to a lot of people around here."

"I guess." Patrick busied himself with his cell phone. "That still doesn't mean he deserved to die."

"I'd also heard about how he treated you." I used the rolling pin to make the blue fondant paper thin. It was going to go over the third and sixth tiers of the seven-tiered cake. The other layers were going to be covered in the brilliant gold fondant accented with some elegant swirls and other gilded accents. Charlotte was going to flip over it.

"He was my boss. I ignored him and did my job." He glanced up for a second before he quickly scrolled the screen of his phone with his thumb. "He was probably just trying to help me because he knew I loved to cook. He even gave me a few pointers. He always told me to follow my heart, not what my dad wants me to do."

"Yeah, but it still didn't give him the right to bully you." I carefully laid the large, flat, rolled-out fondant over the two layers and used the scraper to start to shape the edges to the layers.

"Listen, I only work this hard to help out my family. But you already know that since you went to my house and snooped around. Thanks for tipping off that cop too. My dad wasn't happy when he showed up at the factory."

I opened my mouth to protest, but he continued.

"Next year I'll be going to school on a full scholarship for baseball. I've got to make enough money now to last them until I can come home next summer." He stared at me from under his brows.

"I understand if you killed Emile to protect yourself." I stared back at him.

"Wait." His nose curled and he put his phone down. "Are you accusing me of killing Emile? Is that why you were snooping around at school and here?"

"I'm not accusing anyone. I'm just saying that you have a valid reason for wanting him dead. That's all." I shrugged.

"Listen, lady." Patrick pushed himself from leaning on the kitchen island to a firm stand. "I don't know what you're trying to do here, but you're nuts if you think I killed him. Besides"— his teenager voice cracked—"I got an alibi."

"I thought you were here doing the extra chores for extra money. It would've been the perfect time," I pressed.

"You know that girl you saw me with?" He gnawed on the corner of his lip.

I nodded.

"She's a member's daughter. We're secretly dating. I'm from the wrong side of the tracks. At least that's what her mother said," he scoffed. "Her name is Alice. Alice Devin."

My jaw dropped.

"As in Natalie and Arnold Devin's daughter?" My brows rose.

"Yep. She takes morning tennis lessons before school. I

picked up the extra hours in the morning so we could spend some time alone without her mother here to police her. Her mother thinks I only work in the kitchen after school. She doesn't let Alice come to the RCC at night anymore so she can't be around me." His mouth dropped at the edges. "Alice and I love each other. I'm going to make it big in baseball. Mark my words. Then the Devins will accept me." He hesitated. "We were together that morning."

"Would she tell the cops that too?" I asked.

"Yes. I'm sure she would. Her parents will keep her away forever though." There was real pain on his face. "But if they think I did it, I'm no good without the truth."

"A pack of your gum was found in the refrigerator." I decided to tell them the evidence the police had. "Juicy Tart gum."

"I don't chew anything tart. I have acid reflux and I can't play ball if I chew it. So that wasn't my gum. My doctor would tell you that I can only chew peppermint."

"Do you cook?" I questioned.

"Yeah. I like to cook. Big deal. Emile let me cook for myself a couple of times, and I'm not going to lie; I do cook me breakfast in the mornings when I work early, but no one is here." He shook his head. "I've got to get out of here and study for an exam."

Nothing in my gut told me that Patrick was lying. This only made me mark him off my list of suspects. I continued to think about the crime, and before I knew it, the layers were all covered with their fondant along with all the crisscross designs, overlays, and pearling accents. Though the gold was amazing without any extra features, this was the moment I loved—using the spray gun to make the gold shine and pop even more.

Doing it tonight would allow the edible paint to dry, and all

I'd have to do before the wedding was bring out the cake. I'd put together a perfect plan so I didn't have to see Noah. My promise to Evelyn and my commitment to making sure Charlotte had her dream wedding were almost over.

By the time I'd gotten the cake rolled into the refrigerator, cleaned up my mess, and collected my things, it was almost one in the morning. I headed toward the back hallway. I knew the front doors to the parking lot would be locked, so my best bet would be to go out the back door and around to the car.

There was a light coming from the cracked door of Emile's office. I stuck my head in and put my hand on the light switch to flip it off, thinking someone had left it on, but I stopped when I noticed the ledger book lying out on the desk. I clearly remembered putting it back in the drawer.

I looked over my shoulder to make sure I was alone before I entered his office. I dragged the ledger to the edge of the desk and flipped a couple of pages. The last time it'd been written in was the night before Emile's death. There was nothing new. Evelyn had probably been looking at it for orders or something. Or maybe Noah had taken a look at it. After all, he was the new chef.

"Let it go. You're a pastry chef," I muttered to myself, flipping off the lights on my way out.

My mind must've been playing tricks on me because, when I got to Evelyn's office door, I could have sworn I heard footsteps. I turned around and stood completely still, even holding my breath.

Panic jumped in my head. What if the killer was here? What if the person who ran me off the road had followed me here and waited until everyone was gone so they could kill me?

I sucked in a few breaths, paralyzed, and realized no amount of deep breathing was going to steady my erratic pulse.

"Hello?" I called out when I heard the heavy footsteps. "Who's there?" My voice cracked.

The footsteps sounded like they were coming closer, and the only way for me to escape was to run as fast as I could.

My bag flapped against my leg as I ran around the building. I dragged the strap around to my front and dug my hand in the bag, feeling for the car keys as I tried to keep up the fast pace. I only allowed myself to glance behind me twice so it wouldn't slow me down, but I wanted to be able to duck if someone was going to try to shoot me or capture me.

Thank God the lights in the parking lot were all working and I'd parked right under one. The pavement was hard under my feet as the adrenaline pumped in my veins.

Within mere seconds, I was in the car and zooming as fast as I could out of the parking lot. I didn't bother looking back through the rearview mirror.

Chapter Twenty-Four

That night after my scare at the RCC, I called Bitsy on the way home. I told her how silly I was because I'd made myself scared half to death and wanted her to stay on the phone with me until I made it home. She insisted on calling Carter, but I talked her off that ledge. At least I thought I had until I was watering the flowers in the window flower boxes the next morning and noticed Carter's car was parked a couple of houses down.

Bitsy had called him anyways and he'd spent all night on a stakeout to make sure no one was going to come to the cottage.

After a quick breakfast, I went to take a nice long shower, but it was cut short from a pounding on the front door. I grabbed my robe and threw it on to answer the door.

"Bitsy called and said you were followed last night," Carter said with a stern voice after I opened the door.

Duchess poked her head between my ankles. I bent down and picked her up. "I'm sure it was my active imagination, since I'd just been talking to Patrick about Emile." I held the door open. "Come on in. You can drink a cup of coffee while I get ready."

After he'd come in and sat down at the kitchen table, I set a cup of coffee and the blueberry scones in front of him.

"Make yourself at home. I'm going to get dressed." I scooped some kibble into Duchess's bowl. "I'll tell you everything when I'm done," I called over my shoulder on my way back to my bedroom. I didn't do my usual routine, since I knew Carter was here on official business and I needed to get on with my day. I threw on some clothes and quickly blow-dried my hair.

As soon as I walked back to the kitchen, Carter started to question me. "Did you see any cars in the lot?"

"No." I refilled my mug and topped off his.

* * *

"Seriously." Carter tapped the table with his pen. "I already cleared the kid and his family."

"I heard his dad wasn't happy you showed up at the factory."

"Part of the job. Did you see any other cars last night? Like the truck that ran you off the road?" He continued asking me questions.

"No." I shook my head. "I didn't notice anything. I was only focused on getting to the car."

"You questioned Patrick about killing Emile; then you heard the footsteps?" He hadn't seemed too happy when I'd told him about that when he'd first started to question me about the rest of my night.

"Yes. After I asked Patrick about his love of cooking and where he'd been, he left, and that's when I heard someone following me," I said, and took another sip of coffee.

"Patrick claims that he and Alice are seeing each other."

Carter talked and wrote on his little notepad. "When I asked Alice about that morning, she confessed, but not without her mom grounding her immediately and taking away her phone."

"There's the whole different social class between them. Natalie thinks Patrick isn't good enough for her daughter. And there's the fact that he can't chew tart gum." A big sigh escaped me. "I guess he's not the killer."

*   *   *

There was a knock on the front door.

"You enjoy another scone while I grab the door."

There was a little prance in my step as I went to see who was there. I loved that Carter was enjoying yet another pastry I'd made.

"Noah," I gasped when I opened the front door. "What are you doing here?"

"What are *you* doing here?" His eyes slid past my shoulder.

Carter stood behind me eating one of the scones.

"Sophia and I were just getting up to start our day." Carter yawned and stretched his arms in the air, letting one rest across my shoulder after it floated down. He was good at getting Noah's goat.

"Last night Charlotte invited me to join the wedding after all the food is served, and I wanted to come over and ask you to be my date." Noah tried hard not to look at Carter.

"Oh, man, Sophia is my date. Sorry, bud." Carter shoved the rest of the scone in his mouth.

I gave Noah a sympathetic look before he stalked off down the front porch.

"I'll see you at the RCC," he shouted from the rental car before he hopped in and screeched off.

"That was fun." I turned around and smiled.

"He's so mad. He thinks we're an item. I don't mind you using me." He winked.

"I'm not using you." I held the door open wide.

"You are totally using me to make him mad. Eventually you won't, though. You'll see. Pick you up at five." He shoved past me and walked out the front door. "Delicious scones, by the way."

Playfully I pushed him out the door.

"I've got to get to the RCC to get the cake on display in the ballroom. Get out of here."

I couldn't help watching until his car disappeared before I headed back up to my room to get ready. There wasn't much time before I had to get to the RCC and put the last touches on Charlotte's cake.

With fingers crossed, I prayed that nothing was going to ruin her big day.

A wedding in Rumford was celebrated almost like a big holiday. Charlotte had left no stone unturned. Even the banners hanging from the carriage lights down Main Street were victims to her big day. They read CONGRATULATIONS, BRETT AND CHARLOTTE.

There was a parking spot in front of Small Talk Café. A hot cup of coffee was exactly what I needed. All this wedding stuff had made me think about Noah and how I was going to handle that situation. Not that I wasn't happy that I'd said yes to go to the wedding with Carter. I was absolutely excited about it, though the acceptance was under a false pretense and Carter knew it.

The red dress hung in the back of the car, and I couldn't wait to put it on after I'd put the finishing touches on the cake.

I'd refused to let Bitsy see it. I wanted her to be surprised. The sun was out, and the forecast from the local radio predicted it to be a beautiful day in the Bluegrass State. Charlotte couldn't have ordered a better day if she had put in a request with Mother Nature herself.

The steam from the espresso machine shot up in the air and chatter drifted through the small café. The line was about ten deep and the same grumpy cashier was at the register. She wasn't going to ruin my morning.

"I heard from Bubba down at the feed store that the police are going to arrest Evelyn as soon as the wedding is over." An older woman and a few of her friends were occupying a table with what looked to be tea in the cups.

Oh, no. After the wedding? I gulped and inched a little closer to the table.

"She was always trying to be too big for her britches," another of the women said.

"I think she's a beautiful woman. A shame she never married. Then she could've stayed home, had a few young'uns, and this would've never happened." The third woman nodded as she spoke.

"Beauty is only skin deep, Pricilla. Ugly goes all the way to the bone. You never know what goes on in someone's head." The first lady picked up the cup and extended her pinky. "Some people are just plumb crazy."

The quiet one of the group finally spoke up. "For cryin' out loud, y'all don't be packing no tales where there's no tale to pack."

Any other time, I might've thought this conversation was a little entertaining; not so much today. Even though it was now rumored that Carter was going to wait to make the arrest until after the wedding.

There was no time to waste grabbing coffee. I hopped out of line and hurried back to the car. Before I pulled out and headed toward the RCC, I quickly texted Carter. I wanted to know what his plan was and when he was going to arrest Evelyn.

He didn't text me back between the short drive from the Small Talk Café to the RCC, so I sent him another quick text letting him know I wasn't going to go to the wedding with him if he didn't answer my questions. Charlotte didn't need to see any of that on her big night and have her wedding day ruined. This would completely overshadow her wedding.

The parking lot had orange cones strategically placed with a couple of signs on them stating that the club was closed for the day for a wedding. I couldn't imagine how much Charlotte had had to pay to rent the RCC for the entire day. I pulled around to the back of the building and went in through the back door. The hallways were empty. The kitchen was quiet and Noah was nowhere to be found.

I reached around my back pocket to grab my phone to see if Carter had texted, but my phone wasn't there. I figured I must've left it on the seat when I parked. I set my bag on the island and decided that I'd get started on the cake before heading out to grab my dress and phone out of the car.

The cake was even prettier than I'd anticipated. The gold spray paint had a vibrant shine, and the two blue layers were the perfect accent. With the few hours between now and the wedding, the cake would be at perfect room temperature and easy to cut into for the traditional cake-feeding photo event.

With the RCC still quiet and no one around, I'd be able to

get the cake wheeled into the ballroom and set up exactly where it'd look perfect. I held on to the cart the cake was on and backed it out of the refrigerator. I carefully pushed it across the kitchen and slowly pushed the door open between the ballroom and the kitchen.

The first sight of the ballroom literally took my breath away. Yesterday it had been beautiful, but with all the finishing touches, it was gorgeous. The drapes on the windows had been replaced with ones the same shade of blue Charlotte had picked out for her cake layers. There was a long table with a white cloth along the wall of windows closest to the outdoor courtyard. There were glass hurricane candle holders with gold candles in each of them. I could picture Charlotte and Brett sitting in the middle with all of their attendants sitting alongside them, supporting them at the beginning of their life together. The florist had placed moss-covered round flowerpots filled with white roses on top of the already larger-than-life birdcages. The sides of the tablecloths that were hanging down from the circular guest tables were now pinned up to form a very elegant scalloped edge. It was truly a reception fit for royalty.

For a brief instant, I stood there wondering what my life would've looked like if I'd stayed in Rumford. Who was going to do the weddings? The baby shower cakes? And the other events Rumford put on?

A faint sound from the kitchen brought me out of my deep thoughts. There was no time to dillydally. I had to get the cake in place before they could fit another thing in this room. I wanted it to be the centerpiece of the room aside from Charlotte.

There was a perfect spot in front on the left side of the dance floor and on the same side as the wedding party table. Naturally, all eyes would float to the table and admire the cake. Once I got the cake set in place, I took a rose or two from the arrangements around the room. There were so many flowers you'd never know I'd taken any. I strategically placed the long-stemmed flowers on the table around the cake and the plates.

I took a step back and looked at the cake and the display. It was breathtaking. Pride swelled up in me. It was the prettiest cake I'd ever made. I couldn't have been more proud, and I couldn't wait to see Charlotte's face. She was going to be a beautiful bride.

My mind flipped back to Carter and whether he'd texted me back.

I wheeled the empty cake cart back into the kitchen.

"Hey," I greeted Nick. He jumped. I laughed. "I catch you off guard?"

"You did." His eyes were huge. He was busy tying the tie of his chef's coat around his waist. "I thought I was alone."

"Nope. I wanted to get in here and finish the cake before Noah got here. The less time spent in the same room with him, the happier my life will be." I pushed the cart out of the way.

The kitchen was going to be buzzing like a finely oiled machine in just a short time. Noah would be snapping orders to get it all done, and I wasn't sure how Nick was going to take it.

"Just so you know, he's a stickler for events. This one will mean a lot since he's been trying really hard to get me to forgive him." I walked over and looked into the pot Nick had put on the stove. "What are you making?"

"Just a base for the lamb." He hurried around the kitchen.

I could already feel the stress. It was about go time. Instead of hanging around asking him questions and keeping him from the work Noah had probably barked at him, I headed to the car to grab my dress and phone. There were still a few hours until the wedding, but I could disappear out of the kitchen and hang out in a quiet place until Charlotte arrived. I'd help her and the girls out wherever they needed me.

The parking lot was filling up quickly. The landscape crew was pulling weeds and adding new mulch for the big celebration. It'd warmed up and the sky was a brilliant blue. Not a cloud in sight. A perfect day indeed.

I was looking around the parking lot for the quickest way around the other cars when the back of a truck caught my attention. Images of the night I'd been run off the road clicked in my head. Suddenly I remembered seeing a sticker on the right corner of the back window as the truck sped off. It was the four-leaf clover symbol of the 4-H Club.

Was that the truck? My eyes darted around the parking lot. The landscape workers didn't look up. Like a crazy person, I ran over to the truck and looked inside the window. Nothing was on the seat. There had to be something in there with a name. I focused on the glove box. Bitsy always kept some documents in her glove compartment, like her car insurance. I tried to jerk the door handle open, but the door was locked. I ran around the front of the truck and tried to open the driver door. It was locked too. I took a step back. My brows furrowed. I curled my bottom lip under my top teeth. I felt like this was the truck that had tried to run me over.

Immediately I felt sick to my stomach and took off toward the RCC. Tears stung my eyes. The killer was here and was going to show up at the wedding. This wasn't happening. I ran as fast as I could down the hall to Evelyn's office. There was no time to knock, so I tried to open her door. It was locked, so I ran back to the kitchen to find Nick and call Carter.

"Nick," I gasped, after I'd smacked the swinging door of the kitchen. The door hit the wall and I jumped. "Nick!" I yelled out.

He wasn't in the kitchen where I'd left him. I turned around before I darted around the kitchen, looking in the refrigerator, the freezer, and around the corner to the dishwasher.

A panic ensued. Had the killer already gotten him? A light from Emile's office caught my attention, and without thinking, I immediately headed there.

"Nick?" I pushed the door open. No one was in there. The ledger was sitting out on the desk.

I jumped when my phone rang in my back pocket. Danny from the laundry service was finally calling me back.

"Hello?" I whispered and knelt down next to the desk.

"Is Sophia Cummings there?" he asked.

"It's me, and I needed to know if you talked to Emile the last time you came in."

"No. He wasn't there, which was odd, but that other guy was there," he said.

"Other guy?" I asked. "You mean Nick?"

"Yeah. That's the guy. He signed off on the paperwork, so he should have it." His words sent chills down spine.

"Let me get this straight." I had to make sure, because Nick had said he'd not been to the RCC that morning. "You're telling me that Nick signed for the cleaning service that morning?"

"Yes," he confirmed.

"Thanks." I clicked the phone off and started to dial Carter's number. I stopped when I noticed a pair of shoes stop next to my crouching body.

"Yeah. I'll take that." Nick stood over me with his hand extended out. "You're not calling another person. Ever."

* * *

I winced when he dragged me up to stand by the fatty part of my arm.

He wagged his finger for me to move away from the desk. "I'm guessing you've figured it out."

"Figured what out?" I tried to put on a good act, but tears stained my lids. How could he do this? Was he going to kill me too?

"Sophia." He snickered. "I'm not stupid. I can see it in your eyes. You know I killed Emile."

"I'm going to go." I took a turn toward the door, but he beat me to it.

His hand pushed past me and slammed the door shut.

"I'm afraid you won't be going anywhere unless it's in a body bag." He shrugged.

"Listen, I don't care. I only wanted Charlotte to have her wedding here." I felt like I was going to pass out. The room began to spin. I started to talk really fast. "Just let me go. I won't say a word and I certainly won't be here after today."

I winced from the pinch of his fingers on my skin.

"I can't let you do that. You seem awfully chummy with that sheriff." He shoved me into Emile's chair. The wheels on the chair legs rolled and I was up against the wall.

"I'm not chummy with anyone. I'm a lone wolf. I've been gone for ten years." I nodded, hoping he'd just let me go.

"You're back now, and you know." He walked around the desk and dragged the ledger to him. He tapped the open page with his finger. "Year after year I've shown up here as Emile's sous chef. He was a nasty boss. He never wanted to listen to my ideas. There were so many amazing dishes I wanted to try."

He started to pace back and forth.

"I'm sure you understand how all this works." His eyes lowered. "It was my turn to take over. I'd even written all the ingredients to order in the ledger. I figured Evelyn would fire Emile over it, but she didn't. I came in that morning and he was staring at the menu I'd created. The one I'd created to get him fired, and he laughed in my face. He said that he hadn't told Evelyn that it was me and that I was immediately fired. It was the complete opposite of what I was trying to do. He mocked me. While he read the menu out loud, I picked up the new skillet he'd purchased and I did it. I swung and hit him as hard as I could." He grinned. "After I killed him, I went home to gather my thoughts. I came up with every possible suspect that had great motive. When you started snooping around, I fed those people to you and knew you'd tell that sheriff. I even sent you a very clear message when I ran you off the road. I didn't want to kill you. I only wished you'd stop."

Why was he giving me his confession? Was he trying to clear his conscience before he killed me? My jaw tensed as I bit back tears.

"Today I came in and your ex told Evelyn he was leaving after the wedding. Not taking the job. She offered it to me." He laughed. "But here you are. You figured it out and now I'm afraid I've got to kill you."

"But I asked you to take the job. I even told Evelyn, but you said you didn't want it." I recalled all the conversations I'd had with him over the last few days.

"I couldn't just say yes. Then the cops would've thought I had motive." He ran his hand through his hair. He untied the tie on the apron around his waist. He wrapped the straps around each hand and smacked it taut. "I'm sorry, but I can't let you ruin it for me."

My throat tightened. I lifted my hands around my neck. The look on his face frightened me to my core. I gulped when I remembered I'd been alone with him at the bakery and told him everything I'd learned.

"Now that you know the truth, I'm going to have to silence you." He stepped forward with the strap held out in front of him.

"No! Help!" I screamed, feeling the panic rising within me.

The door of the office burst open.

"Hold it right there!" Carter yelled, his arms out in front with his gun pointed at Nick. "Stop right there, Nick."

Nick hesitated.

I quickly tapped the toes of my feet on the floor, pushing the rolling chair away from the desk.

"Let her go, Nick." Carter stepped forward. He motioned for me to come to him and I took the opportunity to jump out of the chair, rushing to his side. "Are you okay?" he asked, the gun and his eyes still focused on Nick.

"I'm fine," I said in a shaky voice.

Nick dropped his arms to his side, and his chin dropped to his chest. A few more police officers rushed in. One of them grabbed Nick and thrust his arms behind his back, cuffing him.

"You're under the arrest for the murder of Emile . . ." Carter started to arrest Nick.

Noah rushed in and grabbed me, hugging me tight to his body. I burst into tears.

Chapter Twenty-Five

The morning of the wedding might've started a little shaky, but the wedding itself couldn't have been any smoother than a freshly opened jar of Skippy peanut butter.

The cake was the talk of the wedding—after how gorgeous Charlotte looked, of course. The ballroom was glowing from all the candles hanging off the birdcage centerpieces. The entire town of Rumford had come. Even Mayor Pickering looked to be having a good time as he danced with Evelyn Moss. She'd even let her hair down. Literally, her hair was out of the bun and she looked really nice. The smile on her face and the relief in her eyes made my night.

I straightened the cake table up, since I knew it was almost time for the toasts and the cake would be cut soon. It had to be perfect.

"Are you okay?" Carter walked up to me as I moved the plates a little farther to the right side of the cake. I didn't want anything to skew people's view.

"I'm good." *Good* was really an understatement. I was great.

"Who else could pull off a cake this gorgeous while being held at gunpoint?"

"Technically, your cake was already finished before the incident, but I'll give it to you." His smile reached his eyes, making them glisten.

My pulse leapt, my throbbing heart echoing in my ears. I swallowed.

"I . . . ahem." I cleared my throat in hopes it'd clear my head so I could form a complete sentence. "I want to thank you for showing up when you did."

"I wish I could take the credit for it, but honestly, your ex was the one who made the call." Carter's honesty was so refreshing. "He was coming in to start the food for the wedding, and that's when he overheard Nick. He immediately knew to call instead of taking matters into his own hands."

"That's only because he didn't want to get killed." I looked up at the ceiling and rolled my eyes.

"Still, he saved your life." Carter was speaking softly. "The handwriting analysis came back a couple of hours after we arrested Nick, so it would've been too late if Noah hadn't called."

"Handwriting analysis?"

"The writing in the ledgers that you pointed out to me really struck me. I asked Evelyn to tell the staff to write a nice note to the bride and groom about how much fun they had working on all the wedding details when I really just wanted samples of all of their handwriting. Nick's was a perfect match." His eyes softened as he looked at my dress. "You look beautiful tonight."

"Oh, this?" I brushed off the fact that I loved the red dress. "It's from Peacocks and Pansies."

"That's what you bought as a cover so you could question

Ella?" he asked with a slow secret smile that said he knew. "You really did a good job. Next time, though, you need to stick to the baking."

"Next time?" I laughed. "There's not going to be a next time."

The DJ stopped the music and interrupted the line dancing. Charlotte was leading, of course, and Ella was boogying down with her.

"It's time for the happy couple to cut the cake." Suddenly there was a spotlight on me and the cake table.

Carter quickly stepped out of the way. Charlotte and Brett made their way over. I'd already given them the instructions they needed to cut the perfect piece and feed each other. The photographer's camera snapped away as the two gingerly fed each other a dainty piece.

As Charlotte and Brett walked around the ballroom to talk to their guests, a line started to form for a piece of the cake.

"This sure is awfully pretty," Nora, Carter's mom, said when she came up to get her piece.

"Thank you so much." It was nice to get a compliment from her.

"You know. Carter has a big birthday coming up and there's no bakery around here to bake him the perfect chocolate cake for the big day." She was a sly one.

"Did Bitsy put you up to this?" I asked, not putting it past Mama to keep planting that seed in my head because she knew I loved compliments on my cakes.

"No, Carter did," she said. I followed her eyes as they focused on Carter.

He was talking to a group of people he and Brett had gone

to college with. He must've felt me staring at him because he looked over, his mouth splitting into a wide grin.

I turned back to Nora, but she'd walked off.

"I'm sorry." I picked up a plate for the next person in line, not sure how long she'd been standing there. "Here you go. Enjoy."

The banana pudding was snatched up by the kids and the cake was distributed. As much as I tried to stay in the shadow of the event, there wasn't a single woman there who didn't ask me how they could get in touch with me about doing an event or a cake for special occasions.

Charlotte and her father were doing their dance and Brett and his mother followed. I sneaked to the back of the room and leaned up against the wall to enjoy a little moment to myself.

"You ready to blow this joint?" Noah asked from the swinging kitchen door after he pushed his way out.

He ran a hand down my arm. My eyes glanced past his shoulder and the dance floor lights flashed just enough for me to see that Carter was watching Noah and me intently from the other side of the room.

"What?" Noah asked. "Aren't you ready to get back to our life? Our real life that's going to take you further than this little town?"

I looked at him. I took a real long look at him. There were no feelings of romance. The touch of his hand didn't send goose bumps all over my body like it used to, and I wasn't hanging on his every word.

"Don't get me wrong. It's a cute town and all, but this." His eyes darted around the ballroom of the RCC. "Over the past couple of days, I've discovered that this place is about as far as your career will take you in a small town like Rumford. That's why I only signed a temporary contract. You know, to see how I liked it."

I looked around the ballroom. My life was all in this one room. My family and my friends. Even my perfectly baked and decorated wedding cake was in here. My creation.

Charlotte and Madison were talking and laughing about the people dancing all crazy on the dance floor. Never in a million years and no matter how much time had passed between the three of us would they ever be disloyal to our friendship and womanhood.

I looked over at Bitsy and Dad. Bitsy was chatting it up with some of her Garden Club friends while Dad was talking to the members of his golf league. People I'd known forever. People they'd been friends with forever. Even Natalie was snuggled up with Arnold. Ella was dancing with a short bald guy. When she saw me looking, she pointed and mouthed *Grant*.

"You're right." I smiled. "This is as far as my career would go, and you know what?" I sucked in a deep breath and remembered why I'd become a baker. "I'm okay with that." I took my finger and jabbed him right in the middle of his perfectly starched chef's jacket. "You're going to be getting on the big bird back to the city without me, and you can tell The Manhattan to shove it up their derriere."

"Have you lost your mind, Sophia?" His nose curled in disgust. "I saved your life this morning. I'm the one who overheard you and Nick." He jabbed himself in the chest. "I'm the one who called the cops. I could've just walked away, but I didn't because I love you."

"And I'm forever grateful." I shook my head. "But you don't know what love is."

I twirled on the balls of my feet and walked straight over to Charlotte and Madison. Both of them had a look of concern on their faces.

"Madison." I untied the apron from around my waist. "Is that carriage house on Charlotte's street still for sale?"

"I'm sorry." The edges of her lips turned down. "I think I have a buyer."

"Oh." My heart took a dip, because I knew that house was perfect for me. "What about Ford's Bakery?"

"Nope, same buyer." She shrugged.

My shoulders fell. Everything that was going through my head and what I'd dreamed about was crashing to a halt.

"Why are you looking so gloom and doom?" Madison asked. "The buyer is you! The house told me the first day you sat down on that window seat."

She grinned ear to ear.

"And . . ." She reached into her purse and pulled out a set of keys. "I just so happen to have the extra set of house keys right here."

I grabbed the keys and noticed she'd had a keychain with my initials made.

"Thank you." I gave her a huge hug and Charlotte joined in.

"Let me guess." Bitsy stood behind us. "She's agreed to stay?"

"It looks like I am," I said to my parents, whose pride had been poured all over their faces. "And I'm going to reopen Ford's Bakery. Only I'm changing the name."

"To what?" Charlotte begged to know.

"I don't know." I bounced on my toes.

"Did I overhear that you are staying in Rumford?" Carter walked up. There was satisfaction in his eyes. I nodded. A feeling of peace swept over me. "Are you going to sell coffee in the morning?"

"I think I'll have a pot brewing." I smiled, knowing that Carter's handsome face might start my morning off just right.

"I think I just might have to change my first stop of the day." He winked.

"Excuse me." Charlotte's party planner walked over and broke our stare. "It's time for the toast."

Charlotte gave me a big hug and a little squeal before she headed back to the bride-and-groom's table to get ready for the toast.

"Of course." Carter's southern drawl gave me goose bumps. "If you'll excuse me." He gave me one last look at his pearly whites, sending my heart into a-fib before he walked over and took the microphone off the stand. "If I can have your attention."

Carter's voice boomed over the intercom of the ballroom. A wave of silence blanketed the room as conversation hushed and all eyes turned to Carter.

"I've known Charlotte all my life." Carter stood in front of the ballroom with the champagne flute in his hand.

He looked so handsome in his black tuxedo, gelled hair, and freshly shaven face.

"But it wasn't until I met Brett in college that Charlotte and I became friends. If you can believe it, Brett was enrolled in the academy but was too soft to finish," he joked.

Charlotte laughed and Brett just rolled his eyes, muttering under his breath before he smiled, nodded, and flexed both arms.

"That didn't stop Brett and I from being friends. Look at him." He turned to Brett. "Somebody has to protect that pretty face."

Charlotte took her hand and squeezed Brett's jaw, making his lips pucker. She gave him a quick kiss.

"Over a few beers, he opened up to me that he'd met this girl at the campus Laundromat. Of course I teased him, saying he saw what she wore under her clothes and that's what he liked about her." The crowd laughed. "A few weeks later when he asked me to come over to his bachelor pad to meet her, little did I realize it was no longer a bachelor pad. His place was spotless. There weren't empty pizza boxes, empty beer bottles, and clothes all over the floor or stains on the toilet. There was no way this guy was going to be in love, and I was going to find flaws in her to make sure." Carter cocked a brow. He slid his eyes back to the happy couple. "When Charlotte walked into the apartment, we immediately recognized each other."

Charlotte nodded, agreeing with Carter the entire time.

"There was no way I could even think about talking Brett out of loving Charlotte. In high school, Charlotte was exactly what you see. She was kind. She was always happy. She made sure that she said hello to me in the halls, even though we didn't hang around the same crowd." Carter turned and looked over at me. "Charlotte once told me that when she graduated, she wanted to come back to Rumford and make a difference in the community. Her home. The place where part of her heart was. Brett knew that."

I swallowed hard after he took his eyes off me, wondering if that part of his speech was directed toward me.

"Brett spent the last couple of years in college making sure he had a business plan so that when he graduated with his business degree, he could help make the love of his life's dream come true." Carter took a step backward and let his words sink into the crowd. Sniffles broke the silence. Even I teared up. "He wasted no time finding investors with his idea of revitalizing a community that desperately needed it. Within weeks, Brett was buying up property and starting his business right out of the gate. Naturally, Charlotte has been by his side and used her project management degree to work in his office and keep him organized. They work together like a well-oiled machine. Their love is apparent in how they look at each other and how they treat each other."

Carter lifted his arm with the champagne flute in the air.

"Here's to finding not only your soulmate and business partner in life, but moving home to make the community a better place." He lifted the glass higher. "So, let's lift our glasses to finding that one true love and the happily-ever-after that Charlotte and Brett have found." He looked over at me. His eyes held mine as he spoke to the crowd and took a drink.

Chapter
Twenty-Six

The Manhattan had gotten word that I wasn't coming back. The owners tried everything in the world shy of handing me ownership of the place. I knew I'd made the best decision for me because there was a peace inside that I'd not felt in a long time.

Life in Rumford was going to be much different than life in the city the last ten years. A much-needed break and a slow-paced life looked good on me.

I could barely sleep the night after the wedding. There were so many things going through my head. Noah's face when I told him to go stuff it. Carter's face when I told him I was staying. The orders that poured in after a drunken Charlotte announced to her wedding guests that I was staying and opening up a bakery where the old Ford's Bakery was located.

Madison had agreed to meet me early in the morning, though I was sure she was nursing a major hangover. She and Matthew had a babysitter for the night and I wasn't sure they hadn't ended up sleeping in the old swaggin' wagon.

We stood in front of the glass display window of the old bakery.

Madison broke the silence.

"What is it that we say around here?" she asked, and I knew exactly what she was talking about.

"Around here our tea is sweet, our words are long, our days are warm, and our faith is strong." I sucked in a deep breath.

She dangled the bakery keys from her fingertips.

"I have faith. I have faith that you are going to bring this bakery back to life and the line is going to be wrapped around the corner."

"For Goodness' Cakes." The name came to me. Not only was it perfect; it fit my life.

"Adorable." She nodded her head toward the door. "Go on."

I took a step forward with the key facing the lock, sliding it in. With a slight turn of the key, I took a step across the threshold.

Home. I was home in more ways than one.

Red Velvet Crunchies

Do not preheat the oven because the dough has to be chilled for *one hour.*

Ingredients

1 and ½ cups + 1 tablespoon all-purpose flour
¼ cup unsweetened natural cocoa powder
1 teaspoon baking soda
¼ teaspoon salt
½ cup unsalted butter, softened
¾ cup packed light or dark brown sugar
¼ cup granulated sugar
1 large egg, at room temperature[1]
1 tablespoon whole milk
2 teaspoons vanilla extract
1 tablespoon red food coloring, liquid or gel (you might need more, depending on how red you want your cookies to look; I like a *lot*)
1 cup semisweet chocolate chips plus ½ cup for after baking to stick on top for decorations

Directions

1. Whisk the flour, cocoa powder, baking soda, and salt together in a large bowl. Set aside.
2. Use a mixer to beat the butter on high speed until creamy. Beat in the brown sugar and granulated sugar until combined

and creamy. Beat in the egg, milk, and vanilla extract. Once mixed, add the food coloring and beat until combined. Turn the mixer off to add the dry ingredients into the wet ingredients. Mix on low and slowly beat until a very soft dough is formed. Add more food coloring if you'd like the dough to be brighter red, which I do. I eyeball this. On low speed, beat in the chocolate chips. The dough will be sticky.

3. Cover the dough tightly with plastic wrap and chill for at least one hour. It has to be chilled.

4. Preheat oven to 350 degrees.

5. Put parchment paper on two baking sheets and set aside so they are ready for you to place the dough on once you've rolled it into balls.

6. Scoop up 2 tablespoons of dough and roll into a ball. (If you need a photo, please check out Tonyakappes.com, where you will find a photo under "Maymee Bell Recipes.")

7. Place nine balls on each baking sheet. Bake each batch for 10–11 minutes. The cookies may have only spread slightly because the center will be nice and moist. If you want to press down the warm cookie, you can, and it will make crinkles on top. I stick a few chocolate chips on top and in the crinkles for decoration only.

8. Keep the cookies on the baking sheet for 5 minutes before transferring to a wire rack to cool completely.

Surprise Puffs

(The surprise is that each one is filled with a different filling.)

Ingredients

1 cup boiling water
½ cup butter
1 cup flour
½ tsp salt
4 eggs

Filling

After the puffs have cooled completely, you can put in the filling of your choice. I've listed a few choices at the end of the recipe.

Instructions

1. Preheat your oven to 375 degrees.
2. Bring 1 cup water to a boil in a saucepan.
3. Add the butter to the water and stir until it is melted.
4. Add the flour and salt all at once to the water mix.
5. Stir until a ball is formed.
6. Remove from the heat and add one egg. Beat. Let stand for 5 minutes.
7. Add the remaining eggs one at a time, beating after each addition.
8. Let stand for 10 minutes.
9. Drop a heaping tablespoon of dough onto a cookie sheet

with a spoon, or use a pastry bag or ziplock bag to pipe the dough onto the cookie sheet. Make sure the puffs are about 2 inches apart, because they will expand.

10. Bake for 20–30 minutes. Check them around 20 minutes. Don't burn them.

Filling Notes

There are so many possibilities for delicious fillings. Vanilla cream, custard, coconut cream, lemon cream, chocolate cream, and strawberry cream are just a few.

Southern Skillet Apple Pie

Ingredients

2 pounds Granny Smith apples
2 pounds Braeburn apples
2 teaspoons ground cinnamon
¾ cup granulated sugar
2 tablespoons granulated sugar
½ cup butter
1 cup packed light brown sugar
2 packages refrigerated pie crusts
1 egg white

Directions

1. Preheat your oven to 350 degrees.
2. Peel all your apples and cut into ½-inch wedges. Add the cinnamon and ¾ cup granulated sugar together in a bowl and toss your apple wedges around in it.
3. I use a 10-inch round cast-iron skillet, but you can use a square one. Melt your butter in the skillet over medium heat. Add in the brown sugar and stir constantly. Remove it from the heat. Put one of the pie crusts in the skillet over the mixture.
4. Pour your apple mixture into the skillet over the crust.
5. Put the other crust over the skillet (pie mixture) and pinch the edges over the edge of the skillet to seal the pie.
6. In a bowl, mix the egg white until foamy and brush over the

top pie crust. Sprinkle the 2 tablespoons of granulated sugar over the crust. Cut four slits (like an X) in the middle of the crust. This helps the steam to escape from the pie and make the apples tender.

7. Put the skillet in the oven and bake for an hour and ten minutes or until the crust is golden brown. If you've baked for the full time and it's not completely finished, place some foil loosely over the top so it won't burn.

8. Cool for about thirty minutes.

9. You can top it with ice cream!

10. Enjoy!

Banana Pudding Cupcakes

Ingredients

1 ½ cups all-purpose flour
1 cup sugar
1 ½ teaspoons baking powder
½ teaspoon salt
1 stick unsalted butter, room temperature
½ cup sour cream
1 egg, room temperature
2 egg yolks, room temperature
2 teaspoons vanilla extract
⅓ cup vanilla wafer crumbs
1 large container frozen whipped topping, thawed
12 whole vanilla wafers

Pudding Filling

8 ounces cream cheese, room temperature
1 (14-ounce) can sweetened condensed milk
¾ cup whole milk
1 teaspoon vanilla extract
1 (3.4-ounce) box instant vanilla pudding mix
1 ripe banana, cut into thin slices and then diced

Instructions

1. Heat your oven to 350 degrees with your oven rack in the middle of the oven. Line a twelve-cup muffin tin with paper liners.

2. Place the flour, sugar, baking powder, and salt in a large mixing bowl, and use a mixer fitted with a paddle attachment to mix them together.

3. With the mixer on medium speed, add butter, sour cream, egg, egg yolks, and vanilla. Beat for 30 seconds or until the mixture is smooth and satiny.

4. Remove the mixing bowl from the mixer and, using a rubber spatula, scrape down the sides of the bowl. Make sure the batter is mixed evenly.

5. Divide the batter equally among the muffin cups and bake for 18 to 22 minutes. Let them cool before proceeding.

6. Using a spoon or your fingers, create a hollowed-out portion in each cupcake, as you would to make a bread bowl, being careful to leave a layer of cupcake all the way across the bottom.

7. Sprinkle some vanilla wafer crumbs at the bottom of each cupcake "bowl."

8. Using an electric mixer, beat together the cream cheese and sweetened condensed milk for 2–3 minutes. Scrape down the sides of the bowl at least once.

9. Add the milk, vanilla extract, and pudding mix and beat until they are mixed together well. Stir in the bananas by hand. Immediately spoon the pudding mixture into the cupcake holes, leaving enough extra that you can create a layer of pudding spread across the top of the cupcake.

10. Use an offset spatula or a pastry bag fitted with a large tip to add whipped topping on top of the pudding mixture. Garnish with a whole vanilla wafer and more crumbs if desired.

Kentucky Butter Cupcakes

Ingredients

1 cup salted butter, softened
2 cups sugar
4 large eggs
1 tablespoon vanilla extract
3 cups all-purpose flour
1 teaspoon baking powder
½ teaspoon salt (optional; I don't add any since I use salted
    butter)
½ teaspoon baking soda
1 cup buttermilk (or regular milk)

Glaze

⅓ cup salted butter
¾ cup sugar
2 tablespoons water
2 teaspoons vanilla
powdered sugar for dusting (optional)

Instructions

1. Preheat your oven to 350 degrees. Grease muffin tins.
2. Combine all of the cake ingredients in a large mixing bowl.
   Mix with an electric mixer on low speed for 30 seconds,
   then increase the speed and mix for 2–3 minutes.

3. Pour the batter into muffin tins, filling them three-quarters of the way full.
4. Bake 17–19 minutes or until a toothpick inserted in one comes out clean. The tops will be golden brown. Let the cupcakes set in the muffin tins while you prepare the glaze.
5. Prepare the glaze by heating the ingredients on the stovetop in a saucepan over medium heat until the butter is melted.
6. Move the cupcakes to a cooling rack or baking sheet and pour warm glaze over the tops, about a spoonful on each. Dust with powdered sugar if desired.

Kentucky Derby Pie

(from the recipe book of Maymee Bell's own mama, Linda Lowry)

My mama's Derby pie is smack-your-mama good! It's a southern pie with walnuts and chocolate chips. You can use pecans as a substitute for the walnuts, but I really like my walnuts!

Ingredients

½ cup melted butter
1 cup sugar
½ cup flour
2 beaten eggs
1 teaspoon vanilla extract
¾ cup walnuts or pecans (your choice—not both!)
¾ cup chocolate chips (or more if you really want it gooey!)

Directions

1. Mix the ingredients in the order listed. This is very important.
2. Pour the mixture into an unbaked 9-inch pie shell.
3. Bake at 350 degrees for 30 minutes.